BOLT ACTION

Lee slid his right foot back clear of the stirrup, then kicked out hard.

The Irishman was quick for all his size, and might have stepped aside, but for keeping his grip on the bridle. As the man tried his sideways step, the mule shifted and held him.

Lee's kick caught him fair in the middle of his chest and drove the wind out of him with a grunt.

"Don't!" the woman said sharp in Lee's ear. He reached down and yanked the coiled whip from its tie and shook out the long lash. The Irishman let go of the bridle then and did the clever thing. He didn't try to clear the length of the lash—he came in under it, and fast, reaching up for Lee with surprisingly small hands. Lee found, as sometimes happened in such circumstances, that he had all the time he needed, that everything occurred as slowly as in a dream....

TRIGGER GUARD

The bandit saw it coming. Lee saw the flicker in his eyes, but the man was too badly hurt to go tumbling over the countryside as Lee had for the dodge. The bandit stood stock-still (dying, no doubt, from that shot in the chest) and fired the Smith and Wesson as the dagger whacked into his belly—nine inches of broad, double-edged steel—and left him doubled over on his knees, his big revolver fallen into the sand beside him, of no use at all....

D0191679

BUCKSKIN DOUBLE:

BOLT ACTION

TRIGGER GUARD

ROY LeBeau

LEISURE BOOKS NEW YORK CITY

A LEISURE BOOK®

December 2006

Published by

Dorchester Publishing Co., Inc.
200 Madison Avenue
New York, NY 10016

Bolt Action copyright © 1986 by Roy LeBeau
Trigger Guard copyright © 1986 by Roy LeBeau

ISBN 0-8439-2872-7

The name "Leisure Books" and the stylized "L" with design are trademarks of Dorchester Publishing Co., Inc.

Printed in the United States of America.

Visit us on the web at www.dorchesterpub.com.

BOLT ACTION

Nothing special about him, at first glance.

Another drifter down on his luck. Young fellow—but not so young in the face, if you looked close. Worn buckskin jacket, worn clothes. None of them too clean, either.

Riding a mule. Well, a lot of men would say they preferred a riding mule to a horse, particularly in rough deep wooded country like this Pacific Coast timberland. Lot of men would say they favored a mule, but most that talked that way rode horses.

Armed, to be sure. Carried a pistol holstered at his right side. That a little unusual. This was woods country. Rifle country, mainly.

Black snake whip, it looked like, coiled at the saddle-bow where a stockman usually wore his rope.

A hard enough article, most people would say. Dead broke, and way, way down on his luck. Come all the way west and up the coast to the big-tree country, looking for work. Try his hand at jacking, likely, or rafting.

Or firewood cutting.

Or saloon swamping.

Or trouble . . .

Lee gave the mule (which he had never named) another kick, a light one, by way of encouragement. This town, its muddy streets now drying and awash with bright morning light, was, he hoped, Berrytown, named for some forgotten Oregoner who'd lost out down south and had to come up to the Columbia River country.

Not the only one who'd lost out, come to that.

Not the only one.

Took more than a fair fool—and a more than fairly *unlucky* fool at that—to buy land with all his spare cash, then lost that land and his horses. Lose it all to an animal illness.

Hoof-and-mouth.

There was a name to conjure with. That name, embodied, could strip a rich young man (a regular dash, he'd thought himself), could take and strip him of every good he owned, every beast, all horseflesh. And then, with the stock gone, the land to follow after.

The ranch at Rifle River. And Catherine Dowd's Spade Bit. Gone. Gone as so many had gone that winter of '86.

Lost to a Mex disease, a paltry thing that turned a horse's mouth to sores, that turned its

10

hooves to pus and corruption.

One month a rich young dandy, and dangerous. The next, a saddle-bum as busted out as any. All his good men gone to hand it on other spreads, ranches that had been luckier. Sid Sefton . . . Charlie Potts . . . Tough Little Ford. Bud Bent.

Gone. Gone and scattered. Where in the world was he ever to get men like that again? Where in the world—and how—ever to get the property to put them on?

The nameless mule (give it its credit, it could climb) grunted with effort and lunged up a muddy hummock, past a barrel-house festooned along its sagging porch with tramps and drunkards and up into Berrytown for sure.

This town consisted, as far as Lee could make out, of a single large clearing in the forest, a very large clearing, more than a rifle shot across, and the town packed into that raw and muddy space. All fresh-cut peeled timber, slab and pole and plank. Every building green-wood red and yellow, and bleeding sap and 'tine down its boards. The town smelled of wood and sawdust and pitch sap. That, and horse shit, dog shit, and people shit.

The rains in this country—it appeared to Lee that the sky opened up regular as clockwork every afternoon and watered more than its fair share—these rains seemed to make it difficult to keep anything fairly buried, crap and trash included. Odd weather to a man from the mountains.

Not that he was a chooser. A begger, was more like it.

A year on the trail. A long year of haying and carpentering and pig-feeding and wood-splitting, ditch-digging and asking to be allowed to ditch-dig—this long year (which seemed more like five) since the last of the Spade Bit herd had been shot and buried up in the Roughs. Since he and Ford had gotten the telegram from Rifle River . . .

The bay stud and the mares, all sent out to Montana for safety, had carried the infection with them. Like the Bit, the ranch at Rifle River would soon be no horse ranch at all, but a bone yard. A wilderness.

A year ago and more.

And Mister Fancy brought suitably low.

It had occurred to Lee at the time, and since, that there might be some curse about it—some Red Indian curse, perhaps, having to do with the death of a scrawny little Cree girl who'd had no business dying. That death, perhaps, which had occurred under his arm (as Mercutio said).

That death, perhaps, or some other. There were a few from which to choose, if a man's mind ran in that direction as he clung to the shaking rods under some fast freight chuffing up into the Rockies. More likely for his mind to run in that direction then, disliking railroad trains as he did. Perhaps the host of dead his father had put under.

Perhaps not.

In the last part of this last year, his pride considerably reduced, and his imagination more commonsensical, Lee had come to believe that he'd lost Spade Bit, the River ranch, and a fortune in land only to his own carelessness and sheer ill-fortune.

He'd been north when the first horse went down, had not been there to cull the herd hard enough, had not been there to decide. He'd had other business in which the young Cree girl had died for him. More important business, he'd thought at the time.

You live . . . and you learn.

Well, he'd certainly lived. And now, courtesy of a Mexican horse illness, he'd just as certainly learned. Nothing—*nothing*—is certain sure.

Taken him some months just to get used to being poor, a thing most men learned very early, even in this rich and open country. Took him a few months to learn that poor men speak differently, act differently from others, particularly when they speak to, or act before, the rich.

Lee'd learned. The hard way.

Learned that sheriffs and town marshals were not likely to be impressed by some ragged drifter's gun-skill. Were more than prone to have their deputies cover the fellow with shotguns, then beat him into a sort of acceptance of the world as it was.

Surprising, too, what store women set by money—or at least a modicum of it. Youth, good looks, and a rakish air turned out to be less of a draw with the ladies once there was no cash at all to back them.

Living . . . and learning.

A good year of it.

Had had no gun-fights in that time, no lee-way for dangerous or tragical airs. Been too damn busy slopping nesters' hogs, chopping firewood for a paltry feed, bringing in hay at twenty cents a day.

Lee booted the no-name mule along the widest rutty he could find. Saw a rough plank sign calling the way Front Street. Fair enough. Seen almost as many Front Streets as Main Streets.

Busy town, too, from the traffic. Lots of horsemen, but more wagons and wains. Fair amount of men on foot. Women, too—decent women, by the sad, work-worn look of their faces.

Some kids. Lee had seen a good number of town kids up in this northwest. Appeared the townfolks bounced the bedsprings more than most. Had more leisure for it, likely, in this green, rain-soaked country. Lee had never seen land as rich for growing as down in the Willamette. More like chocolate cake than dirt.

Lee reined the mule out across the traffic, heading toward a resort across the ruts, a two-story log lash-up with a sign nailed across the front: *The American Eagle.*

Got a cussing-out from a wagoneer, getting across.

Lee'd bought the mule for fifteen dollars from a woman greengrocer in Eugene, Oregon. He'd worked for this lady three weeks, crating potatoes, freighting green goods. Damned hard work. He'd had seven dollars and nineteen cents saved. Hard saved. Saved out of food. Saved out of a needed pair of brogan shoes. The shoes he had worn then, still wore, were broken along the sole. His foot showed for an instant every time he stepped.

Had that seven dollars, and the change, and earned eighteen dollars working for the lady greengrocer in those three weeks—really only earned fifteen dollars and some, but had picked through the spoiled stuff and been allowed to peddle that on his own. The lady greengrocer had been tough but fair enough, if you worked an honest twelve hours a day for her.

Lee'd probably been foolish to buy the mule —couldn't really afford the animal, and had to ride bareback for more than a week, bareback with rope halter before he had managed a McClellan with a broken tree. Cost him seventy-five cents.

Probably foolish to buy the beast, but he was damned tired of walking and begging rides. Not much respect given to a man outside of the cities who had to walk or beg rides.

Lee swung down off the mule with a grunt of relief (the McClellan was a brute of a seat) went to his head, and tied him off to the saloon hitch.

Slipped the keeper-loop off the Bisley Colt's

hammer as he went up the resort's steps. Habit, more than anything, doing that.

The lady greengrocer hadn't let Lee wear his revolver at work. "My customers don't care to be frightened by an armed rough, Mister Morgan. Put that piece away—or, better yet, sell the thing for a decent pair of shoes!"

Lee hadn't sold the Colt's. Probably should have. The lady greengrocer hadn't noticed the broad blade dagger in Lee's belt under his shirt. Or if she had, had chosen not to mention it. Hadn't mentioned the whip, either; likely she thought that only a proper tool for a loader and drover to sport.

The American Eagle was a solid dive; none of your bust-out barrel-house here. Place was suitably dim, lit by a few kerosene lamps, yellow light flaring softly against the wash of bright sunlight through the bat-wing doors.

Good long bar. True mahogany, it looked like. Pleasant brasswork, and a series of really prime mirrors sported behind it. Bottles stacked most artistically along the glass.

One barkeep. A tall drink of water, looked like a lunger. Appeared to rough his cheeks for seeming's sake.

The deep, low ceilinged room smelled of stale beer and fresh sweat. Could be a fellow had failed to hold his water, too, sometime in the last few days. Faint smell of piss in the air. Deep sawdust, though. Lee's brogans kicked up a heap of it at every step. No shortage of sawdust in Berrytown or environs.

"You'll be havin'?" The barkeep looked concerned for his free lunch, having taken in Lee Morgan top to toe and not found him likely customer material.

Lee leaned against the front door end of the bar. It was the real McCoy. Mahogany, and with a sweet grain to it. He thought he might afford a nickel.

"A nickel pull-beer," he said, and the lunger barkeep nodded a 'might have known it,' and strolled down to draw the drink.

Not many men in the place. They'd be out working, this time of day. There was no other man standing at the bar.

Lee saw a middle-aged woman—a gambler, she looked like—dealing cards to two clerks and a lounger at a table in the back. The woman was fat as a Christmas goose, and seemed, in the dim light and at a distance, to have a face hard as stone.

Lee wouldn't have given much for the chance of the clerks and lounger coming up winners. The woman gambler wore black bombazine and a yellow straw hat with a wide brim, to shade her eyes. Her fat little hands shifted the cards before her as neatly as one of Mister Singer's new sewing machines stitched a seam, and just about as quickly.

A few other men, those not gambling. Business people—lumber buyers and sawmill men, he supposed—who could afford a late fried-egg breakfast. Maybe a pounded beefsteak with their eggs. Those fellows were sitting at two

17

tables against the wall, chatting, at ease . . . money in their pockets.

Near the free lunch.

The barkeep brought Lee his mug of beer, a good deal of it foam, and watched in weary disapproval as Lee strolled across to the free lunch.

It was a pretty good spread, and new laid-out. A plate of cold sliced beef, a bowl of boiled eggs. Some German slaw, and a crock of pigs feet in pickling. Some radishes and spring onions in a dish. A half wheel of yellow cheese . . . sliced rye bread.

Pretty good spread. Lee could have gone through it like a herd of hogs. His last meal had been a snared rabbit the day before on the ride upcountry. Meal before that had been a breakfast of boiled horse-oats.

He could feel the barkeep's eye on him, waiting to see what he'd cadge for his nickel beer. How many times had Lee sat in comfort in a place and seen ragged tramps pitched out into the street for piling one plate and then trying another for their one nickel beer . . .

Many times. And had usually laughed about it.

He reached over the crock of pigs feet, the bowl of eggs, and picked up two pieces of rye, then forked a slice of beef and a slice of cheese between them, smeared that with mustard, and carried this modest sandwich away to a corner table, his gut grinding with hunger.

Might have been smarter to forget his pride.

Might have been smarter to do as those other tramps had done—stack his plate and gobble— and then let them throw him where they pleased. Might have been smarter . . .

Lee sat and watched the morning traffic through the *Eagle's* engraved front window glass. He sipped at his beer to make it last, and took slow, careful bites of the sandwich. The beef and cheese, the crusty rye, all tasted so good they made his jaws ache as he chewed.

· *Money.*

Money was what he wanted. Other things as well, but money first.

There was a clock over the bar, its pendulum swinging with a miniature Union battle flag attached. Just after nine o'clock in the morning. Late to be seeking a day's work. A week's work, if he could get it. A bed, too, if that could be had, or at least some sacking in a shed. This was poor country for sleeping out. Too wet. The damp slid up into a man's bones if he slept too many ditches.

The night before, Lee had wakened at moon-rise to find that some short rain had already fallen in a gentle drift, and soaked his jacket and trousers through the threadbare blanket he'd swaddled in. The ditch he lay in was slick with mud, and had been bone dry when he'd lain down.

Poor country for sleeping out. Poorer yet, if you couldn't keep a fire going for the regular rain. And this was high Spring, God only knew how wet the country was in winter. A slicker would have helped, to be sure, if Lee'd had the five dollars to buy one.

A day's work, or a week's work or more. And shelter to go with it. Then, perhaps, a look at a local bank or freight office.

Lee was considering, had considered for some time, what way he might achieve some capital, a sum of money sufficient for a start in business. Day-laboring was surely not the way.

Professor Riles had once quoted some French writer. " . . . Behind every great fortune, there is a crime." Something to that effect. Lee was more than slightly certain that the Frenchman was right. And, that being so, it seemed sensible to delay no longer, but commit his crime and get on with fortune-making.

He had no notion of its being easy. He'd seen the law in operation, and knew that sheriffs and town marshals (now that they had the advantage of the telegraph) had organized their posses in the last few years so that even clever road agents found themselves chased into smaller and smaller circles, worn down, then run down, then killed. Lawmen were often impatient with the law, and oftener were influenced by this or that group of rich men—ranchers, further east. Lumbermen, no doubt, out here.

Had no notion at all of its being easy.

But necessary, perhaps if a man were to start making his way again, starting from scratch.

Less than scratch. And it wouldn't be the first time.

How had his father paid for the ranch at Rifle River? Had Buckskin Frank Leslie earned that cash in any other way than with his gun? Not likely. And Lee's mother, that gentle little lady, who'd been a whore . . . What but crimes, at least as the law saw them, had gone to the buying and building of the ranch at Rifle River?

And Dowd? How had the little Canadian's father made his fortune? How had Dowd increased it? In no perfect legal way, for certain. And out of that (or those) crimes had come Spade Bit.

It was, perhaps, a little late for a start, and robbery with a revolver not a subtle method. But a man got weary of working for seventy-five cents a day. Got more weary of the tone in other men's voices . . . women's voices . . . when they talked to a man who worked twelve hours a day for those pennies.

Very weary of that.

The last bite of sandwich tasted as good as the first. The beer was gone. Lee couldn't remember the last swallow of beer. He saw the barkeep standing at the far end of the bar, watching him, watching to see that Lee didn't stroll back to the free lunch, forgetting to buy another nickel beer. It was the sort of look that made Lee weary.

* * *

21

The day was bright, cloudless, as hot as days were likely to get in this country, the sky a wide, flat plate of silver-blue. A hot, hot bright sun . . .

"Five miles out of town, maybe six," the barkeep had said. "The camp on the Rusty—that being a river, the Rusty. They're hirin', I think." Lee's reward, apparently, for not having charged the free lunch. Regarded now as an honest working man, fit to be helped to another honest day's work; maybe a week's work.

The mule was deep into his plugging half-trot; it was a ground eater, but hard on the tailbone. The trail was more of a track than a way, narrow and deep rutted between walls of green. Didn't have far to look for a tree in this country. A heaven for timber cutters. Pretty country, too, at least when the sun was shining.

Small butterflies orange as harvest moons came swirling out around the mule. There were white wildflowers at the sides of the track. Flat blossoms grew on them like clusters of lace. Butterflies and lacy flowers. Rich country, and pretty, when the sun was shining.

Lee rode easy, relaxing to the mule's lumpy pace—damn thing seemed to have five legs! It was true that most men grubbed hard for their living, and raised families doing it. Gritted their teeth, got up in the dark, worked their twelve hours (with Sundays off) picked up their pay—five dollars, seven dollars—at the end of the week, spent a dollar or two getting drunk, went home to beat their wives or screw them. Then, on Sunday, sleep late, play with their kids. Tell their wives they're sorry, give them the rest of the money for the rent, for food.

A good enough life for most men. And, to be fair, plenty of good men among them, neither drunks nor wife-beaters. Good enough men. But not men who had been princes on the mountain range, who had held miles of land beneath their horse's hooves. Had a dozen wranglers, gunmen at their call. Not men who'd lived the sporting life, had bought a slave girl in San Francisco. Had found love, doing it.

Not men with a father like his.

No, what he could not earn with his back he would take. And God help the man in his way.

A mile and more further on, the narrow track commenced to widen, break, and slowly vanish into a broadening meadow as full of flowers and butterflies as the trail-side had been. It was a hot day for this north country, hot and hard green under a white-hot sun. More butterflies than Lee recalled seeing before, the orange ones and some brown and white ones. Clouds of the brown and white ones . . .

The meadow reached a stretch, rolling out far and far to a distant line of trees. Open country if only for a while. It reminded Lee of the mountains, of that open country. He could have turned his head, looked back, and seen one of this country's mountains. "More properly volcanoes," old Riles would have said, And not, in any case, the same as the wall of the Rockies above Spade Bit. The end wall of the world, that rank of mountains looked.

It occured to Lee for the first time that he might not see those mountains again. He hadn't thought of that before for some reason, had, like a child, somehow assumed that what had been must always be so. That the past could not be finally past. Could not be lost forever.

You live, and you learn.

Likely, he would never ride Spade Bit again. Never raise horses.

Damn place was owned by people from Chicago now, anyway. Men with considering eyes, and fine attorneys. Had their hired men on there raising beef.

Lee—or more accurately, the mule—found the track again past a crowd of cloud of berry bushes, and went ambling along. He should hit the lumber camp with the sun just past straight up. Might, if there was no work, be offered some beans and bacon instead.

He saw the horse's head first, just above some shrub or other ahead. Something was the matter with the horse. It held its head oddly.

Lee drew the Bisley Colt's and slid off the mule. He would have given a good deal to have the big Sharps in his hand. He'd sold that wonderful rifle to buy himself a blanket, a steak diner, and a bottle of whiskey. He'd still been a fool, when he'd done that. Had been a fool not to have cleared off with a few thousand dollars, too. He could have kept that much back; the bankers in Boise and Denver wouldn't have minded.

Could have, but didn't. Too proud not to pay all his debt.

Lee left the mule standing (give the ugly thing credit, it stayed put) and started walking toward that oddly standing horse. A sorrel, it seemed, standing still, tossing its head.

He could smell the flowers beneath his shoes. Wished he'd had the money for practice ammunition . . .

Heard a woman scream, up ahead. Heard her sobbing. He surely wished to God he'd had the money for that practice ammunition . . .

He ran toward that oddly standing horse.

He cleared the cloudberry brush at a dead run breasting through it, the Colt's held high. His heart was pounding hard.

The horse was tangled in harness. Behind it, down a steep ditch, a surrey lay splintered on its side.

Where in hell was the *woman?*

Then he saw her. A flash of white stuff—her dress, distant through the grass and berry brush. A fair pistol shot away. Seemed to be running, falling. Lee saw white hair. An old woman out here injured, screaming.

He holstered the Colt's and ran after her.

He caught her staggering, stumbling through flowers in the hot sunlight as if she were blind. Got her by the arm and held her.

25

Held her still when she yelped in surprise, and swung her around to face him.

Lee froze at the look of her.

White, white face—white as white paper. White hair flowing down . . . must have come unpinned when she'd lost her hat.

And *red eyes*. Eyes as bright and red as rubies, as blood.

She was no old woman. She was young. She struggled briefly in his hands, and Lee saw tears on her face. Her hair flowed down like snow.

"The sun!" she said. "The *sun!*" and bent her head, buried it against his chest.

An albino. A pure albino! And the sun was killing her.

"Oh, help me!" she cried, and clung to him as if he were the tree of life.

Lee got his old Stetson on her, led her stumbling back to the ditched surrey. She side-slipped, or the sorrel had shied, gone into the ditch and cracked the rear axle, knocked the rig over and spilled her out. Must have dazed her . . . lost her hat. Then she was lost indeed— sun struck, blind, and wandering.

Lee made her sit down and be still; she was trembling, weeping. Skin white as new milk. Eyes red as rubies. Hard to tell, so inhuman were those colors, whether she was pretty. A long, fine face, long jaw. A high-bridged nose. Not very pretty. A lady's face.

"Thank you," she said, and squinted up at him from under the brim of his Stetson.

"You're very kind." Then she closed those remarkable eyes and bowed her head.

Strange creature . . . Strange way to have to live, always in fear of the sun, always going swaddled and shaded in daylight. Free of that only by the light of the moon. Safe in that silvered, shadowed dark.

Lee unpinned the linch, loosed the harness, and led the sorrel off, checked his legs. No harm that he could feel. Left fore a little hot, but that might be nothing. A handsome animal; a stepper, and no plug. Well-mannered, too; no jumpy airs about him.

A lady in a fine rig drawn by a fine harness-horse. A snow-white lady out on her own . . .

Lee searched around the rig, poking through the high grass for her hat, but didn't find it. Down in the ditch, though, silver ear-pieces shining in the sun-light, he found a small pair of spectacles, the round lenses smoked to black.

He brought those to her, and she put them on with murmurs of relief. "Thank you . . . very kind . . ." Her white hands were long, slender, nervous. She adjusted the spectacles, then tucked her hands into a fold of her skirt, as if even in the surrey's shadow the light was too great for them. Putting on the smoked-glass spectacles appeared to have calmed her, eased her. Lee supposed she'd taken a hard fall when the surrey went over. Damned high-sprung things. Not the best rig for rough country.

She looked up at him (small, round black

lenses against a long, white fine-boned face) and forced a smile. "My name is Nancy Lorena Parker." She took a slender hand out of the folds of her skirt, and held it out to shake.

Cool hand . . . bony . . . fragile.

"Lee Morgan," he said.

"You have a hard hand, Mister Morgan." She withdrew her hand from his, tucked it back into her dress. She had a soft voice. An eastern voice, Lee thought. That cool drawl to it. Calm, now that she was covered from the sun . . . had her smoked glasses on. "I wonder," she said, "I wonder if you were riding to Berrytown (pronounced *Berryton*), Mister Morgan."

"No, Ma'am, the other way. I was going out to the camp at Rusty River."

"Oh," she said, "the Rostov—that would do. If you could speak to Micky, Micky Daley, and ask him to send someone to set up the surrey . . . "

"There's no fixing it," Lee said, "without putting in another axle. You better come on with me. I'll take you back to town, if you'd like. If you don't mind riding pillion on a mule." Truth was, he'd heard a tone in her voice he didn't much care for. Something of the lady-of-the-manor, talking down to a rough fellow with several day's growth of beard.

If so, a clever lady, and a noticer.

"No, Mister Morgan, I wouldn't mind at all. I'd be pleased to ride behind you, if you'd be kind enough to allow me . . . " It was difficult to tell whether she was being satiric. The smoked glasses were blank as obsidian. "I'm afraid I've already been a trouble to you."

"Not a bit," Lee said.

"My home is near the Rostov camp . . . If you could take me there?"

"Be my pleasure," Lee said, with a sudden vision, not unpleasant, of himself, the mule, and this odd fairy-tale figure of a lady, all journeying through this handsome country. A small adventure, almost enough to keep his mind off his belly. That single sandwich was feeling more and more lonely . . .

Nancy Lorena Parker, shaded by his Stetson, bespectacled, long white hands tucked into the folds of her skirt, made no bones about being hoisted aboard the mule's butt. Appeared, in fact, comfortable on the animal, somewhat relishing her adventure.

Lee got the notion that Nancy Lorena Parker didn't get about much—understandable, in view of that crippling albinism. A curse of colorlessness . . . eyes like an Easter rabbit's. What such a state must have meant to the woman as a child, a young girl.

He booted—*broganed* would be more accurate—the mule into motion, felt the woman's slender arms slide around his waist as the beast fell into its odd rocking gait. The sorrel whickered after them as they went by—likely thought it was abandoned forever—and the woman called back over her shoulder to him.

"Oh, easy . . . easy, Handsome Nat! You're not forgotten!"

They rode on, the lady's arms light as smoke around Lee's waist, for more than another mile. Rode on through the high grass with its spangled decorations of butterflies, more and more tangled shrubbery of berry bushes (Lee wondered if Berrytown hadn't been named for these, rather than a possibly mythical pioneer) and finally deeper into a well-defined roadway, rutted and stone-filled in its lower passages, where apparently it flooded.

"There will be a small turning off to the right," she said, her breath touching the back of his right ear in the lightest possible way.

When Lee turned the mule there, it balked and shuffled to a stop. He'd noticed before that the animal didn't like turning right, probably had developed that dislike from some injury or mistreatment, and mule-like, had never forgotten it. Would *never* forget it, was the truth of the matter.

Lee sighed, gathered the reins in a good grip, and drummed the beast's ribs with his heels as hard as he could. The mule muttered, farted, and lurched into motion; Lee felt the woman's slight weight press against him, then away, as the mule achieved his awkward trot.

"What an undecided animal," she said gaily. "You must never be certain you'll get where you're going, Mister Morgan."

"I would certain have described a great circle to the left, up from Oregon, if he didn't

30

have somewhat tender ribs," Lee said.

"Has he no name?"

"Nameless."

"Is he? Then 'Nameless' shall *be* his name."

"The lady wishes . . ." Lee said, reining the new-named animal down a dark and narrow track. Soft, dark green mosses under hoof, dark green pines and hemlocks at arm's length on either side. This sort of track made him nervous, as railroad trains made him nervous— as if there might be in the next railroad car ahead a small dapper man in a fine suit of clothes. A small smiling man, with bright, mad eyes . . .

And in this track, so close and overgrown in green, perhaps a round and gleeful woodsman perched high as any bird, a fine-honed hatchet in his hand . . .

It was such imaginings, such ancient terrors, that likely made Lee act the fool.

The close brush crashed to Lee's right and a man came jumping out, reaching for the mule's bridle.

"Hold here, you!" This man, very wide in the shoulder, a tight gray sweater-jacket on him, had the long upper lip of an Irishman. He'd stopped his shout as Lee turned in the saddle toward him, the Bisley Colt's already drawn.

Lee would certainly have killed the fellow, but the albino woman, quicker than most ladies would have been, had her hand already on his gun-arm, was calling to him as a woman might call to a distant child, or to a sleeping

31

one to wake it from some nightmare. "Don't kill him! Oh, *don't!*"

They stood frozen like that, the rider, his face a mask of murder; the snow-skinned woman seated behind him calling to him; and the Irishman, big and heavy-boned, standing stock still in the narrow way, his right hand still up to the mule's bridle.

The Irishman was cool enough. He stood still under Lee's revolver muzzle, staring up with eyes as hard and green as malachite. Eyes hooded by busted brows, ridges of scar tissue where fists had struck and battered at him. This wide-shouldered fist-fighter then gripped the mule's bridle and dragged the animal's head down.

"You'll be puttin' dat piece away, cowboy, or usin' it. And to hell wit youse, either way!"

"Don't kill him," the woman said. Her hand was still on Lee's arm.

"I won't," Lee said. "I won't. Let go my arm." Ashamed of himself. To have been so startled by nothing but some Irish bruiser. Memories had made him a coward, it seemed. Made him play the fool.

He slid the Bisley Colt's back into its holster.

The big Irishman spit just past Lee's stirruped shoe and kept his grip on the mule's bridle.

"Micky, this man has helped me; I tipped the surrey out of the trace. Mister Morgan, this is a . . . friend, Micky Daley."

"An' him?"

"This man helped me."

"This scut?" The Irishman pulled the mule's head down a little more. "Youse ain't supposed to be out of the house at all."

Lee was done being embarrassed over drawing on the man.

"Mind your manners when you speak to a lady," he said to the Irishman. "And take your hand off that bridle."

The hard green eyes on him again.

"An' you'll do what if I don't? Will you be pullin' out your pistol to frighten me, then?"

"Micky—please . . ."

"Never you fear, Missy. This one'll take no offense. You'll not be takin' offense, now, will you, gunman?"

"I take no offense at all," Lee said, beginning to see some humor in this. "I had no business drawing on you, no need to, either." He slid his right foot back clear of the stirrup, then kicked out hard.

The Irishman was quick, for all his size, and might have stepped aside, but for keeping his grip on the bridle. As the man tried his sideways step, the mule shifted and held him.

Lee's kick caught him fair in the middle of his chest and drove the wind out of him with a grunt.

"*Don't!*" the woman said sharp in Lee's ear. He reached down and yanked the coiled whip from its tie and shook out the long lash. The Irishman let go the bridle then and did the

33

clever thing. He didn't try to clear the length of the lash—he came in under it, and fast, reaching up for Lee with surprisingly small hands. Lee found, as sometimes happened in such circumstances, that he had all the time he needed, that everything occurred as slowly as in a dream.

The woman still crying out, still plucking at him, he reversed his grip on the lead-loaded handle of the whip, raised it, and struck down across the Irishman's head as the fellow reached up and almost grasped him.

The weighted butt of the handle smacked into the man's skull with the sound a bar-keeper's wet towel made slapping mahogany.

The Irishman crouched motionless, for an instant, his hands still reaching. Then, as Lee raised the whip handle again, the man brought his arms up to guard himself . . . and all this so slowly that Lee seemed to have all the time there was to stare down at the fellow's short-cropped ginger hair, the beginnings of a bald spot at the top.

Lee leaned out further from the saddle (give the mule its credit; it would stand) and reaching, swung the whip butt down, beyond the Irishman's blocking hands, and caught him smartly over the back of his head. This time the sound was harder, with more *crack* to it. Wood on wood, it sounded.

The Irishman made some sort of sound and bent at one knee. His right hand fell away from the side of his head; the hand was shaking very rapidly. Result of the blow, Lee assumed.

The man's position was such, now, that Lee could see his left temple bare of any protection. Lee felt better than he had in some time. He had wanted work suited to him and here it was. The woman was striking at him, slapping at his back.

Not enough to disturb.

He raised the lead-loaded handle, and watched the Irishman's bare temple all the while. He thought that surely he would break the fellow's skull with this blow. If not this one, then the next.

He swung the whip-butt down with all his strength, swung it starting from the muscles at the small of his back, then his left side, and then from his belly. The strength of his arm was the least of it.

Staring up at him—seeing, as he must, even in that instant trip-hammer of motion, that Lee would kill him—the Irishman, his right arm shaking, wagging out as helpless as a baby's, lifted his chin and spit up at the man above him.

Not much of a spit. A dribble was what it was, and ran down his spade chin.

Lee could not stop the blow, could not because it was already an accomplished thing. Could not, because he was not in perfect agreement with himself to stop it.

But he turned it. And his muscles cramped with the effort.

The whip handle caught the Irishman's left

arm, where it still was raised, crooked, above his head, and struck and snapped the long forearm bones. The force of the blow knocked the fellow down.

"Be damned to youse!" The Irishman shouted, rolling in the green. He got half up onto his other elbow. "Be damned to ya, ya dirty fucker!" He struggled, tangled in vines at the track's edge. Rolled almost under the mule's hooves.

Lee was no longer angry. Wondered why he had been angry before. "I told you to guard your tongue before a lady," he said, leaned down out of the saddle, and struck the Irishman sharply across his broken arm with the whip handle.

The man cried out at that, then lay still.

Nancy Lorena Parker, silent now, slid off the mule and bent over the fellow, clucking as if he were a lap dog gone sick from chocolates. She plucked at him as she had at Lee, trying to comfort him, to turn him, to do him good.

It was apparent there was to be no riding away and leaving this foul-mouthed Irishman unsuccored. Lee swung off Nameless, and went to help her.

The Irishman, that last blow being, apparently, more than he could bear, had gone into a Celtic faint, and was only roused when Lee put the woman gently aside, took the man under his arms (the left flopped like a puppet's) and dragged him well to the side of the track and into soft greenery.

The Irishman cursed Lee then, and lifted his right hand to hit at him, but Lee pushed it away. Fellow had spirit enough, if not manners.

"Micky," the white-skinned woman said, "I'm so sorry! So sorry you should have been hurt like this . . ."

"Doin' me job," the Irishman said, shrugging Lee away, and trying to sit up. "The bloody t'anks I get!" He managed to sit up then, his long, rawboned face gone as white as the woman's in his pain. "An' I'll be seein' youse, me foine cowboy. I'll be seein' youse again, an' then Sweet Jasus help ya!"

There was not much funny in that nor in the look on his face. Centuries of bitter no-forgetting, in that face . . .

"You and the Pope's ass," Lee said, to see what the fellow would say to that, then apologized to the lady for his language.

But the Irishman would rise to no bait. He had had his say, and now sat, legs spraddled, in a deep blanket of vines and grass, cradling his broken left arm in his unbroken right.

"Mister Daley—*Micky*—please come on to the house. I'll send Lucy for Mister Quarles at the camp."

"I can get to the bloody camp on me own." The Irishman gritted his teeth, managed to get a leg under him, knelt up, and then, with a considerable effort, climbed to his feet. Stood swaying, looking at Lee with a face still as stone. Green eyes harder than stone. "But I thank 'ee anyway, Ma'am." Kept watching Lee, thought, as if he were engraving his features on some copper plate at the back of his own aching skull. He was not swaying now. Stood straight enough, steady enough on his feet.

No broken head-piece, then. Just the broken arm.

"Then get trotting to that camp, and get doctored," Lee said to him. "And the next time you're rough with me, or rude to this lady, I'll kill you." This with a smile, to show the fellow it wasn't temper talking.

"Micky . . ." The woman's face was white as bleached muslin, distraught, except for the twin round darkness of her spectacles.

The Irishman paid no heed to either of them. He turned his sweatered back and tramped off down the narrow track quite steadily, seeming, from the set of his shoulders, wide as a door, to be nursing his broken arm as a mother might her baby, as he trudged away.

Something occurred to Lee which ought to have occurred to him before. The woman was standing staring after the Irishman, still seemed worried over him; or something else.

"You didn't take that surrey out this path. Too narrow a way."

She turned those small round lenses to him, black as night.

"No. I went out north, out to the pike. And I was foolish to do it. Foolish to think that Daley wouldn't find it out . . ." She appeared to decide she'd said enough, and stood silent for a moment, staring at Lee in much the same way the injured Irishman had.

"I apologize for that brawl," Lee said. "I doubt all that was called for—just for some rough words."

Silence at that, though. Only that continued long look. Then she essayed a smile, managed it, brought one snow-white hand up from her dress to touch her pale-lipped mouth as if to assure herself she was smiling, and said, "You couldn't be blamed. Daley . . . Daley is set here as a sort of watchdog, a . . . a sort of Cerberus, you see. But I thought he would be at the camp today . . ."

Lee coiled the blacksnake whip and went to fasten it to his saddle-bow. The mule, disinterested in noise and struggle, was cropping at the grass growing deep beside the trail.

"Come—I'll help you up," he said.

"We can walk," she said. "I'd rather walk. It isn't far at all, now."

"All right." Lee drew the rein over Nameless's head and led him out, the mule following with no fuss at all. The woman walked to catch up—appeared to be a good walker (long stride on her, under the white material of her dress). Lee could see why she wore white. The contrast of any darker color would make her skin look like a corpse's.

"Well . . ." she said, sounding as if she'd put the distress and violence of the fight behind her, "well, this has been an afternoon it would be difficult to forget! An adventure! I believe that any woman would regard it as a genuine adventure—rescued from a wreck, *and* a guardian-keeper—and all before lunch!"

She sounded gay as a schoolgirl, and nearly skipped along at Lee's side, her white cheeks just slightly flushed with pink as she walked.

Lee had the notion that Miss Nancy Lorena Parker did not, or was not allowed to, get about very much. Perhaps because of her health . . . perhaps some other reason. The Irishman—Daley—was an odd sort of nurse for a lady.

"An adventure," she'd said. That was true enough; he'd thought the same himself even before the trouble with the Irishman. An adventure . . . before lunch. Lee found himself more interested now in the lunch. For a solid meal of good food, he'd be happy to skull any number of rude Hibernians.

Worse things to be doing, for a man with only a few dollars to his name. Worse things to be doing then walking down a narrow way, green close on either side and a Nameless mule trailing, with a lively woman, white as iced-cream, and very odd.

And all, he hoped, tending toward that lunch.

CHAPTER TWO

CHAPTER TWO

"Would you care for more chicken?" she said. "Lucy has a way with chicken, I believe. Some Indian herbs or other. She bakes it."

Lee swallowed the considerable bite that was in his mouth, then nodded and said it certainly was choice. Very particular chicken indeed.

They sat in fine-carved satin-seated chairs with lion-claw feet at either side of a Chinese table, in a wonderfully elegant drawing room with yellow silk curtains. This was a rich room —rich in comfort, rich in look, rich in odor. It smelled of money and the pride of money.

An odd room, in an odd house. Very odd, to be found deep in north-west woods, weeks from Portland, weeks from Seattle.

They'd walked another quarter of a mile along that narrow trace, the mule plodding behind. Nancy Lorena Parker chatted of this and that, as easy and thoughtless as if she were not an oddity . . . as if she had not been upset in

43

her carriage . . . had not met a wanderer, hungry, unshaven, armed. Had not been braced in the way by an Irish bruiser.

Had not seen that man beaten down and bone-broken.

Cheerful as a singing bird, Nancy Parker had strolled, chatting, her white face lively behind the black spectacles. Lee walking beside, leading Nameless and exchanging pleasantries, his belly growling now and then like a cougar up a tree.

Then the green-closed track had come to a trellis of grape vines—catawbas, perhaps—and gone on under that and out onto a wide and wider stretch of close-cropped grass, so cropped and fine-grown, cut so close, that Lee might have supposed it a house lawn.

They walked up this stretch, the woman still talking in her fine dry eastern drawl, walked on up the stretch, the mule thumping along behind, until Lee looked up ahead to a slight rise and saw the house.

He stood stock still then, the mule shuffling to a stop behind him. The woman, speaking of Seattle, walked on a few paces till she noticed he'd stopped, then stopped herself, looked back, and smiled.

"It is a sight, is it not?"

It was, indeed.

It was big, in the first place—a tall two stories, and with wings at either side. Thirty rooms, it must have had, and asphalt shingling the only dark thing about it. The rest of it was white, white as the woman's skin, shaped in New England style of clapboard, and trimmed and finished and decorated with lacey gingerbread as fine-carved, snowy, and clean as the icing on a Chicago wedding cake.

Lee had seen houses as fine, houses the like, with turrets and verandas up high and wide, wide porches below. Had seen houses as fine, but none finer. Unless the stone mansions on Nob Hill . . . But those were mansions. This was a house.

And buried deep, deep within a wood.

"More chicken, Mister Morgan?" Here, in the soft shadows of her home in the curtained room, she had taken off her smoked glass spectacles, set them aside on a small occasional table bearing a filigreed brass lamp. Her eyes shone deep red. They were like living rubies in her face.

She looked an ivory figure, long and thin and white, set with those two rare stones for decorations.

Lee had finally had enough of the chicken. Enough, too, of the sugared rolls, the lemonade (the lemons up from California, like as not, at a hell of a price), the hot potato salad, hot biscuits (beaten biscuits, by the size and taste of them), the creamed herring. A wild cherry tart . . .

The three of them had been greeted at the house's porch by a small, slight Indian woman with cleaner cut features than most. Brown eyes, pitch black hair streaked with grey, done in pigtails down her back. This woman wore a neat long black housekeeper's dress, like a white woman.

"Lucy, I've brought a guest home for lunch. A famished guest, I believe."

The Indian woman had looked at Lee with lively curiosity—appeared amused at his appearance no doubt—and the mule. "Hokay!" she'd said. "I fix big lunch!"

And so she had. Another Indian, an old man named Charlie, had come 'round to take the mule out back to the stable. Both these Indians—the same West Coast tribe as far as Lee could tell (both had the same tattoos, strippled lines marked down their cheeks, as if they'd wept blue tears) both of them dressed in white people's clothes—seemed more at ease with whites than most Redskins were. Lucy was a better cook, too, than most Indian women Lee had known. She cooked as well as a colored woman might, if this lunch was any sample.

The wild cherry tart was one of the finest articles of baking that Lee had ever put into his mouth. He had two large pieces, though the second one nearly made him sick from fullness. The cherries tasted warm from the tree; the crust (it only had a bottom crust) tasted of toasted butter.

It was the best food he'd had in more than a year. The *most* food, too, at a sitting.

The red-eyed woman sat back in her chair, nibbled this or that, and watched him eat. She leaned forward to pour more coffee for him.

"May I ask a somewhat personal question, Mister Morgan?"

"Yes, ma'am."

"Are you . . . well, you seem to be a dangerous man. You certainly dealt roughly with Micky Daley, and he is accounted a dangerous man hereabouts." She offered him the sugar (ground to powder in a small silver bowl). "You seemed very adept . . ."

"Something of a bully, is what you mean?"

"No. No, I didn't. Not at all." She looked down, translucent alabaster lids covering those ruby eyes. She was not a pretty woman, really. Her wrists were thin as a child's. "I meant that you could kill a man—would have killed Micky Daley, wouldn't you? but you decided not to."

A personal conversation, then, and if Lee hadn't been drunk with the rich food and the steaming coffee, it would have seemed stranger.

"He tried to spit at me, knowing he was a dead man. I liked him for that."

"Yes," she said, and set her coffee cup down on the Chinese table. "Yes, I see. But you weren't afraid. He startled you, but then you weren't *afraid* of him."

Lee thought the lady had been badly upset by the fight, more than she'd let on, apparently. Odd how women who faced the most terrible danger and agonies in childbirth, the event a desperate one of blood and fear, were none the less confounded by a simple country brawl, an ordinary beating.

"No need for me to be," Lee said. "I have a knack for that sort of thing. That fellow was strong enough, and had sand . . ."

"But not . . . a knack?"

Lee laughed. "Enough, likely, to knock my ears off in a fist fight."

"I think not," the red-eyed woman said, and put down her coffee cup. "Would you like to see this house? Do you think it handsome?"

"You have a wonderful home," Lee said, and got up out of his chair with a slight grunt. Suddenly he felt shabby, unshaven, trail-dirty. Talk of this house had done that, he supposed.

"This is not my home," she said. Standing, she was only a few inches shorter than he. "This is George Petroff's house."

She led the way out of the drawing room, across the entrance hall, and up a wide, burgundy carpeted flight of stairs.

She stopped on the landing, and turned to face him. "Have you heard of Mister Petroff, Mister Morgan?"

"No, I haven't."

"Mister Petroff's father was the Russian governor of Alaska and of some of this coast as well." She turned and started up the next flight.

"I thought the British used to own this territory," Lee said, following her.

"Mister Petroff doesn't recognize their claim, either, as his father did not." At the top of the staircase, she turned right, and led Lee down a wide corridor, carpeted and decorated on either wall with prints and pictures, small gilt sconces on slender stands. There were fern plants here and there along the walls placed in large brass pots.

They had passed four doors on either side, when Nancy Parker paused at a fifth (on the left) opened it, and walked in.

It was not an entrance to a room, as he had thought. It gave onto a short hallway that ended in glassed double doors. Her shoes, invisible beneath her skirts, tapped crisply on the hardwood flooring, were silent on a small Turkish rug, then tapped again till she reached the double doors, paused to take her folded spectacles from a pocket of her dress, a wide-brim straw hat from a stand, then opened the doors and stepped outside into sunlight and tree shadow as Lee followed her through.

It was a balcony, open, unroofed, that appeared to run clear 'round the west side of the house's second story. The white-painted palings of the rail were carved as elaborately as may be, each one a small slender replica of a tropic palm tree, scaly bark, leaf-fronds, and all.

Below them was the lawn, half hidden, at this height, by great hemlocks and spruce that towered on up past the balcony to throw wide shadows down upon the house. Beyond was forest, an Afghan plaid of light greens and dark greens, and other greens darker still. The

49

forest seemed to roll out almost forever, but there was, in the distance, something shining in the sun.

"The Rostov—The Rusty, it's called now."

"River."

"Yes—and the only feasible carrier for big timber out of these forests."

It was a view and a half, and the highest Lee had yet gotten of this country. Air went with it, fresh and pine-scented, faintly hazed with spring pollen from the shrubs and woods grasses. Refreshing, after the perfumes and sachets, the pot-pourri that perfumed the house . . .

The afternoon sun blazed down as if to compensate by this temporary brightness, for all the rainy, dark days to come. Even in summer, Lee'd been told, this country stayed wet, stayed dark and cloudy.

Nancy Lorena Parker stood beside him, looking out into all the brightness through her smoked glass spectacles. Dark and cloudy, for her always. Or else she'd burn up in the sun, as evening moths did in kerosene lamps.

"I own two thousand acres of prime timber, Mister Morgan." One slilm, white hand rose from her skirt to point to the northwest. The hand was laced with veins definite and dark blue as if a child, playing with an ink pen, had etched them. "That small piece of timber was a . . . gift, from Mister Petroff. Not so rich a gift, after all, since only a few acres of it border the river . . ." The white blue-veined hand swept

50

further north, pointing along the angle of the corner of the house.

"Now, however, George has bought—for a huge sum of money—the rights to seventy thousand acres to the north of his old sections. Timber that runs right back to the slopes of the Cascades."

She was silent after saying that. Thinking, Lee supposed—or dreaming. Great sums of money, great stretches of land often interrupted conversations temporarily by their mention while people contemplated them, dreamed of them . . .

"Handsome property," Lee said. And didn't care to say what he'd often wished to say when he'd been given his orders by this foreman, or that ditcher, that greengrocer.

I have owned as much—and more beautiful.

"Yes," she said, and turned her blank spectacular gaze on him. "Fine property." She tucked her naked white hand back into the folds of her dress. "Mister Petroff," she said, "makes few mistakes—very few in a business way. But there is no man who is perfect, dearly though some like to believe it of themselves. No man is perfect—at anything. And when he paid a great fortune for that seventy thousand acres of wonderful first-growth, Mister Petroff forgot that I owned two thousand acres on the east bank of the Rusty."

"You cut him off," Lee said. "You bar him from the river!" He was amused to feel his heart thumping, as if this opportunity was his to take advantage of, to hold a timber baron cold to ransom. To hold him . . . to press him 'till he squealed . . .

"Yes," she said. "I do." Then turned from Lee to look out over the country again. "Or I could, if it were possible."

"He can't skid around—he can't drag his timber to water another way?"

"He could," she said, staring out over the miles of green to the glint of the distant river. "If he cared to take two years and more to blast through a granite bluff." She smiled and shook her head. "It's unlikely George would chose to do that."

"Then it strikes me you've got him," Lee said.

"Then it strikes you wrong, Mister Morgan. For I do *not* have him." She still looked away, talking out to the shining day. She smiled. "George Petroff has *me*. Has had me since I was . . . since a friend of his discovered me." She walked to the balcony rail, stood looking down.

"I was a teacher in a school for children in St. Louis . . . blind or deaf ones. It seemed as good a life as any, for someone with my peculiarity."

She turned to look at Lee, and he smiled into his reflections in her spectacles.

"Not more peculiar. Striking, I would say."

"Very kind . . . very neat. What a strange sort of a man you are, Mister Morgan! I've no doubt you've killed men; you came within an ace of killing Micky Daley this morning.

You're penniless, mounted on a mule, but you have the manners—and the table manners—of a gentleman. And now you compliment an albino lady as if she were rose-cheeked Lillian Russell! A man of parts."

Nothing a man could say to that sort of thing. It was a kind of talk that ladies used when they wished to hear their own voices on a subject. Besides, it seemed to Lee there was business mentioned before his compliment had upset her.

"*Striking,*" the white lady said, and threw her head back like a laundress and laughed. Her gums, her tongue, were pale as ivory. When she stopped laughing, she said, "In New Haven, children used to throw stones at me in the street. Stones—and, on occasion, horse manure. Once an Italian woman attacked me with a knife; she thought I'd cursed her daughter, given her a cancer of the breast by my evil eye." She smiled at Lee. "Striking? Yes, I suppose George's friend thought I was that. He brought George to the school for a visit. George spoke to me once classes were done—the principal hoped, I suppose, for a charitable donation—George spoke to me, explained what he enjoyed (and what he paid for it) and left his card."

She stopped talking then for a moment, and looked out and down through the air to the wide lawn beneath, as if she'd dropped something and was trying to locate it.

Lee had nothing to say.

"Mister Petroff is a . . . collector of oddities. In . . . women. He told me once, he'd paid an Albanian a hundred pounds to . . . for the use of a girl for one week. The girl had been born a monster, you see. She had neither arms nor legs. George told me she was disappointing. A watering pot, he called her. Said she'd leaked at both ends the whole week . . ."

She turned from the balcony rail. "You see before you, Mister Morgan, the last—as of this date—of a series of very odd . . . very *striking* ladies in service to George Petroff. I could tell you . . . Did you know that he had a Digger Indian girl deafened (she was already blind and mute) so that she would be *perfect*? And before you blame George, before you judge Mister Petroff too harshly, you should know that it was the girl's mother, who, for payment of seventy-five dollars, pushed needles into her daughter's ears."

She stood for a moment after that, gazing at Lee as if she expected some considerable response to such a tale—and tragic enough, it was. But Lee had known too many whores (too many ladies, as well) to be shocked by what any man (or any woman, either) might prefer to be partnered by in bed. Petroff's tastes were, of course, unfortunate, if this red-eyed woman was telling the truth.

It was certainly more unfortunate for Nancy Lorena Parker to have been picked out and chosen by a man for her oddity. Enough of a circumstance to twist any woman's heart.

"A sad fellow," Lee said.

"Yes, indeed—and due, I hope, to be far sadder." The brim of her straw hat threw a dark slanting shadow across her face. "I would like to ask you an odd question, Mister Morgan —an impertinant one, you may believe . . ."

"Ask away."

"Well, then—have you any experience of business at all?"

An odd conversation, with a snow-white lady (a kept lady, it appeared) on an upper balcony overlooking a wilderness of timber.

"I have had—not too fortunately, as you can see."

She would not be diverted. "Of what kind?"

"I have owned two ranches and run them."

Nancy Parker drew a deep pleased breath, brought her narrow white hands out into sight, made a delicate fist of the left, and pounded it gently into her open right hand.

"Then tell me," she said. "What is the greatest difficulty a rancher experiences, in the usual way?"

A woman as odd as her looks, apparently.

"In the north, winter feeding."

She nodded, the shadow of her hat brim riding up and down her long white face. "And the second greatest difficulty?"

"Maintaining an open range."

"And the third?"

"The banks."

The woman laughed. "You have that, at least, in common with George Petroff. Or

55

had—he has his own bank, now. Found it easier borrowing."

"And would you like to know how I came to my present pass? About the loss of those two ranches?"

It still disturbed him, he found, to talk about it. Made him angry.

"No," she said. "I am sorry."

"Oh, it's quite all right," Lee said. "Hoof-and-mouth killed my stock. I was . . . doing something else at the time."

"I am sorry," she said.

A bird flew up into the hemlock branches that dropped high above the balcony. Lee caught the flash of red out of the corner of his eye. Red against the green. Nothing but green in this country; a man began to long for the grey of granite, black mud . . . any other color.

Lee thought, perhaps, that Nancy Parker had something in mind in nature of a payment for that fine lunch. The morning's adventure had turned to talk of money. Talk of business . . .

This odd man . . . Petroff.

"Mister Morgan," the pale woman said and made the same frail decisive strike at her delicate hand with a delicate fist. "Mister Morgan, I am in need of a partner in that timber land."

The red bird flirted its tail in the hemlock's foliage, then flew away. No song to be sung there, apparently. Perhaps it wasn't a singing sort of a bird.

Lee's father had certainly hired his gun, if that was what the lady intended for him, and it seemed to be. Amusing that Lee had thought such doings beneath him at one time. Of course, now that he had been contemplating an armed robbery of some sort, the notion of using his revolver to make his money seemed more in the natural course of things. More respectable. And he had, to be sure, used weapons many times to *keep* what he had.

It seemed to split hairs to argue he shouldn't do the same to attain property in the first place. Unless she had something else in mind . . .

"What sort of a partner?" Lee said. "And for what part?"

"I will deed one half of my interest in that river-edge land to you, Mister Morgan." Black, gleaming circles of her spectacles. "And, I presume, you will do what you must to protect your property."

Despite himself, Lee felt his heart thumping as if he'd run for his life. A half interest in that land was wealth for sure, if he could hold it . . . if she meant it, and wasn't a mad woman kept here confined for her madness. If there *was* river land, and a George Petroff who must have it . . .

"Protect my share, then—and yours, of course, incidentally."

"Of course. My interest would become your interest, Mister Morgan. Against all others."

Lee went to hitch a ham onto the balcony

rail, and half sat there, resting. He'd learned some time ago, that haste in business, and business this seemed to be, meant waste indeed.

She turned to watch him, the shade of her hat brim shifting its angle across her white face.

"There are men who could be hired to protect your interests and for a good deal less than a half share."

"Possibly. I know none such, and do not see how I could trust such a man not to be—influenced by George. Or frightened away. George has frightened away many men, and, I believe, has killed other men who were not frightened away."

"A desperate man, then. As well as specific in his tastes."

"Delicately put," she said, and smiled under the shade of her hat. "Yes, as well as that, George is a determined man. He is *determined* about anything that he owns, or wishes to own. It is, I believe, a sort of mania with him."

"I've known plenty with that mania," Lee said, "and damned determined, too, if you'll excuse my language."

"Perhaps," she said. "I have known only George Petroff, of that type."

"Well, you know two of them now."

She laughed at that, showing, for an instant, her white teeth, her ivory tongue. "Then I've chosen well? You accept?"

Lee felt the excitement of great good fortune

flowing through him like the captive lightning medicine-show men could start through a man's hands and hair with their copper globes. The house, the white railing, the whiter woman standing before him with her spectacles and straw hat . . . the air and light of the early afternoon . . . all shone around him, brighter and clearer, as if his eyes had grown as keen as a hawk's.

If it was a dream, he didn't care to break it.

"I'll take the offer," he said. "A fifty-percent interest on that land. If you'll trust me with it."

"Oh, I don't trust you, Mister Morgan—I don't know you well enough for that! I doubt I shall ever know a man well enough to trust him with valuable property—with my only property. It is simply that I have no choice. It is you, or no one. And Mister Petroff will be back from Tamisket tomorrow."

"For lack of better, then."

"That is it precisely, Mister Morgan. Without your possible aid, George Petroff would have my note to that property by evening tomorrow."

"By force?"

"By any way he chose, Mister Morgan. As it is, it will be you he exercises his determination upon. And for that I am, believe me, profoundly grateful."

She turned smoothly as an actress and went back inside through the glass double doors; Lee rose from the railing, and went after her.

In the house's cool shade, she talked while going down the hall. "I'll write you your bill of sale, Mister Morgan—have you a dollar?"

"Yes."

"Then that will suffice for the purchase of one thousand acres of prime timber, inextricable from mine. A *real* half-interest, I believe I've heard it called . . ."

"That's what it's called."

Down the long corridor, to the head of the staircase. She had a considerable stride for a woman. Went with her long face. Lee found he was getting used to her color—or lack of it.

"I will write out a plain paper. Lucy can witness it; she's a Christian, and has been taught to read . . ."

"You do not have to give away half your property, to interest me," Lee said, and regretted it the moment the words left his mouth. "I mean that some lesser share—say, a quarter, or a fifth . . ." and felt himself more the fool the more he'd said.

Nancy Parker stopped on the stairs, and looked back up at him, unpinning her hat as she did. She'd taken her spectacles off before. Eyes as red as wine was by candlelight. "Goodness," she said," what a thing to say!" She smiled up at him. "You are either a romancer, or an honest man, Mister Morgan. I trust that neither will handicap you in dealing with George." And went on down the stairs, her hat swinging in her hand, her floss-white hair like a ghost's in the dim stairwell's light.

"Don't think," she said, taking his dollar, and motioning the Indian woman to sign both copies she had handwritten on the same Chinese table where they had lunched, "don't think to make this agreement, Mister Morgan, then simply trot off to Seattle, or nearer, to Berrytown, to appeal to the law."

"I don't imagine that would be much use."

"Good. Because it would be of no use at all. Mister Petroff is a Democrat, a mover and shaker in Territory politics, I understand. In any case, he fears no law—except perhaps the Federal people, since the marshal is a Republican. It is believed locally, however, that the marshal is a venal man. And if that is true, then George need not fear him, either."

"No surprises for me there," Lee said. "I expected to have to work for my share." He took his copy from the table after the Indian woman had signed it with a clear enough hand (the good penmanship, the tall, looping t's and l's of a missionary school). One page, and a document which would give a San Francisco lawyer fits. But neatly written, clearly dated, signed and witnessed; it would stand in any territorial court in the West, providing it couldn't be proved one of the signers were drunk, or held at gunpoint (or, in Texas, paying a gambling debt).

It would do.

And Lee Morgan owned land again. An interest in land, at any rate, for whatever the traffic would bear. If he could hold it.

He folded the paper, placed it carefully in his snap-top purse, then in his jacket pocket.

"I'll want to get a copy of this made and filed in town at the land office. Have you any objection, ma'am?"

"None at all. I believe it a wise precaution." She sat back in her chair, and seemed to regard Lee with some satisfaction. "Partner," she said, and smiled.

"I'll be guided by your wishes," Lee said, "as regards this property. Do you want to work it for timber or hold it for sale?"

Her ruby eyes grew bright as a child's with a secret. "Oh, I think . . . for sale," she said.

"You wouldn't mind letting Petroff have it, then?"

"Not at all," she said, gleeful. "He may have it for—what do you say, partner? Three hundred thousand dollars?"

Enough money even split in half to live very well on for very long. Enough money to buy back both ranches. Spade Bit . . . Rifle River . . .

Lee felt almost sick with pleasure. He had them back, and in this fantastic manner. In this fairy-tale fashion. *He had them back!*

And, in the proper fairy-tale way, he had only to defeat the dragon to win all.

"That sum is agreeable to me," he said. "If Petroff—or someone else—will pay it."

"Oh, no one else will even try—they will be

afraid to. Wentworth Company has the capital, I understand, but they would not go against George in this. No one will try to buy against George. He'd kill them.''

"And can he wait us out? Can he winter over, get his timber cut, and wait for a year or so to market it?'' A serious question. Lee had no notion that he could outwait a man who nearly owned the territory. Time would lie on Petroff's side, not Lee's and this odd lady's.

"No,'' she said, and Lee saw her narrow hands grip the upholstered arms of her chair, white against yellow damask. "No, he can't wait to raft his timber down, not from the Cascades. He owes those men a million dollars and more in notes. He must timber that land or lose it.''

Nancy Lorena Parker was near vibrating with joy at this. Lee wondered which cause she had to hate Petroff the worse—his purchase and use of her, or her own oddity, that had persuaded him?

In any case, Petroff had apparently not found it possible to love his albino lady, nor she to love him. Perhaps she hated him for this, more than for the other. Lee was not fool enough to suppose that he could ever know any woman's heart down to the quick. Certainly not such a creature's as this. Long, slight, bony lady—a virgin, like as not, before Petroff got her into his house in the woods, and likely exercised upon her some variations not usually employed upon decent women.

She must have dreamed of her fairy-tale as well (to change from oddity to lady loved by this timber prince). That dream had not come true.

Nor might his, unless he was quick and careful.

"I'll need a loan, partner, against future profits, if you have the cash money."

"I believe that I can advance you two hundred and sixty dollars, Mister Morgan, if you can tell me why that's necessary."

"It's necessary because neither the land-office clerk, nor some jack attorney in Berry-town to do the needs, nor your Mister Petroff is going to take very seriously a man whose toes are poking from his brogans and who, for transport, uses a spavined mule."

She made an amused face, perked down at his shoes, and said, "I take your point, partner. I will risk a year of hoarded pin money (Mister Petroff doesn't believe in spoiling)—I will risk my pin money on you."

"I won't waste it," Lee said. "I'll repay it on sale."

"On sale," she said, and put her hand up to touch lightly at her pale lips, a gesture Lee had seen her make before. "I only hope that George doesn't kill us both prior to any sale taking place."

"That difficulty will be my part in the business, partner."

"Yes . . . yes, I suppose that it will." The albino woman looked suddenly tired. Her long white face, handsome enough, if not pretty, suddenly seemed slightly roughened, fallen a little from its fine texture to something faintly coarser, ivory turned to shot silk. "George will not be come till late tomorrow," she said. "I suppose it would not be too improper for you, as a business acquaintance, to be my guest for dinner, to stay in the east wing if you chose. It's a long ride back to town, Mister Morgan, and would be a late start for you."

"I'll stay till morning," Lee said, "if that won't inconvenience you—won't make things more difficult with Petroff. You might prefer to come into town with me, then. He's unlikely to make it pleasant for you when he learns of this property matter."

A tired smile at this. Lee supposed that the day's events—the carriage wreck, the wandering, sun-struck, then the fight with that fool Irishman—had all been too much for her. Might, in fact, have left her too unsteady to be sensible about this timber business.

She was a clever woman.

"I gather you're concerned that I might have bitten off more than I can chew with this business, Mister Morgan, even if you are certain of being able to chew it. Let me put you at ease." She sat straighter in her chair, those odd inhuman eyes (rich red, black pupiled) fixed on him. "I know precisely what I'm doing, and I've thought of doing it ever since George, so uncharacteristically, made me that small gift of land. It was a Christmas gift. I don't suppose it ever occured to him that I might *use* that land, certainly not in any manner that might inconvenience him."

She closed those remarkable eyes (Lee was somewhat relieved to have her gaze off him) and leaned back, weary. "Among other very good reasons, Mister Morgan, I have a motive of profit. I intend to be able to support myself. I intend to be able to live alone, and in comfort, without the aid of a man."

Nothing to say to that. Not surprising that such a creature, having, Lee supposed, been treated as a creature, would prefer her own company, and in comfort, if she could achieve it.

"Do you find all this very strange, Mister Morgan?"

"New, but not so very strange. And, to be blunt, damn good luck for me."

She opened her eyes. "You are a rather odd individual yourself, you know, as a specimen of a man. Oh, not *physically*. But in other ways. I suppose that is why you seemed such a heaven sent . . . partner."

"Doubt I was sent by heaven," Lee said, and she laughed.

CHAPTER THREE

Dinner was a plain meal, though very good. Venison, green peas, greens, and white-flour rolls. Little new potatoes, cold with pickles for a side dish. Baked apples for dessert, and vanilla-bean iced-cream to put on them. Lee had two servings of those . . . some of the best iced-cream he'd tasted.

He'd eaten near as much as he had at lunch, though more slowly. Neither he nor Nancy Parker had much to say throughout. Worried, likely, the two of them. What worried her, unless it was simple apprehension, Lee couldn't tell. What worried Lee was losing through some stupidity this most extraordinary fortune. One hundred and fifty thousand dollars, near as made no difference. His earned share.

If Petroff would pay it—truly had no option but to pay it. If the man *could* pay it. He might, unknown to Nancy Parker, have spent himself into a corner (as Lee had on the wide lands above the Bit) and be unable to pay the sum for that access strip.

Be funny if all they accomplished was to ruin the fellow without enriching themselves. Happened to other business tricksters before them. Killing the goose for the golden eggs . . .

Petroff himself figured small in Lee's thoughts. No matter that he might be formidable. Lee had known a number of formidable men—his own father the most dangerous, in his curioiusly gentle way.

All of these men were dead. Though by no means all at Lee's hand.

No man living who couldn't be whipped, one way or another, at business or whatever or, if not whipped, then killed.

Petroff's grandfather had apparently been what the Spaniards called a "grandee," one of the Tsar's governors, and Petroff appeared to fancy he was the like. Well, the man could fancy what he chose—could purchase an oddity of a lady to do with what he wished, as much relying, Lee supposed, on her loneliness and need for caring, as on his money and his Irish guard, and fear.

This clever man, though, had proved less than clever, giving the woman that crucial strip of timber—had not, apparently, thought what that access to the river might mean to him if ever he purchased timber this side of the Rusty.

Clever or mistaken, cruel or tender, George

Petroff now stood between Lee and a fortune. It seemed doubtful to Lee that any man at all would stand secure in *that* position.

The dinner had been simple, but prime. That Indian woman, Lucy, was a cook and a half. Lee felt afterward as if wrinkles in his belly's interior, accumulated through a year of slim rations or none at all, had finally been starched and ironed out.

He had gotten up from the table, and made his manners to his pale hostess—a sight to behold in a crimson dinner gown (crimson velvet, wine-red eyes, frost-white hair), said good-night, and retired behind the elderly Indian, Charlie, up the broad staircase, then down the corridor a fair distance east past more than four or five other bedroom doors, at last to his, a big, handsome room, with blue French paper on its walls. The paper was printed with small wading birds and white flowers against the blue. A wide bed, a highboy dresser, wash stand, an armchair and occasional table with an oil lamp on it. This with two tall windows looking out over the back of the house's grounds. A cabin there, and the long low roof of the stables. Both of those buildings as fine and spanking white as the house itself. Graveled drive to the stables.

Better than nice.

"Handsome room," Lee said to the Indian who, like his female counterpart, had finer features than most redskins. Some dose of white blood in both of them, Lee supposed.

"Guest room, east wing," old Charlie had said, to nail down its identification with the compliment. "That mule no damn good," he added. "Son-of-a-bitch bites."

This was news to Lee, though not terribly surprising. He could only suppose that the animal had liked him all this while, and so had not practiced biting. It was touching, in its way, being the unknowing object of a mule's affections.

Charlie had then brought up all Lee's plunder, and pretty slight, sad stuff it was, all crowded into a small tent-cloth sack. A clean shirt—or as clean as soaking in a flooded ditch could render it—a pair of socks equally spotless, and trousers of the same material as the sack, something dirty.

Charlie had taken Lee's trail clothes then and there, Lee stripping off to hand them over, taken them down to be scrubbed back of the kitchen. Apparently there were other Indians at work in Petroff's woods.

Charlie was back sooner than expected. Lee was standing naked, recalling dinner, wishing for a tub full of hot water, when he came in with just that article, and pushed it into the room resting on a soft of low, small, wheeled trolley. The tub, a copper hip bath, swayed precariously on this contraption, its steaming water rocking as the trolley rolled over the door sill and into Lee's room. It was a clever way to transport bath water, better by a long shot than having some girl haul hot bucket after bucket. The old Indian grunted as he pushed the thing along the carpet, then paused to spread out some sort of small tarpaulin and shoved the whole kit-and-kaboodle onto that.

"I'll come and get," he said, gestured to the towel and cake of milled soap on the washstand, and walked out, swinging the door closed behind him.

The bath was as good as the dinner had been. Either it was the custom of the house to so welcome a traveler, or Nancy Parker had decided that Lee needed one and as soon as possible. Lee gave not a damn which.

He slid the Bisley Colt's out of its holster, and laid the piece on the canvas, just within reach of the tub. It was certainly possible that George Petroff might decide to return home early from wherever. It was even possible—the thought occurred to Lee as he carefully lowered himself into the bath (the water was hot as blazes, hoisted straight up from the kitchen by dumb-waiter, like as not)—it occurred to him that Nancy Parker might even have planned just such a surprise return with an eye, perhaps, to having a certain ragged drifter (kindly giving lodging) shoot and murder one George Petroff and then properly to be hanged for it.

Lee didn't intend any such domestic entanglements, nor such tricky ones. If, in the remote possibility, the lady had planned such a charade (and all the talk of timber land being but bait) Lee would damn well not cooperate. If

73

he showed all unexpectedly, George Petroff might well be shot, but not mortally. Wing the fellow and high-tail it out of the territory, if that was the plot.

Business was one thing and killing business, too. House-murders were something else. Not much profit there, but the noose.

The bath water was very hot and richly comforting. The milled soap smelled of lilacs. Lee hadn't had a proper hot-water bath in two . . . no, three months. Bath-house in Sacremento. After that, nothing but farm ponds and rain barrels. Ditches, sometimes.

He eased deeper into the bath, felt the water soak into him, steam its way into his bones. The bones of his back clicked softly, a delicate, felt sound, as his back muscles relaxed. He lathered thick, working up a white foam of bubbles and suds along his arms, under his armpits. Reached under water to soap his cock, his ass. Then ran the soap along his legs, scrubbed at his feet with it. Lathered his face, his hair, worked his fingers deep along his scalp, worked the scented soapsuds in. Even bored out his ears with soapy fingers, rubbed the foam well into several day's growth of beard. Have to shave that. No good appearing the tramp in Berrytown. Not now.

Paved with suds, smelling to high heavens of lilacs, Lee grunted with pleasure, stuck his feet in the air, and slid down all the way into the copper tub, head under water, to blow bubbles up into the foamy water.

Then he heaved up, the water still fine and hot, splashed and rinsed—the tarpaulin beneath the trolley a better than good idea—and washed the last of the suds off him, near as he was able. Traces of runs of foam still clung to him, still floated in white rafts atop the bath water.

He was contemplating the coming pleasures of sleep, considering whether these were worth the trouble of climbing out of the bath, when the door-latch clicked, and the door swung open. Old Charlie, for the tub, Lee supposed, but reached out, picked up the Colt's and thumbed the hammer back, just the same. He'd have to lock that door or brace it shut to get a good night's sleep in this house . . .

The small Indian woman, Lucy, came bustling in, carrying a thick white towel folded over her arm, and Lee's brogans, cleaned and polished as well as such weary and broken leather might be.

She stared at Lee a moment, watched him put the revolver down, then nodded, stopped to drape the towel over the armchair near him, and went to put the brogans at the side of the bed.

"Those are no-good shoes," she said. "Worthless."

"I know it," Lee said, not ashamed to be seen naked in a bathing-tub, if the woman wasn't ashamed to see him. "But they'll have to do 'till I get better."

"Mule no good, either," the woman said,

75

standing looking at him, and apparently in no hurry to leave.

"Not a damn bit of good," Lee said, feeling something guilty, though, to be talking down an animal that had carried him so far and without biting him, too, though that was apparently its nature.

"You goin' to fight Mister?"

'Mister' seemed to mean George Petroff. Not many secrets could be kept from house servants, even if Nancy Parker had tried.

"No," Lee said. "Business." The bath water was cooling.

"*Ha, ha, ha!*" The small woman had learned to mimic white people's harsh laughter. Indians—Indian women, at least—usually giggled. Of course, this one had white blood in her. That must make a difference.

"I take tub away," the woman said, and stood waiting, having apparently made all the comment she cared to about Lee's doing business with Mister George Petroff. Lee supposed his shoes and his mule had united to place him mighty low on the totem pole.

And this woman appeared to have no intention of leaving without the damn tub.

So be it, and to hell with her. Lee'd heard that Englishmen bathed, screwed, and shit before servants, male or female, as if those people were empty air.

He gripped the sides of the tub, and heaved himself up onto his feet, feeling curiously weak after the steam and heat of the water. He stepped out of the foam-rucked water onto the tarpaulin, and reached for the towel she'd brought. Thicker, softer stuff than the washstand cloth.

The woman stood staring at him as she had before, didn't seem to care to dissolve into empty air, either. Nice-looking woman, in her way. No spring chicken, to be sure; a woman grown. Handsome face, pretty, well-cut nose, delicate mouth. Eyes her best feature, though —brown eyes, big brown eyes rather than the usual Indian black. If she'd been a white woman, her skin something lighter than light honey-brown, she'd have been considered a looker . . .

Beautiful hair. Rich long black hair . . . fine threads of drawn silver. Her hair reminded him . . .

Damn the woman.

Lee stopped toweling himself. "Why don't you wait outside," he said. "I'd like privacy."

She stood staring at him a moment more, then shrugged.

"I dry you dry," she said, came over, took the towel. Lee tried to hold onto it like a fool, and she jerked it smartly out of his grip. "I done this plenty times," she said, stepped behind him, and commenced to scrub away at his back, brisk as a hospital ward nurse.

His options being to seize this slight woman and toss her out his room door, or be still and be ministered to, Lee decided on the latter. He stood like a horse under currying, shifting slightly from foot to foot, as the little woman worked at him.

Felt well enough. Soft towel . . . strong, small hands. Felt good.

She dried the long muscles of his back, stretched up (he supposed—he couldn't see her) to towel the moisture from his hair, gently rub the back of his neck dry, then down the slope of his shoulders, his arms.

Her hands left him, then, for a moment. Then Lee felt them on the muscles at the back of his thighs. More steady strokes with the softness of the towel down to his ankles, his feet. She tapped at his ankles, first the left, then the right, and Lee dutifully lifted his feet in turn to be neatly dried, heel to toe.

Her hands, the towel were off him again. Then Lee felt a gentle touch at his buttocks. Her hand resting on him there, then the towel stroking at him . . . soft, circling strokes. He felt her hand on him again, gripping him gently for a moment. Then she pried his buttocks apart, drew the cloth up lightly between them. Drying him as if he were a baby. An infant with no secrets at all . . .

He felt her hands on his hips, tugging to turn him.

Lee turned to face her, not embarrassed that his cock was nearly at a stand. Those had been woman's hands upon him, as womanly as could be, and their owner must have expected what she could now see.

And appeared to do so.

The small woman stood looking at Lee's privates in the same direct way she'd stared at his face before. She looked for a moment—he was swollen half-erect, the cock-head already dark red with blood—then she bent with a soft grunt to towel the front of his legs. The same slow, steady, gentle strokes as before.

She finished, stood up, and reached to dry his face with quick neat little patting motions . . . his throat . . . and down and across his chest.

It was remarkable with what pleasures a man could give himself up into gentle hands. Lee shifted and moved slightly under the Indian woman's ministrations, and was more and more pleased. He began to feel there was some knowledge of her growing in him; that her touch, her closeness was allowing him to know her.

An illusion, possibly, one he was seized with, one most men were seized with when they touched a handsome woman, or were touched, caressed by her.

"You're beautiful," he said, like a Reuben at a carnival, but didn't feel too much of a fool for saying it. She *was* beautiful, now that he had a closer look at her. The small features better than fine. She skin like sun-darkened satin, crumpled delicately here and there by what must be forty years or more of living. Her teeth were bad . . . stained. But Indian Lucy was, in her small slight, honey-skinned way, a beauty. Lee marveled that he had missed it after so many weeks with nothing to console him but his hand. (The two dollars that might have gone to a whore, having, when pushed came to shove, gone for two dinners.) Likely he'd been distracted by Nancy Parker. Difficult to take careful notice of another woman, when that extraordinary lack of color, a whole creature of polished silver, red-eyed, stood before you. Though now he came to realize it, she had not the essential fine looks this older Indian woman had. Halfbreed woman, more likely.

She was running the toweling slightly over Lee's belly now; he could feel the small pressures of her fingers through the cloth. Rubbing at him, passing gently over his skin, tracing the lines of muscle across his belly.

"Strong," she said, and stopped rubbing at him. She looked down at his cock. It was up, straining oak hard, and full to bursting with blood. She moved her arm so that her right forearm touched the head of it, only very lightly. Accidently, more than likely. Then she turned to toss the damp towel across the copper tub's near rim.

"You like Miz Parker?" she said, and turned back, looking up at him with that same attentive stare.

"Yes," Lee said.

The Indian woman nodded. Then reached out with both her hands, and gently gripped Lee's cock. She squeezed the thick shaft of it, bending her head to watch what she was doing. She slowly drew her hands up and toward her, as if to milk him of what his privates held.

Lee made a sound in his throat, but stood still.

"She do this," the Breed woman said, then corrected herself. "*Does* this. She does this." The woman looked up from what she was doing, and watched Lee's face.

"She does this for Mister . . . " The small, slender, work-roughened hands moved and moved on Lee, squeezing quite hard, then gently caressing it . . . stroking the length of him lightly with her fingers. "She does this for Mister . . ." The woman suddenly put out a small dark-pink tongue. "She lick his ass for him. I see her do that many time." The small tongue made a licking motion. "Mister makes me and Charlie watch, sometime. She lick his ass for him. She lick my ass, too. Mister told to me pee once. She drink that up . . ." The small woman opened her mouth wide, to show Lee how Nancy Parker had received her urine. "You like to watch that?"

"I suppose so," Lee said.

The small woman nodded, not surprised, then suddenly knelt before him, looked up into his eyes, then opened her mouth wide, and directing him with her clutching hands, took the swollen head of his organ to her lips, and began very gently, as if it were a rare and expensive sweet, to lick and suck at the tip of it. As she kissed at it, suckling, licking—pausing at times to hold still, stop what she was doing, and look up into his face—she gradually worked more and more of his cock into her mouth, though still only the head of it, so that her cheeks bulged out, straining, crammed with it.

Some drops of jism oozed from Lee's cock then and the small woman seemed pleased with that. She pulled her head back slightly, lapping and probing with the tip of her tongue.

Lee reached out and put his hands into her hair to hold her to him, but the woman shook her head sharply, took her mouth from him and leaned back.

She stood up suddenly, then bent down again, gripped the hems of her long black dress and her white petticoats, and drew them abruptly to her waist. She wore black high-button shoes, black cotton stockings and showed, above her garters, small, slim honey-brown thighs smooth and narrow as a girl's. Her cunt was bare, naked but for a shadow of black fur.

Lee got his hand on her there though she reached down to try to stop him, gripped her, and holding her still at the nape of her neck with his other hand, gently worked a finger up into her.

She was stickly, small, and tight, and she struggled a little as his finger went up all the way. She twisted in his arms, a strong little woman, smelling of sweat and laundry soap—a smell of fish-glue about her as well, from where he had his finger. Lee picked her up off the floor, carried her over to the bed and put her down on the coverlet.

She clawed at his arm as he held her down with one hand and slowly pushed a second finger up into her. He could smell her more strongly now.

After a moment, she lay still, clutching at the arm holding her down, staring up at him.

"I won't hurt you. I'm not going to hurt you."

Still holding her quiet, Lee slowly pulled his fingers out of her, out of her sticky tightness, then brought them up to his face, to her mouth. He drew his damp fingertips along her lips, though she tried to turn her head aside on the pillow. He held his fingers, moist, rich with her smell, against her lips, until she opened her mouth just a little, and slowly he slid the fingers into her—felt the soft moving wet of her tongue as she licked them.

She sucked on his fingers and lay still beneath him in a foam of linen and black dress material and lace-edged petticoats. He felt her flesh, her bones with his weight as he pressed down upon her. She was slight as a child, and lay like one, quiet now, licking her liquid off his fingers. She stared up into his eyes as she did it.

Lee leaned back off her for a moment, reached down, gathered her skirt and her underskirts in his hands and slowly furled them back up, gathering the cloth about her

83

narrow waist. When her spraddled thighs were exposed, her crotch, her cunt laid bare, he reached down again, slid his hands under her smooth, cool buttocks (narrow and small—hardly any ass to her) and gripped them. Then he lifted her hips raising her privates as her legs lay slack, spread wide beneath him. He lifted her, held her with one hand, and put his other hand on the small scant-haired mound of her cunt.

He spread her open with his fingers, and she softly parted, split wide as a small sliced steak cooked bloody rare.

Lee knelt, looking into the woman's secrets, the pinks and reds, the narrow liquid hole just showing deep. She looked juicy as a broken melon. He bent down to sniff, to inhale the rich, salty, ripe smell of her.

Then he buried his face in it.

The Breed woman grunted in surprise, and her hips jerked under him, but Lee held her hard, each meagre buttock a smooth, cool handful. He held her hard, and drove his mouth against her, licking at her, into her, biting at her meat gently, thrusting his tongue out so that it hurt at the root—the better to get further up into her, to taste what she had hidden.

It must have frightened her, for Lee felt her kicking out on either side a time or two, and felt her hands reaching down, clutching at his hair. But he paid no heed. It had been too damn long a wait without the *otherness* of a woman against him—something wealthier to the skin and lips and hands than mule hide and saddle leather, than lard-fry dinners, than crates and bridle reins, pick handles and whip handle.

Too damn long to wait for better than those to feel, smell, touch.

He had it now. And might have a fortune, too. But the timberland and cash could be never. The woman was now, here, with him.

The little Breed was settling now, feeling he wouldn't hurt her; feeling more than that. It was a woman's sex that Lee was into and, under his lips and tongue, it spread wider than a girl's (ran longer, too—split the Breed's crotch near down to her small dark smudge of an asshole. It was a feast of a thing, and Lee bent to the enjoyment of it, licking the soft furred lips as a cat cleans her kittens, lapping at the slippery flesh between them, curling his tongue deeper into her to catch what flowed there.

The woman said something in Indian, and Lee felt her fingers clench harder in his hair. Her buttocks, her hips suddenly heaved in his hands, and Lee gripped her fiercely to hold her to his mouth. He wasn't near finished. He sucked at her, drawing the wet warm meat up against his lips—gently put his teeth to her, biting delicately, then sliding his tongue deep into her again.

The Breed called out as if for help in some dangerous strait, wrenched at Lee's hair, and kicked out to either side. He held her and wouldn't let her go, worked at her, licked at her.

She gasped in a great breath of air, bucked beneath him, and drew her knees up high, doubling them to her breasts, presenting herself to Lee open as a book round, and split, and soaking. His face was smeared with her. He raised up on stiffened arms, leaned up above her. Her fine honey-colored face had gone darker, congested, blurred with pleasure close to agony. Her dark eyes were great as a deer's.

Lee's heart was hammering like a donkey-engine. He felt he could shove his hand deep up inside her, his hand and then his arm, and seize her living heart. He felt that he knew her to her bones.

He knelt up straighter, his cock paining him, his stones aching—fumbled to grasp himself— and placed the tip just at her. Then, unable to wait an instant, feeling that nothing could make him wait an instant more, he thrust his hips forward with all his strength.

His cock ran up along the hot, slick trench and socketed into her to the root all at once, and with a soft, wet, smacking sound.

The woman shouted and twisted under his weight as he came down upon her. Lee felt every movement of muscle and bone within her, every twist and heave. It was a sort of dance she did, as if she were dying, or were struggling to ward death away. He felt it all in his cock, as if that swollen, sliding, thrusting thing had become her backbone, the foundation of her.

Her body squeezed down upon that intruding staff that slid and thrust, that rammed into her, then pulled back, then thrust in again. Her body squeezed and clutched at it, wet, oily, and hot, and Lee drove into her again and again as she moaned and called out loud, as if she were in danger.

She was a strong little woman, for all her slightness, and Lee rode her as he would a rank pony—balancing, easing, bearing upon her with his weight. She was sweating, soaking the crumpled cloth bunched between them as she bucked and struggled in her pleasure. Only her throat, her effort-darkened face, were bare above the stuff and collar of her dress. Below . . . below the buttoned blouse, the tight-laced waist, revealed in a blossom of tossed-back white linen and lace, two slender light brown thighs strained wide. Between them was heat and hair, wet red meat and pumping, as Lee fucked into her with all his strength, seeming, thick, straining cock and all, to be too big, too massive for her, for the delicate soaked fork of her groin, the small, swollen, hair-ringed hole that stretched around him as he struck.

Suddenly, she stopped crying out. As Lee moved faster and then faster again, the sounds of their flesh meeting smacking through the room, she began to grunt as with a terrible effort, gritting her teeth, grunting hoarse, deep, desperate sounds, as if she were giving birth.

Lee felt her suddenly stop moving, stop struggling, stop bucking up against him. Instead, her body trembled, trembled in a fine, continuous tremor. And he felt her hands clutching, gripping at his shoulders hard enough to hurt.

A high, keening sound came from her—a note hardly human, a glassy pitch of pleasure almost beyond hearing. Lee felt something within her suddenly clench, grasp him like a fist, hold and hold again. Staring down, half blind with the sweetness of it, Lee saw her look up and into him as if her eyes had been some great physician's probe, or more, the eyes of God almighty.

He groaned to be so known, and came into her as though it were blood flooding out of him. It felt too fine to bear, a joy that hurt him to the backbone. He came and came as if a year and more of loneliness was spurting out of him, pouring into her.

Loved her—as always, in that state. Found this small Breed woman, Lucy, altogether lovable.

And she must have felt something of the same. Her slender arms were around him, holding him to her tight as baling wire. They both lay still, the slight woman taking all Lee's weight, soaked in each other's sweat. She smelled of a wonderful rich winy scent—sweat

88

and flowery woman, and the odor of her sex.

Their breathing slowly eased, became quieter, but still they breathed together for a while.

She murmured something finally, and Lee grunted with the effort and lifted himself off her, felt the damp parting as his cock slid free.

He got off the bed, stood beside it, and looked down at her. She lay quiet in the rumpled lace of her petticoats, made no effort to cover herself, to hide the slick wetness of her crotch, the pearly run of jissom on her thigh. She was watching him with the same direct, candid gaze as before.

"You are fine man," she said, raised one hand, made a circle of thumb and forefinger, then brought up her other hand to thrust a finger in and out of the circle. "You are fine man for fuckin'."

Lee laughed.

"You're some shakes yourself, my dear."

The Breed woman smiled. Despite her stained teeth, the smile enhanced her beauty. "You good for that," she said, sat up and arranged her skirts. "Don't know," she tapped her forehead with a finger "don't know if you a deep man up here—enough to be fightin' Mister."

"I won't be fighting him," Lee said. "Unless he wishes a fight. Unless he interferes with my business . . ."

The small woman said something in Indian and got up, smoothing her skirts. She went to the copper tub, dipped a corner of the towel into the water, and came to Lee without cleaning herself. Just as she had before, she commenced to minister to him, washing his chest and belly, using the damp towel gently to clean his privates. It was a pleasant way of doing.

Lee looked down at her small bent head as she tended to him, her black hair mussed, faintly striped with silver, small curls still plastered in perspiration at the back of her neck. *What lovely creatures handsome women were . . . Each of them a particular beauty.*

"Thank you," he said to her, as she patted lightly at him. She glanced up, smiling. "For me I do—not for you."

CHAPTER FOUR

Lee rode Nameless out at sunup, down the graveled drive from the stables, old Charlie not seeming saddened to see the mule on his way. "Son-of-a-bitch bites . . ."

Lee'd risen at still dark, dressed, and gone down to the kitchens (in his experience, the first part of any house to wake) and found the small housekeeper, Lucy, looking neat as out of a band-box, drinking black coffee and talking with a fat Indian woman who was scooping fine-gauge anthracite coal into a huge, greased indoor range.

The women hadn't seemed surprised to see him up, and Lucy had poured Lee a cup of coffee, then gotten a handful of eggs from the food safe, gone to the stove, and made Lee the finest French eggs he'd ever tasted. She mixed and fried them in a small, buttered tinned pan, added a sprinkle of green stuff, slid them from one side to another, tossed the pan to fold the eggs over as they finished cooking, then slid them onto a plate.

These wonderful eggs, three thick slices of ham—purple-salty country cured, not pale hotel stuff—four biscuits with strawberry preserves (the biscuits belonging to the day before, but reheated in the oven, and almost good as new) and two more cups of coffee to finish, all made a breakfast fit to follow the lunch and dinner the day of before. Lee felt some slight guiltiness as he finished his coffee, considering it was George Petroff's hospitality he was enjoying—and him preparing to nail the fellow, whatever it took.

Some guiltiness, but not enough to bring the breakfast up again.

The Breed woman had had his war-bag ready for him as well, his worn trail clothes cleaned and steam ironed, and folded small to be stuffed into the canvas. As good as a wife, Indian Lucy was proving to be.

Lee stood from the table and picked up his goods. He took the small Breed's honey-brown hand, bowed, then thanked her as if she'd been a lady, then found a bit-piece in his purse and handed it to the fat woman, who giggled, ducked, and tucked it into her garter.

The Breed watched Lee as he went to the kitchen door and out; there was no expression on her face.

Lee had assumed that Nancy Parker would not be up and about at dawn—had in fact decided he'd rather not see her before he left. The danger of her telling him she'd changed her mind . . . begging him to hand that paper back to her . . . It had crossed his mind.

And another thing. The matters the Breed woman had mentioned in her heat. Lee found he preferred not seeing the albino just now . . . embarrassed for her, he supposed. To speak to her, knowing how Petroff had used her, the stunts he'd put her to. Of course, the Breed could have lied—if she could have imagined such lies . . .

He'd gone out to the stable, given old Charlie a bit coin for his bites (one bite actually, on the upper left arm; Nameless had tried for a second, and missed.) It felt odd to be giving out coins, as if he had money (as he did, of course, money advanced by Nancy Parker to her partner). Business money, though, that was. Not really his. And would never sit down easy in his pocket, not till he began to earn it.

He mounted the mule on the graveled drive, and was engaged in booting the animal into motion when he saw Nancy Parker, in white morning dress, picture hat and veil, come down the wide steps from the big house's back verandah, and lift a gloved hand to him.

Lee wrestled Nameless in that direction, booting all the while, and managed to approach her.

"A difficult relationship, partner." Her pale face shone glimmering through her veil in the dawn's light. The morning was brightening, beginning to glow. That slanting new-risen sunlight made reflecting shade and shadows through the fine weave of her veil. Her eyes were dark orange through the mesh.

"Rewarding enough," Lee said. "He hasn't bitten me."

She laughed, and Lee bent forward from the saddle to see her face more clearly. "You're certain you don't wish to come into the town with me? This matter is bound to become unpleasant . . ."

"I look forward to it," she said. "And I can assure you, that leaving this house would not promote my safety in the least. Quite the contrary. George has odd notions . . . of propriety."

Damn sure he did, Lee thought. Well, she knew the fellow best.

"If he changes his notions of . . . propriety, and I believe he will as matters progress in this business, you come into town. I'll see you safe."

She curtsied to him, the lace trim of her dress stirring in a morning breeze. "As you command, sir," she said. "*Partner.*"

Lee held out his hand, and she took it. "I do want you to know, Ma'am, that I appreciate . . ."

" . . . an opportunity to be shot?"

" . . . this, or any opportunity at all. Win or lose—and I believe we'll win—I intend to make this fellow dance."

Her hand lay in his as light as a leaf. The breeze molded her veil to her face. "Yes," she said, "I believe that you will." She took her hand away, and though it was gloved, tucked it into the folds of her skirt out of habit, to keep it from the burgeoning light.

Lee hauled the mule's head around and commenced the kicking necessary to stir Nameless into motion. He spoke over his shoulder "And your hospitality. Thank you for that!" The mule ambled on its way, as if it had decided on its own hook to take a stroll, not under any influence of kicking.

Nancy Parker called after him, "Hospitality here is more a matter of Lucy than myself."

Lee didn't know for certain what she meant by that.

He turned in the saddle to wave, then settled back to steer Nameless clear of a bed of flowers, a course the animal appeared determined on. Lee thought he'd wait till well out onto the road to Berrytown before he dwelt on the reference to Lucy's hospitality. Would wait longer than that before he dwelt on what the Breed woman had said in her heat, the performances that George Petroff might (and might not) have required of pale Nancy Parker. The vision of those . . . exercises. Of Nancy Parker, white as new snow, thin and naked, crouched, bent, stretched, mouth open . . .

He would wait a while before thinking of that.

The day came in with trumpets, clear, vibrating with light. The skies were a fine-grained dazzling blue, only smeared a little with streaks of distant white, and much further than those clouds, the faint notch of a volcano's peak to the west. As the sun rose higher, the breeze that had stirred Nancy Parker's veil had grown into a strumming wind that tossed the tall grasses, the red and yellow flowers—some daisies and batchelor buttons among them that grew up with the grass to the grass's height.

The wind had come up, held for an hour or so, tugging at Lee's Stetson, blowing the long smoke-blackened fringe along his jacket hem, then had slowly subsided and let a spring morning turn to summer noon, sunny, still, and hot.

Lee drew his revolver as Nameless five-footed along, and fired it at twigs and stobs as he came past. He missed his first shot at a knot-tipped twig tipping a willow branch, then settled down and commenced to hit. Ammunition cost money, and he'd hoarded what rounds for the Colt's he'd had, but it seemed that now was a reasonable time to spend them.

He fired across the mule's neck—the animal didn't appear to notice the weapon's blast just past his ear—and clipped the head off a spring flower six feet off the track. The flower'd been pink, very pale, with a small stack of petals not taller than a man's finger, all on a stalk two feet and more in height. There were naturalists, Lee supposed, who could have ridden Nameless, or, if they were lucky, some finer beast, along this track and named each and every plant and animal they saw.

Wonderful thing to be able to do . . .

Professor Riles would have said considerably more wonderful than a knowledge of horse ranching, skill with a revolver, and the last smatterings of Latin, history, and mathematics retained from Riles's academy. Hard to disagree with Riles—but then, it always had been.

Lee, the Bisley drawn, tried a two-handed hold, sighting on a black bark sapling some hundred feet off. Got a good hit, too. It did give a steadier bead . . . might be more accurate shooting for the pot, if a revolver was all you had. Way too slow for exchanging fire with an armed man who knew his business. Might do, though, for law officers dealing with fools and drunks. They'd have time, then, to take their fancy hold.

Lee stood in the stirrups, drew and replaced the Bisley in its holster a few times. Drew as fast as he could, forcing his arm, his wrist. Must be a comic sight, a saddle-bum standing in his stirrups atop a mule, practicing his draw like some fool pimple-face kid.

" . . . Any draw with an angle to it," or something of the sort. Catherine Dowd had told him once that his father had said that. God knows Buckskin Frank Leslie should have known what he was talking about . . .

Lee eased off, relaxed his wrist as he drew, allowed his arm to weary. "No angles . . ."

Easy to say, hard to do. He'd tried many times to remember his father's draw against Curry. But he hadn't seen it—perhaps a flicker from the corner of his eye, then Curry shot and dying, still firing back into gunsmoke in that instant.

Too fast . . . too damn fast to see it all.

Slow enough, after, to see the dying. Lee remembered that well enough. Remembered shooting Curry through the head to put the little man out of his agony. Remembered his father looking weary, a blot of blood at his shirt front. Holstering his revolver, lying down, then, to die.

Remembered that well enough. Enough to wake him in the night with cold sweats sometimes. His father in his arms . . . smaller; he had seemed smaller than before.

Lee stood in the stirrups again, drew and put five fast shots into a small stump well down the track, then rode on through the haze of powder smoke, sat back in the saddle, reloaded the Bisley Colt's and holstered it. His ears buzzed slightly from the gunshots. The scent of powder, of hot gun oil hung on the air; the weight and warmth of the curved walnut grip still printed itself in the palm of his right hand.

The pleasantries of target practice.

He rode into the great clearing of Berrytown just after noon, into the bustle and noise, the rip and whine of bucksaws, shouts of teamsters, all the buzzing, rattling noises of a town busy on business. Timber business, mostly. Huge creaking drays laden with man-tall stacks of sawn wood, still green, still oozing sap, carved their slow way along deep rutted streets. The sun, shining bright and hot today as it had the day before to blind and discomfit Nancy Parker, sparkled on drops of sap and tree-glue dripping from these loads as Lee booted the mule on by. This animal, which had not objected to Lee's shooting practice, objected strenuously to the *crack* of the teamsters' whips, and sidled and danced like a restive thoroughbred under this commotion.

Lot of men in the streets . . . boys. Not many women. Whores would still be asleep. Respectable ladies and workmen's wives would be home, overseeing lunch in the better places, fixing a midday dinner in the shanties.

A newspaper boy was calling out on a corner across the drag and Lee waved to him, shouted for a paper (couldn't hurt to learn the town and territory a bit better) but the boy hadn't heard him and strolled off up another street, still hollering at the top of his lungs for the *Eagle*, or the *Bugle*—it was hard to tell.

Lee gallumphed along, keeping Nameless in order as best he might, and looking through the mix and tangle of every sort of tradesmen's signs hammered up hung or strung along the boardwalks for one that credibly stated "Dry Goods," and finally found that article on his side of the street alongside a China Bakery at the corner of a cross street called Constitution.

Lee hauled the mule over just under the edge of the walk, and reached up to loop the rein over a member beam. It was quite a high walk. Apparently Berrytown stood nearly submerged when the winter rains came down to mix a mud.

Lee swung off, took a wide way around Nameless's hind quarters (might not be caring to bite Lee, might have no such prohibition on kicking) and walked up the boardwalk steps past a jostling jack in calico shirt, corduroy trousers and thick caulked boots, past a whiff of Chinese baking, sweet and odd, smelling of honey and carraway seeds, and into "Sloan's Drygoods Emporium."

Lee never knew if he were waited upon by Sloan himself. The fellow that served him, a long drink of water with no teeth in front, top or bottom, never introduced himself, apparently not expecting any repeat custom from a saddle-bum of Lee's description. He did brighten more and more as Lee bought, but not enough to shake hands or give his name.

The place was smaller than its sign signified, and not stocked to the nines, but it sufficed. Lee tried three pairs of boots, and then bought the second he'd put on, a rough-out pair of high-leg cowhides, hard wearing, and just easy enough to walk in without wincing. He bought two cotton shirts, a brown check, and a blue stripe, and a four-in-hand necktie, dark red. He bought a new pair of underwear short pants, a cotton undervest to match, three new pairs of wool socks, grey, and two pairs of trousers, one of dark brown wool and one of Mister Levi's blue canvas work trousers.

The Stetson was worn, but of quality; he'd keep it.

Keep the old buckskin jacket, too, greasy and black with camp-fire smoke. Keep it.

The long drink of water who might have been Mister Sloan tried to sell Lee a bearskin coat for the coming winter. Winter coming in about five months. Maybe six.

Lee refused the bearskin coat and bought instead a fine blue bandanna big enough to wrap a baby in and some left over, then asked the fellow to tote up. No-teeth took his time, licking at the tip of his pencil stub, and figuring on the back of a delivery bill once, twice, and a third time to be sure.

Sixty-six dollars and fourteen cents. Lee could see he had to deal with boom-town prices; his partner's advance wouldn't be lasting him long.

He asked to look at the bill himself, couldn't make head nor tail of the fellow's figuring, and decided to let it go and pay.

He then changed into the new underwear, the brown checked shirt and brown wool trousers, new socks and the new boots behind the fellow's counter. The toothless man had attempted some small protest at this proceeding, but had subsided when Lee threatened to read over the bill again.

Came out of that store at last, some lighter

in the purse and nicer on the person—a saddle-tramp no more, at least not to look at (appearing more a veteran drover out of work, or a very small-running rancher in town to beg a loan at the bank). Came out a new man, in any event, and went right next door to purchase a small round cake with orange-colored icing from a small Chinese man, came out to the walk again to eat that (it reminded him of someone he had known) and to watch for some sensible-looking man to pass.

Lee had finished the cake and watched for a minute or so afterward, when he saw a big man carrying a big belly before him, tucked into a figured vest, and fronting a square, red, hard-looking face atop that. He seemed to be no fool, and down-right.

"Say, Mister!"

Fellow stopped walking, turned, and gave Lee the eye.

"Say what?" he said. Not friendly, not un-friendly.

"I'm fresh in this town," Lee said, raising his voice a little against the bustle and foot-steps pounding past on the walk, "and I'm looking for a reasonable livery and a hotel or put-up for myself."

The big man looked Lee up and down in a manner that would have been insulting if Lee hadn't invited it.

"Purvey's Livery and Rents," he said, and swung a large thumb up between them, aiming further down the street. Then he considered for a moment, said, "The Columbia's all right, if you don't mind late music downstairs."

"I don't," Lee said. "Much obliged."

"You'll find the Columbia over on Second Street. Purvey'll tell you where."

"Obliged again," Lee said. "Saved me some looking."

The big man nodded, looked to be considering tipping his Derby hat, decided not to apparently, turned and went on his way.

Lee walked down to the street, unhitched Nameless, mounted him, and kicked him out into the traffic.

He saw Purvey's sign a few minutes later—a few minutes and a bad stall in traffic later (a beer dray and lumber wagon had come to a disagreement at a crossing, their respective drivers dismounting to complain and then to fist-fight).

Purvey's had not been built as a stable-livery; rather, it had been recently knocked out, cleared, and re-arranged from the apparent wreckage of two houses and their yards. Pieces of broken siding, planks, members and frames, and a busted-back parlor sofa all stood mournful alongside a corral of nailed house-siding.

Even so, jury-built, the place did its duty—one house cleared, back torn out for stable stalls; the other house, on the left of the corral, boarded for grain bins here, gapped for passage there.

No question who Purvey was. A squat-built,

lively young man with dark red hair and a barkeep's mustache to match, engaged, as Lee booted Nameless onto the premises, in chivvying two carpenters into activity on a second corral (like the first, apparently being made of torn-away house siding).

Still, though busy and shouting, his fists clenched as if he intended to box both the carpenters down in the next moment, Purvey had an eye for a beast brought within his ken.

"You there!" he shouted at Lee, as if a customer brought trouble for sure. "What in God's name do you intend? You surely don't plan to board that beast with me! Nor, I hope, sell it!" The squat fellow came swaggering over, his fists still clenched from his talk with the carpenters, who, with a casual air, Purvey's attention distracted, had recommenced their work, slow as the hour hand on a two-dollar watch.

"A damn mule," Purvey said, surveying Nameless from a few feet away. "Looks like a biter."

"Got a temper more like a draft horse," Lee lied as he dismounted, hoping that Purvey wouldn't step too close to the animal's head. "Name's Daisy."

"Gut-buster, you mean." Purvey, a contrary man, ignored Lee's wishes and stepped up to Nameless's head, apparently to look at his teeth.

"Four years old," Lee said.

"I'll just look for myself, Mister, if you don't mind."

And, as if he'd heard and understood the stableman's intention, Nameless then and there helped him out by curling his lip like a dog, showing the man his teeth, then thrusting out his head quick as a wink, and using them.

"*Oh! Jesus!*"

Purvey was quick enough—quick enough so that Lee supposed he might be a pretty fair fist-fighter (whence that constant clenching). He jerked back almost as suddenly as Nameless had taken his snap at him. Back *almost* far enough.

The mule's teeth just caught a pinch of the flesh of his left arm, right above the elbow and seemed to have given it a considerable chew, because Purvey, once he yanked his arm away, commenced to curse like a sailor and do a small dance.

Lee noticed though that he made no move to kick at the beast, or pick up a piece of scantling (as many a handler might have) to punish the mule. Might have been Lee standing there that discouraged him, but Lee thought not. Fellow appeared to like animals, which might save the sale.

"You lied to me, you son-of-a-bitch," Purvey said. Fighting words and more was not a mule sale the subject and object between them.

"Damn right," Lee said. "You suppose I'm fool enough to tell the truth about this bait?"

"I knew this jackass was a biter; he had the goddamn look in his goddamn eye!"

"More fool you, then, for standing in close," Lee said. "Listen to me, now—if you can't handle a difficult animal, even though he's got character, even though he's a bull for staying and a bear for work, then I'll thank you to point me the way to a dealer who knows mules, *fine* mules, and can handle them!" Having delivered this hard infield hit, he waited to see what Purvey would say to catch and return it.

"That's good," squat Purvey said (behind him, the tortoise carpenters were amused at his having been bit). "That's a nice ploy, Mister. Now, let me tell you this: there is no better judge of a goddamn mule in this part of the country than I am! And that includes a bad fault of behavior that might injure a child or woman wasn't looking for it that just happened to pass by, such as biting!"

"Oh, an expert on the mule, are you?"

"You say damn right, Mister Whatever-your-name-is!"

"Then you'll likely know how this animal was bred—and out of what?" Lee made a face as scornful as an actor's in a stage duel.

"So I do, Mister Smarty-pants!" and Purvey hauled off a little way, and circled 'round, and gave Nameless a once-over as thorough as a physician's.

"This here mule," he said, (several hostlers and hangers-on had gathered to see the fun) " . . . this here mule was bred out of a Spanish jack . . . see those fine legs? that's Spanish blood in a mule." He circled around a bit more, staying well clear, Lee noticed, of the animal's hind feet, fine or not. "This here mule," Purvey said, coming back to Nameless's head, but not close, ". . . this here mule was bred out of a Spanish Jack and a Morgan-mustang cross mare."

"I'll be damned," Lee said. "I will be damned! Now how in the world did you know the truth of that?"

"Hoo-*eee!*" The bystanders were much impressed with Purvey for calling that. Fact he'd been bit seemed small potatoes now. A *Morgan-mustang cross mare!* Called that right on the money. Man knew stock, no saying he didn't!

"How could a man tell that from just looking?" Lee said.

"It's *quality* tells, Mister," Purvey said. And went on to dig his grave a little deeper. "Hindquarters say Morgan blood—that short strong back says mustang. If you knew stock, you'd know what I'm talking about."

"Well," Lee said, "if you're right, this high quality mule is worth sixty dollars of anybody's money."

"Twenty!" Purvey snapped, and turned red.

"Oh, no, not with these fine legs. Not with these Morgan quarters, this strong, short . . ."

"Thirty, and not a red cent more!" Someone looking on laughed, and Purvey swung 'round, his fists clenched. "We're doin' business here!

No loafers needed to look on!"

"I take your good judgment, Purvey. The animal has the breeding. Forty-five dollars."

"Thirty-five—and if you don't take it, you can haul that crow-bait out of my yard!"

"Thirty-five? With these fine legs? That back?" Lee shook his head. "Sorry; I have it on the word of the best judge of mule-flesh in the Territory. This animal has the blood and bone that makes for class! Forty, or I'll call the man who judged him a liar—or a fool."

More laughter from the laughter in the crowd. "Gotcher by the shorts, Purvey!"

"He bites," Purvey said, driven to the wall.

"Nonsense. Kisses rough, is what he does! And knows a man that knows a mule!"

Purvey only smiled, while others laughed, but then he said, "All right, you son-of-a-bitch, I'll give you the forty just to get you off my property."

Pleased at this price, which was ten and more dollars than he'd expected, Lee went to the mule's ear, said "Kiss him again, Nameless," and saw Purvey, alert, take a half-step back.

Out of the crowd, and wary now, Lee found Purvey a hard bargainer on horseflesh.

"That's a cute trick," he said to Lee, in the cool of the stable, "leading a man to show off and make a fool of himself bloating a bargain. I'll remember it."

"It's a good mule; you won't be the loser by

110

it." Lee was looking over a wall-eyed roan that jerked its head high whenever he waved a hand past it.

"That mule of yours is going to the army. Those fools take good care of them and no-one gives a damn if a private gets mule-bit."

"This roan is more than half blind."

"Oh, know horses, do you?"

"I've raised them."

"Wouldn't care to guess at the roan's breeding, though? Count off its good points?"

"I'm not that sort of a fool," Lee said, smiling to show there was no offense. "Show me another horse—and not one, please, that'll dump me if a chicken trots under its nose."

"Well, now listen," Purvey said. "Listen to me, now. If you want a really fine animal . . ." and led away into the gloom in the direction of a stall that held a bay horse, otherwise solid, that suffered serious swellings from glanders.

"My time is worth something," Lee said, after that, "even if yours isn't."

"Well, now," Purvey said. "I do have a rough one. Mighty rough, but tough as leather."

"Show him," Lee said. And was introduced, three stalls down, to a narrow-backed paint, slab-sided as a picket fence, but well enough ribbed-up to go.

"Spots is the name," Purvey said.

"Trot him out."

In the corral, Lee saddled the horse, which stood quiet as death, mounted, and rode the animal around at a walk, then a trot. It was rough-gaited enough.

"Open up," he said, and when the bars had been slid back, spurred the horse out of the yard and down the side of the rutted street at a run, scattering stray dogs and causing pedestrians and wagoneers to curse at him as he went by.

The beast could run. A hard, fast, pounding gallop. Lee spurred him down the street, up another at a hard right turn, again a right turn on the next (the horse keeping its head down, cold-blooded as nevermind) and finally around to Main again, lining out for the livery, licking the animal left and right with the reins.

The hard, driving gallop never slackened until they swung, in a rattle of hooves and haze of dust followed by unkind shouts from the street into Purvey's livery again.

Lee hauled the paint down, slid off him fast, and went to press his ear to the horse's chest.

It was a narrow chest with a bit too much bone, bit too little muscle. Narrow, but with no noise in it. The animal's wind was well enough.

Lee stroked down the paint's legs, lifted his hooves. Hooves were the best thing about him. Seemed hard as stone.

Lee went to his head (the loafers had gathered again, had knowledgable comments of their own) checked his teeth, snapped fingers at each side of him to ware for deafness, watched to see if his eyes were clear.

A healthy, ugly little horse. A splitter to ride, too, on any long journey . . .

"How much?"

"One hundred dollars even."

"Humorous," Lee said. "That's a good one. Eddie Foy couldn't tell a better one than that."

And so it went, back and forth for a while. Then Lee groaned, reached for his purse, counted back Purvey's forty dollars, added twenty-five more, and took a bill of sale for *"One paint horse, six years old, spotted brown and white with blaze on forehead. No bad habits."*

These monies and paper exchanged, Lee, feeling it had been almost a fair bargain, shook hands with Purvey, who had a considerable grip on him, and walked back 'round the paint to mount him.

Walked a little too close, apparently.

The next instant, he was down in the dust, having rolled there to be missed by the quickest, hardest kick he'd ever seen a horse kick. The goddamned thing was a back-end brute! Like to kill a man if he came within range!

Lee got up out of the dust to a chorus of pleasure from the loafers who were happy to see anyone japed, more than a little angry.

"What do you mean by that 'no bad habits' shit?" he said to Purvey, looking a little dangerous, and dusting himself off.

"Now, now," Purvey said. "The little fella

was just tryin' to pat you on the back by way of congratulations for the purchase! He *is* a rough patter . . ."

Great pleasure to the gallery.

CHAPTER FIVE

Lee found the Columbia on Second Street. Purvey'd told him where.

It looked a cheerful kennel—weathered board-and-batten built, a narrow two stories high, with house windows along the front rather than figured plate glass. A tall beak-nosed whore stood just clear of the front door (a plain house door, rather than fancy bat-wings) raising her beer mug in toast to two layabout dandies in scruffs and dented Derby hats. These three citizens looked more than several sheets to the wind, and it not too far past noon. One of the men, an Irish-looking sort, began a lively jig to the piano music leaking from indoors, and danced, his arms correctly crossed, back and forth across the boardwalk as Lee rode up on the slab-sided paint.

This all looked like home-away-from-home to Lee. Not a day before he had been a rag-dressed drifter on a contrary mule, yet here he was, mounted after a fashion (and, after a fashion, well-mounted; the small horse was a tough enough article), neatly dressed, if no dude, well fed (and intending more good feeding) and, all in all, ready to see the elephant and rustle the son-of-a-bitch if he had to.

He almost pitied Mister Petroff.

Lee tied the paint off to a hitch post level with the boardwalk's planks—it seemed Second Street rode a little drier than Main when winter came—swung down, unlaced his war-bag, climbed the steps, and crossed the boardwalk to the Columbia's door. The beaky whore gave him the eye as he went by; the dancing Irishman skipped 'round him as he walked. As nice a saloon greeting as a man could wish for, except maybe drinks on the house.

The Columbia was a whitewashed place with more light in it than most resorts. The owner had chopped the front of the ceiling away to allow the front rank of second story windows. Sunlight streamed down from them and lit the place near like a theater. Bright at this time of day, in any case.

A thin crowd of undoubted regulars leaned along the bar—light oak; wouldn't be much mahogany in this neck of the woods.

A bony barkeep, no bigger than he had to be to reach the slide and serve, appeared to be the owner. He had, beside a compensating great

118

handle-bar mustache, a certain relaxed, proprietary air, as if he could pull from the cash box whenever he chose and not sneak it.

This fellow, while serving a mixed drink of some kind to an old man, noticed Lee walk in, and fixed him with that quick judging glance which is the barkeeper's stock in trade.

"Say there! You a new fish in town?" In a friendly enough fashion.

"New as fresh paint," Lee said.

The barman waggled his great mustachios. "Then get yourself over here and pick up a beer." For a slight man, he had a sonorous voice—a quartet singer, Lee supposed. "It'll be your first, and on the house."

"I'll take it," Lee said, and slid up to the wood alongside the old man—a trapper-looking sort, with a full grey beard (cleaner than most of those articles), a worn suit of greasy buckskin, an old-fashioned Dragoon Colt's worn for a left-hand cross draw, and a Massachusetts Green River knife in a blue beaded sheath.

Looked the real article, if long past his beaver-catching prime.

"Go ahead and jostle me," the old man said, "Youth will take its liberties with wisdom . . ."

Said friendly enough, with a sigh.

The old man turned to Lee, and gave him the once-over with watery eyes the same shade of grey as his beard. "New blood," the old man said, and held out the hand that wasn't holding his beer. "Mine's Bill Tatum."

"Morgan," Lee said.

"Any first? Or would your rather conceal it?"

"Lee."

The old trapper appeared to chew that over, half closing his eyes the better to consider. "I know that name," he said and, aside to the proprietor sliding down the bar with Lee's first and last free beer, "Nothing to the bad, Nat, mind, some revolver murder or other east in Idaho Territory. Nothing to the bad." He glanced back at Lee and winked.

A type. Playing the ancient outspoken gaffer. Lee had seen numerous of these, but not many that still went armed and seemed not too decrepit to use their iron, if given time to pull it.

"Never heard of a Tatum, though," Lee said, "except for old Ira Tatum, was whipped for pig stealing down in Tradition. Didn't cure him of it, though, from what I've heard."

Old trapper didn't blink. This sort of japing was checkers and chess to him, apparently. "My uncle Ira," he said, "a romantic boy, and stubborn. Will love an English pig wherever he can find one—don't care for the French."

"Not much use at Lundy's Lane, then," Lee said.

"No use whatsoever," the old man said, smiled and held out his hand again. "And I do love a jokester."

These saloon pleasantries put on like a familiar jacket, Lee asked the proprietor

120

(speaking loud to clear the mustachios) for the chances of a room, perhaps for a week, perhaps longer, and was informed that two were cleared, the best being a generous chamber on the second floor rear.

"A palace," the old man said.

"A dollar and a bit a night," said the proprietor, "and as near no bugs as coal oil and elbow grease can provide."

"I'll see it," Lee said, and was guided up the stairs by the same big-nosed hooker who'd been carousing by the boardwalk door. This woman also, though forbidding to look at— more the maiden schoolmistress she seemed than a down whore—nonetheless proved as jolly as most in this resort, and was good company up the stairs, animadiverting on the charms of cocks bent to the left versus those tending to the right. Straight members weren't even in it.

This hawk-nosed creature was fearfully drunk and staggered down a narrow white-washed hallway beckoning Lee on, opened a narrow deal door to the left, and stepped back to usher him in.

It was a cubby, seven foot by four and a half, but mopped and whitewashed clean. A tiny window looked out into the alley, and Lee, peering through its real glass panes, saw the dancing Irishman of before, his jigging ended, lying asleep on a sawdust heap.

"Isn't this plumb fine," the schoolmistress said to him, her nose hanging over his

121

shoulder, aimed at a slender wooden cot taking up most of the space. A thin horsehair mattress covered almost every slat. "Isn't this fine?" Lee was surprised to find that he could distinguish not only beer on her breath, but a distinct variety of other spirits. Rum, for certain sure, and rye-whiskey. Lemons, too. She must have drunk toddies . . .

A hand as big as a man's, emerging suddenly from a frilled sateen sleeve, slipped around Lee's waist, and commenced to fiddle with his trouser flies.

"Do you think a gift of two dollars too great," the schoolmistress said, breathing heavily into Lee's right ear, "for intimacy?"

"Certainly wouldn't be," Lee said, "with such a lady," and turned to give her cheek a pinch, "but I'm poxed with the Silver Lady, and still mercurizing for it."

"God damnit to hell!" the schoolmistress said, and took her hand off him. "Isn't there a clean-cocked man left who cares for a woman and can please her? Nothing but corn-hole sissies and drain-pipes!" She whirled and flounced, and was gone in a storm of rustling sateen, stale beer and burped rye. Lee heard her receding down the hallway, ricocheting off one side wall as she went.

He dumped his war-bag on the cot, went to the small window again to see if it opened (it did), then walked out into the hall and closed the thin-panelled door behind him. Theft didn't seem to be a serious problem at the Columbia

Hotel, likely because there wasn't much among its patrons to steal, and what might be worth the effort being generally kept on the owner's person, not left in a cubby.

Back downstairs and at the bar for his second—and first paid-for beer, Lee gave the proprietor three dollars and change for three nights' lodging, exchanged a turn or two with the elderly trapper (apparently a fixture of the place) and took his mug of beer to the free lunch table to fix himself a thick sandwich of corned beef and sour pickle. He found another table by one of the front windows, and sat in peace to eat and drink, still digesting, in a bright beam of sunlight from the second story windows above, his startling good fortune.

A pale lady, and a piece of land.

Good fortune for him—or should turn out to be, unless he was too careless or too slow to seize it. Good fortune, too, for the local freight company, or any other company that might have had cash to be stolen at gunpoint. For sure as God made little green apples, he intended to ride out of this country with considerably more cash than he'd had riding in.

Lee finished the last bite of the sandwich—a good lunch, though the bread (a seeded rye) had been slightly stale. A better than good lunch spread for a place like this—not exactly the Republic, in Kansas City. Swallowed his last bite, washed that down with a final gulp of beer, withheld his hand from a dozy fly crawling in small circles in the beer-ring on the

sunny table top, stood up, nodded to the group
of steadies at the bar, and walked on through,
past the piano, where a very fat man sat in his
shirtsleeves, his buttocks overflowing the
small stool, playing (soft pedal) some Mississippi ragged-time tune—and so on out the
back, down the steps past the ice-chest, across
the alley (the Irishman still decorating it) to
the outhouse.

A new animal to ride, new clothes, a clean
room, a cold beer, a solid lunch, another cold
beer and finally, a thorough crap.

Little more that a man could reasonably ask
of life, Lee supposed. Perhaps a cigar . . . And
the way to the Territory Territorial land office
in this town. He supposed a man might reasonably ask that, as well.

The land office was a stretch, and Lee might
have ridden it, but he felt like a walk and felt as
well it might be sensible to know Berrytown a
bit beyond Purvey's Livery and the Columbia.

He'd stabled the paint across the alley from
the hotel, forked down some fodder and poured
a number ten can of grain into the stall's bin.
Then he set out to see the town and to do some
business.

Lee thought he'd had good directions from
Mister Peabody, the monicker of the
Columbia's barkeep and proprietor, but either
the man had erred or Lee had (and probably,
the latter, since his new boots were giving him
what-for), so that he had to stop passers-by to

ask the way more than once. It was odd, how much easier it was to find one's way about on horseback. Perhaps the extra height had something to do with that, or some confidence in going . . .

However, after inquiring of a young sport wearing a checkered suit and decorated with oiled Burnsides from here to there, Lee walked (limped) down a way crowded with stacks of stored lumber and hardware, took a corner to the left, and saw the sign for the land office across the street. Eighth Street, that was.

There was a group at the office doorway, but most of them not in line to be served. Using the position so near the seat and registry of real estate and land dealing as a sort of forum, Lee supposed, from which their own opinions might carry more weight. Some remarks on acres versus hectares, on top lay and bottom lay, on well-watered and dust-bone dry (if there was such in this country) were rattled past Lee's ears like musket fire as he shouldered up the boardwalk steps through clouds of cigar smoke and argument, resolving to get a cigar for himself when he finished his business.

In the gloom of the office, two couples of young people waited to be served, as alike as pairs of peas in pods. Men—boys, really—all gangle and Adam's apples, wearing the roughest sort of work clothes. Their women, young wives, by the thin brass rings both sported on their fingers, both equally interchangeable, short, plump, with mouse-brown hair and mouse-brown eyes, one in gingham, the other in calico. One had more freckles than the other though, and giggled less.

The charms of these respectable young women fresh off some farm or hard-scrabble ranch had always escaped him. Nothing to speak of, awkward to lay, eager only for a nest, and a mean nest rather than none. Had always seemed to him that, given a choice, a sensible man deciding he should marry would be better off offering for a handsome whore who'd seen the elephant and had more to give a man than debts and a reluctant cooze.

"Mister, you can come on front and center, if you wish—these folks are waiting for file stuff." The chief office clerk sat behind a good oak desk, looking across at Lee with what once had been military sternness. This fellow, square-faced, square-bearded, short and stout-shouldered, still wore his old cavalry shirt (wash-worn blue, a sergeant's stripes still visible in stitching-ghosts along his sleeves) and looked to fancy himself some image of old Ulysses Grant, gruff, sawed-off, and knotty. Retired Army men and often non-commissioned men at that so featured in Territorial governments that they'd become a joke, bringing their Army manner and manners to government business.

Still, this one was a card. Behind him, as he sat stern and poker-spined, a sallow little clerk of lesser pull or the wrong party was delving in files for whatever paperwork the young couples required.

"Speak up on your business, Bud—we have matters to attend to!" No-nonsense blue eyes, addressing a simple civilian. Fellow happily sporting all the weight of government behind him.

Lee took out his purse, took the land-sale paper out of that, and leaned to hand it over the oak to this stern ex-sergeant.

The man took the paper, glanced at it, started to say something, perhaps ask Lee a question, then suddenly stopped and read it again. He put the paper down on his desk, got up from what looked like a mighty comfortable wide split cane chair, and went to what appeared a map of the county. Lee saw it was a survey of some kind, full of contours, cross-hatching, scales and compass roses.

The Sergeant took a good look at that, traced part of it with a blunt finger, came back to his desk, sat down, put his hand protectively on Lee's paper, and gave Lee a hard look.

"This property is in Mister G. Petroff's title."

"This property *was*. It was transferred to Miss Nancy Parker by deed outright, and registered here. So the lady told me."

The Sergeant Clerk got up again, went to a file case, shouldering his slavey aside without a how-de-do, and riffled through the paper there as neatly as a gambler playing cards.

He found, after a few moments, what he wished to find, pulled it out to read, read it again, and put it back. Then he came back to his desk, and said, "That appears to be correct."

"And that," Lee said, pointing to his deed still resting by the man's hand, "is a legal paper and bill of sale and I would like it registered and stamped."

"Now hold on," the ex-sergeant said, apparently not caring for Lee's tone . . . apparently not caring to register this particular agreement, either. "Now, just you hold on, Mister," he glanced down at the deed paper again. "We got regulations here. How do I know who the hell you are? How do I know Miss Parker has sold this stretch free-will? I'd sure . . ."

"That's law-court business, and later on," Lee said, "and no damn business of a land-office. I've brought you a deed of sale, signed and dated. Your business is to register it."

"Don't you tell me my business, Bub! I'm doin' nothin' with this here paper until a judge says it's okay! And that's . . ."

"You mean till George Petroff says it's okay." Lee's throat felt tight as a hanged man's but he intended to keep the lid on his temper; he determined to avoid trouble now, if he could.

"That did it," the ex-sergeant said, and he stood up out of his chair. "You get your sorry ass out of this office, and pronto!"

Hold hard, now. Hold hard . . .

"Give me my deed, and I'll take the damn thing to a judge, then." *Hold hard* . . . The ex-sergeant's slavey was standing still by the file cabinets, listening to this scandal with both ears on the stretch. Lee heard a nervous giggle from one of the young women behind him.

The ex-sergeant picked that paper up, opened a side drawer in his desk, and slipped it in there. There was a small revolver lying in the drawer as well among a raft of steel-nib pens.

"I want no trouble here," Lee said. "You just hand me back my property."

"I will hold this paper till a Territorial court says otherwise," the ex-sergeant said, and left he desk drawer open, the small revolver showing. "If this is a valid deed of sale, it'll be returned to you."

Lee put his hand on the butt of the Bisley Colt's.

"I want no trouble," he said.

"Oh, be damned to you!" said the ex-sergeant, now red in the face. "You believe you may come into a government office and play the bully?" He reached deliberately into the desk's drawer to grasp the small revolver. Apparently he saw no need to hurry.

Lee drew the Colt's, leaned far over the desk, raised the revolver and brought it down as hard as he could upon the man's hand as it closed upon that small pistol in the drawer.

There was a sudden cracking noise of splintering wood, and perhaps bone as well, and the ex-sergeant shouted in pain and reached out with his other hand to grapple with Lee.

Lee let him do so, paying no heed to that, but swung the Bisley Colt's again with all his strength, sweeping the weapon's weight across to catch the struggling man at the side of his head with a loud, dull knocking sound, as if a man had struck at a stump with a hammer.

The Chief Clerk let go Lee's jacket collar (which was the grip he'd gotten) took a slow step back into his cane-bottom chair, seemed to catch his leg in it somehow, tripped and fell to the floor.

Shouts and squeals from behind Lee. The slavey stared pop-eyed from his files—staring down at the ex-sergeant crawling on the floor behind his fine oak desk, and Lee heard a step behind him. He turned as quick as he could, hammer back, and ready to kill a man. But there was only one of the boys, goggling, stumbling back to be beside his wife. The two young women were now continuously piping, like shore birds, standing stock still, staring at the Colt's, and uttering cries. The one with freckles had gone sufficiently white in the face that she looked to have been spattered with brown ink across it.

"Be quiet," Lee said. "This has nothing to do with you. *Leave me alone!*"

An odd thing to say, but they appeared to understand him, and were quiet and still.

"Now you . . ." Lee turned to the beaten Chief Clerk, who was sitting on the floor beside his fallen chair. Blood had run to cover the man's left ear, and Lee supposed the gunsight had cut him there. The man was blinking, but looking alertly enough at Lee to seem to have his senses back. The other clerk made a move to go to the fellow's aid, but Lee waved him back with the barrel of the Colt's.

"You thought to make a mark of me?" Lee said to the sitting man. "That won't be done—not by the likes of you." He leaned over the desk again as the man attempted to get to his knees, and struck him with the revolver a third time, hitting him in the mouth, but not so hard, breaking a tooth or two perhaps and cutting the fellow's lip. The Chief Clerk bent his face down to the floor, and put up a hand to ward off another blow. He made a soft spitting sound. Lee saw he had broken a bone in the man's forefinger when he'd struck at his hand in the drawer. If he'd seen that before, he wouldn't have hit the man the third time.

"Now listen to me," Lee said. "I want my property; I want my paper returned to me, and I want the sale registered and the paper stamped."

He drew a deep breath, and tasted tin in his mouth.

Lee leaned over the desk again—the son-of-a-bitch wasn't so badly hurt he couldn't reply—but the slavey at that jumped forward from the file cabinet to crouch over his Chief and stare up at Lee as if he was the devil come hot from hell.

"You daren't hit him again!" this odd man said, hovering over his boss like a prairie hen over a chick. "You daren't!"

Seemed the man had tender feelings for the ex-sergeant, and some guts, too, however lilac they might be.

Under that fragile aegis, the Chief Clerk stirred and mumbled, and Lee felt some ashamed; felt tired, too. One of the women behind him was commencing to cry.

"Pick up my deed," Lee said to the brave sissy. "Pick it up, stamp it, and file a note of transfer. Do it right now."

The office door opened as he said it, and Lee turned to see two young couples scuttle out and a tall man with a thin, dour-looking face walk into the office, glance at the revolver in Lee's hand, the disarray behind the desk, then, with no change of expression, turn on his heel and walk back out.

Lee turned back to the clerks. "Do what I told you," he said. "Do it right now." The ex-sergeant was sitting up, blood on his left ear, blood on his beard, looking pale and ill. He had nothing to say.

"I won't hurt your friend," Lee said to the brave sissy. "Go on and take care of that paper." He watched while the fellow went and did his stamping and registering and note-filing. When the sissy brought Lee's deed back to him, the ex-sergeant was up and back into his chair, still with nothing to say, sitting with his head bowed—from pain and from shame at being beaten, Lee supposed. He holstered the Colt's.

Lee took his paper back, folded it, tucked it carefully into his snap-clasp purse, and put that away in his jacket pocket. "Listen to me," he said to the two of them. "I regret this matter came to violence, but you would have it so. You know damn well this is a legal paper; you chose to play a game for Mister Petroff. Don't play another game for him. Don't lose that register-note. Don't misplace it."

He walked to the door, stopped there, turned, and said, "Do that, and I'll kill you both."

The men outside the office seemed to have no more land deals to discuss. They stood on the boardwalk steps as still as monuments, watching as Lee appeared in the land office doorway, and continued to watch him, silent, as he walked down the steps past them and out into the street.

Eighth Street was crowded with people hurrying, minding their own business, jostling along. Lee walked with that crowd, allowed himself to drift with the flow of men and women moving on their ways.

It was restful. No one noticed him . . . no one even glanced his way. He'd thought, leaving the land office, that they might have sent for the town marshal or constable, have some deputies run after him.

Not so. Or not yet.

He'd have to clean the revolver tonight—

fool's doings, hitting a man with a fine weapon. Many a pistol barrel bent off true by that trick.

Hadn't had to strike the third time at all. The first, when the man reached in that drawer for the gun, that didn't count. Deserved what he'd gotten for that. Second time . . . yes. But not the third. "Ride your temper or it'll ride you . . ." A true enough saying. But fancy that brave clerk, running to shelter the fool of an ex-sergeant. He'd get no thanks for that.

And marshal or not, constable or not, the business was done. *Done.* The deed of sale from Nancy Parker was registered and noted. It would take a judge, a high-court judge and a six-month case to void that.

Lee doubted Petroff had six months to wait to timber off that section, to clear a skid road to the river, to start moving his logs onto water. Lee doubted the man could wait that long, not with million dollar debts owing. No. No waiting for six months.

Mister High-and-mighty, who so enjoyed his tricks with odd ladies, who so remembered his grandfather's glory days in service to the Russian Czar, was about to come a cropper. Had already done so unless he could deal with Lee Morgan, or deal him out.

The high ranch at Rifle River was waiting for the purchase . . . for the sounds, in only a few months, of the hoofbeats of Lee's horse as he rode in to claim his own.

Rifle River, and Spade Bit.

He'd change his brands. Change them to Double-R . . . the two ranches. Riding animals, work, and maybe draft. Breed the finest horse-flesh west of old Kentucky . . .

Build with good wood, alright. Build those two ranches richer than before, side them with lumber money from George Petroff's timberland. Get his men back, first thing. The best there were. Sid, Charlie, Little Ford, McCorkle. Get them all back, and then go horse-buying. The finest studs, and mares so perfect a human man might find himself enamoured of them. There'd be mornings then, more perfect than in the old days. Sunnier mornings . . . some rain in the afternoon.

He saw the Columbia's sign further down the street—had walked back to the place through an unfamiliar town, dreaming of good times to come. An old man's trick, to be that drifty. Some two-for-a-nickel constable might have come up on him, taken him flat-footed as a brain-loose prizefighter.

Might do not to dream for a while or Petroff might step into that dream.

Old Tatum was still standing at the Columbia's bar when Lee walked into the place. A new bunch of daylight drinkers surrounded the old man, and a new sudser was working the bar.

Tatum waved and Lee waved back but kept on going across the room to the stairs, weary as if his new boots were made of lead. Had the paper, though, and registered. Let someone try and take it, if they were feeling lucky. *Very* lucky.

He walked slowly down the whitewashed hallway, and his narrow cot in his narrow room was calling him to sleep.

He woke at dark, surprised he'd needed to sleep that way, as if he'd been drunk or just back from roundup, and lay in shadows, thinking about his luck . . . the two land-office clerks.

No visit from the law, at any rate. Lee doubted there'd be one—the ex-sergeant wouldn't care to explain in court why he'd refused to register a legal land transfer. The local law had probably learned to steer clear of big property fights in any case. The winner would be their friend, regardless.

No visit from the law, and some hours of sleep on a horse-hair mattress felt hard as a board. Lee sat up and reached to the washstand for the oil lamp (coal oil, it would be at the Columbia) took his match safe out of his trouser pocket and scratched a lucifer on the wall, slid up the chimney and lit the lamp on the first try. Good cotton wick.

He set the lamp back on the washstand, reached down to the floor for the Bisley Colt's, slid it out of the holster, unloaded it, and reached further under the cot for his war-bag, the patches and gun oil.

Sat in lamplight—not the first time a man had done it, not the first time he'd done it—

and cleaned the stains of blood off the weapon's barrel, front sight. Took the cylinder out, thought of unscrewing the side plate and decided not, and sat polishing and oiling lightly. Restful work. And it took a time. Only thing lacking was some boiling water to work the last of the powder-cake from the revolver's bore. Still, got most of it. A few smudges there. Maybe pour some coffee down through in the morning, get those out.

Re-assembled, the Colt's illustrated its fine action with a click and a click as he thumbed the hammer and triggered its release. It sounded as if a creature was speaking, so precise and neat, so definite were those mechanical responses, its leverages, springs, and accommodations.

The revolver done and holstered, Lee reached into his right boot-top for his knife, stropped the blade a time or two along his boot leather, tested the razor double-edges with his thumb, wiped a drop of oil along the blade each side, then slid the weapon back into its sheath.

Mister George Petroff would have returned to his handsome house by now, would likely have been told the way the land lay by Nancy Parker. She had struck Lee as mighty eager to do just that.

And what might the man do then?

Kill her. He might kill her, planning to deal with Lee in his good time. Lee thought, himself, that in such a situation he would be strongly tempted to do just that. To get rid of the woman, to cut that portion of the Gordian knot, at least. Might do that, when he knew more of her new partner. When he could be certain it was just the two of them in it and not, for example, a ploy by the men who'd sold him that Cascades land to begin with. Would be clever of them to take his first payments and then arrange it so that he could make no more, and must return the land to them.

If he were in Petroff's place, Lee would find the answer to that possibility, before proceeding against the albino woman and whatever drifting adventurer had "happened" to come upon her.

No—there'd be no killing at the handsome house tonight.

Tomorrow, Petroff would come in to Berrytown to send his telegrams to his agent and that one and to the Pinkertons, perhaps, to try and discover what plans those original sellers might have against him. To discover from the Pinkertons what they knew of a man named Lee Morgan—or who called himself so.

Tomorrow.

Time enough for as good a dinner as the Columbia could serve, for a whiskey or two, perhaps a dance with that beak-nose whore. Then to sleep again, and up with the sun.

Perhaps they had, downstairs behind the bar, a box of cigars worth smoking. In all the excitement of the day, mule-dealing and horse-dealing, the trouble at the land office . . . in all that he'd forgotten to buy himself a cigar. And damned if it hadn't been many months since he'd smoked anything of the sort, discounting one chewed butt he found himself picking up out of an alley's dirt in Sacremento. There'd been more shame than pleasure to that sotweed.

There'd be no more of that, whatever this timber thing turned to.

No more of that.

Lee stood up, stretched so that his bones cracked, easing out the kinks a daytime sleep had left in his muscles, bent over to blow out the lamp, and left his room to the dusk light still glowing at the window.

"Well, you've slept away the best part of the day," Mister Peabody said from his post behind the bar. He set a rye whiskey, neat, down on the oak before Lee with not the faintest *click* to betray it. Peabody had set out a deal of whiskey glasses in his career.

"How is that?"

"Why, man, the Omak Wildcats came to town to play, and got the bejesus whipped out of them!"

"Baseball . . ."

"Yes indeed, and some of the neatest sandlot you'd ever have seen. Norris Mack hit a ball far enough, and damn near hard enough to clear the Canada border, that's all!"

"Berrytown won big then?"

"Not only big," Peabody said, "but for the first time in a coon's age. We had Mack, and we had Wheelwright pitching, was what made the difference."

"You win money on that game, Mister Peabody?"

"You are damned right I did!" Peabody went up the bar to answer a call for three beers, drew them, leveled them, served them, cashboxed the change and returned. "But it was only fair," he said. "The good Lord knows I've lost enough on the Speedsters over the years. Mack made the difference, is what it was—showed that Omak bohunk what was what!"

"My congratulations to the home team," Lee said, and sipped at his whiskey. The liquor had been only lightly watered. "Say, now, you wouldn't happen to have any Havanas, would you? Rum soaked tips?"

"I believe I do," Peabody said, and slid down the oak to mix a martini cocktail for a dandy-dude trying to impress a pale little whore with a wall eye and feathers in her hat. "I'll see if any are left," Peabody said on his way back up the bar to two shouting jacks thumping for service.

The Columbia was jumping, full of pipe and cigar smoke, sweat smell, the scent of cheap perfumes, beer, whiskey, neat's foot oil, damp wool and a roar of voices, all threaded through by a lively small band of musicians—banjo, piano, trap drums and kazoo—playing Kansas City music for all they were worth against the back wall of the place.

Three hundred people at least crowded in out

of evening dark into the lights and noise and music as if they'd been moths of the larger sort, and mightily attracted. There were some sights to see from a vantage point at the center of the long bar. Dancing, for one, some various styles of that: shimmies, cake-walks, bugs and hops. A neatly dressed dwarf with black oiled hair (the fellow not more than a yard tall) was prancing like a pony, playing paddle hands with a flat-faced whore, a Polish woman she looked like, who'd had her nose broken once. The dwarf, all stumpy thighs and hips, was nonetheless a fair dancer, and had some class to him. Wore, Lee noticed, high heel high-button shoes to give himself an extra inch or so.

Jacks filled the place like soda—foaming up in shouts and laughter here and there, dealing each other fists full of cards incomprehensible, stomping on the sawdusted flooring in thick high-laced caulked boots, shaking their fists at each other in mock threats as they played. Cosying whores on their laps—foreign girls mostly, Lee noticed, big-boned Swedes, fat Indians, more of the flat-faced Polacks. A few American girls, and those not choice. The jacks, many foreign themselves, Finns and Norwegians and such, appeared not to mind.

There was no sign of the big-nosed woman who'd shown Lee up the stairs. Likely she was already back up there on business, and would soon return.

"Now, here you are, you lucky fellow," Peabody said, returning again to hand a cigar near a foot long over the bar. "This one and one more is all I have left of these beauties."

"Hold the other for me, too," Lee said. "What do they run?"

"I'll have to charge you two bits for the both," Peabody said. "These are not simply your ordinary nasty rope."

"Sold and hold," Lee said, and Peabody nodded, dropped a lucifer on the bar for him, and slid away sideways to where a gentleman of some sort in an English cap was tapping on the oak, politely, for a beer.

"You'd be Morgan, I suppose."

Lee looked for the voice for an instant, then glanced down to his left and saw the dwarf staring up at him with pretty long-lashed blue eyes set in a Spanish face.

"Yes," Lee said. "And you?"

"Pauley Pruitt." The dwarf held up a broad little stub-fingered hand. His coat parted as Lee shook his hand, and Lee saw a narrow-headed hatchet, a tomahawk sort of thing, the handle thrust down through the little man's belt. "I gather you aren't a lumberer."

"No," Lee said. "I did raise horses."

"Clean work," said the dwarf, "much like jacking in that. Outside work at least—not shit work, like in the mines or clerking in a store."

"I agree with that," Lee said.

The dwarf—Mister Pruitt—reached up to the bar to grasp his beer mug. "I have been in carny work. You know what that is?"

142

"Yes." Lee saw the little man's collar was wilted with sweat from his dancing. The dwarf had a grown man's head; it looked odd topping such a diminutive body. "Yes. It always appeared to me a tough way to earn a living."

"Not so," said Mister Pruitt, and took a swig of his beer. "Not so at all."

Lee heard a clatter at a table near by, glanced there and saw a lumberjack, more than half drunk, bending down to pick up a fallen double-bit ax, prop its handle against the table edge.

"Seems peculiar," he said to the dwarf, "bringing tools into a saloon . . ."

"Would," the dwarf said, sipping at his beer, looking up into Lee's face. (Struck Lee the little man must get mighty tired of looking up.) "Would be, but we had a contest after the game—chopping steps, pole climbing, tossing axes. You never saw a choppers' shivaree?"

"I haven't."

"Missed some fine blade-work, then. Only the Canucks and some Australians as good, I believe." He tapped the hatchet head at his belt. "I'm a trimmer, myself—lop the small stuff when she's down. Light ax, usually, but this for fine work."

"You in the contest?"

"No," the dwarf said. "My arms are too short for speed work. Not that I don't earn my pay. I do. And find it easier on my spirit than displaying my curiosity to a crowd of rubes." He finished his beer then with a gulp and a swallow. A thirsty little man.

"No pleasure to any man to be stared at," Lee said, and Mister Pruitt nodded his large head in agreement. He was looking off across the smokey room—looking for someone, he seemed to be. The little man had a strong odor of Bay Rum and dirty linen.

"No pleasure to get an arm broke, either," he said, still gazing out into the crowd. He looked up at Lee. "No pleasure to get an arm broke by some nasty drifting ranny with a whip," he said, and added, "I'll hold that fine cigar for you, if you like."

Lee heard boot steps pounding and turned from the bar to see the big Irishman, Micky Daley, driving through the crowd toward him, battering through the crowd like a big ship through rough weather. His left arm, (wrapped and clubbed in plaster-of-paris) was bound to his broad, sweatered chest and in his good right hand, he carried, light as a Malacca cane, a bright-edged double-bitted ax.

"You're a fool and a dead one!" Lee called to Daley as the man charged in. Lee went for the Bisley Colt's. *Ware the dwarf,* he thought as he reached—thought too late and felt the revolver lifting away. He struck down hard as he could, hit the dwarf's wrist and saw the Colt's spin to the floor to skitter under stampeding feet, people scrambling out of the Irishman's path, out of the bright circumference of the axe's swing.

The oak bar stood behind Lee. Men packed

him in on either side. The ax blade was up, poising, the polished steel, the double cresent of razor edges seeming to gather all light, and Lee bent double, kicked off the bar for his start, and lunged forward under the descending ax.

He reached down to his right boot as he went, trying for the knife there, and just missed it as he drove full tilt into the Irishman's gut, a belly dense and solid as a sack of cement. Just then, in that very instant, the helve of the falling ax caught Lee fairly down and across his back, pounded the wind out of him, and knocked him to his knees.

The ax blade sank in splintering wood beside his right foot. Lee, red dots dancing in his sight, ignored it, reached back again in his boot top there, fingered the knife handle, then had it clear and in his hand.

The ax helve was off his back, he thought. He felt the floorboards rebound as the weighty head was twisted free. Above him—wool trousers, a wide brown belt—Lee heard the Irishman grunt in a breath as the ax rose high again.

Leaning up from the sawdust, all sound muffled, in the slowest of motions it seemed, Lee thrust out his arm and carefully pushed the length of his broad dagger's blade up into Daley's crotch. Halfway in, or perhaps a little more than half, Lee felt a sudden harder resistance (some strip of bone or gristle), and had to thrust again, very strongly, to split

145

that, or pass it by.

Then the knife was in up to Green River.

Lee, still not breathing, still not able to breathe, got a foot under him, lunged up and put his left arm around the Irishman's waist like a lover while he hauled up hard on the handle of the blade-sunk knife. The same something, he thought, that had given him pause before seemed to halt the blade from running up, and Lee and the Irishman reeled drunkenly across the room, the ax blade wagging high above them, the Irishman (though Lee never heard it) snarling, showing his teeth like a huge and furious dog.

Lee's back felt broken. He was amazed to be standing on his feet. He saw, as the two of them, engripped, staggered against a table and upset it, a circle of shouting faces, bearded, mustached, howling at him. The knife wouldn't budge from its lodgement, and Lee gripped the handle harder, twisted it with all the power of his wrist until he felt his wrist bones ache and seem to separate. The Irishman's right arm swung down and brought the ax down with it, flailing at Lee's legs.

It was in jumping to the side, dancing like a dude whose toes were being shot at by cowboys, that Lee felt the dagger blade jolt up and deeper into meat, free of bone.

He clutched the Irishman close at that, and rowed on the handle of the knife, put his shoulder, the pain of his battered back, into it.

The knife blade suddenly slid and skidded

then—sliced across to Daley's hip, caught at his broad belt, then clipped through that and flew free of Lee's grip, so slippery and spurting was the blood.

Lee thought that it had cut him, somehow, as it fell. Had slashed the back of his left leg. He tried to jump away from there as if his knife had gone mad, had a life of its own and was cutting to kill him. The pain in his leg was cool and deep.

Lee jumped and spun and tripped away, turning to try and catch the thing before it could cut him again. He had forgotten the Irishman. That man had gone, somewhere.

The dwarf, looking more intent, was standing just to face him as Lee turned. The little man had his hatchet in his hand, and had hacked Lee with it. Lee saw his own blood, as clear as anything was ever seen—a thin curve of pretty red that bordered delicately the deeper cresent of the blade.

The dwarf cried out, *"Here!"* and swung the hatchet at Lee's face.

Lee stumbled back, remembering the Irishman, wishing he could turn for an instant to find where the Irishman had gone. The hatchet blade made the tiniest gusty sound of air as it missed his face by very little. It was odd, but that small quick breath of wind, hardly perceptible, seemed to refresh Lee, to give him some swift sort of rest.

He stepped forward, trying to find out if his injured leg, which felt oddly heavy, would support him, and kicked with his other as hard as he could. The toe of his right boot struck Mister Pruitt on his bulky, small, misshapen knee, and Lee felt something, the dwarf's kneecap perhaps, break at the blow.

Mister Pruitt shouted and swung his hatchet again, but Lee set himself, kicked the little man in the chest and sent him stumbling back, flailing his empty hand and the hatchet both. A grown man would have saved himself then and not fallen, broken knees or not, but Mister Pruitt, so small, his thick, strange legs so short, so ill-proportioned, could not do so.

He staggered back, waddling as he went; his leg folded, and he fell.

Lee, limping after him, caught Mister Pruitt still struggling to get up, and stomped down upon him—drove his boot heel down with all his weight behind it into the dwarf's belly. The little man screamed like a woman and tried to thrash away, tried to strike up with the hatchet, but Lee paid no heed to that. He raised his booted foot again (his injured leg supported him well enough; it felt solid, stiff and dead as a column of brick) raised his boot and stomping down once, and then again, felt the high boot heel strike into the little man's chest, felt something in there break like kindling.

Mister Pruitt, staring up at him, opened his mouth to scream, perhaps, but was only able to produce his tongue. This thrust from the dwarf's mouth like a separate living thing and turned darker as it did, swelling. Then Mister Pruitt's legs began a slow stumpy shambling dance as he lay there, the heels of his high-button boots tapping and rattling aimlessly on the floor.

Standing astride this dying little man, Lee remembered the Irishman, and turned to look for him. But there was no such to be seen—only a ring of silent faces, that had been shouting a few moments before, and, away toward the side of the room, a long thick wet strand of red-blue rope, splashed with small puddles of blood, that led to a cluster of white-faced men staring down at a knottier coil heaped between some fellow's spraddled legs.

The Columbia rang with silence. The long room, smoky, smelly, full of the heat of men and women, ached with silence.

Then Bill Tatum, looking older than he had in the glare of the kerosene chandeliers, came down from the far end of the bar, took Lee gently by the arm, said, "Now, now—I'm old enough to be your father and then some; don't hackle at me. You just come along now. You just come along . . ."

He supported Lee, limping, up the stairs, talking nonsense all the while, and the jacks below, who might have thought of getting a rope and hanging Lee with it for killing two of their own, apparently could not make up their minds to do so.

CHAPTER SIX

"Son, you're a fool for luck," Bill Tatum said. He'd brought Lee a lunch of beef stew and new potatoes. "A clever man just don't go 'round killin' jacks in a lumberjack town!"

"I appreciate your help there last night, Mister Tatum."

"An' well you should! I will swear I never saw as fine a fight as that, 'cept once—and that was watching Mike Fink gouge a man on the flats in Saint Louis when I was a kid. You are certainly hell on wheels in a do, Morgan. You as good with a pistol?"

"I believe I'm better," Lee said, "though I don't feel it now." In fact, beef stew or not, he felt much less than well for revolver work or any other. A woman named Meg Gaines, a hospital attendant nurse (or so she claimed) had come in with Tatum late in the night, unwrapped the trapper's clumsy bandaging, cleaned the injury—"You're lucky this blow

didn't cut your hamstring, young man!"—
cleaned the injury with what felt to be a hot
poker, but was in fact only a series of swabs
dipped in spirits, and then, unsatisfied, had sat
down on the edge of the cot, threaded up a
heavy, curved needle, and proceeded to sew
away, heedless of Lee's curses.

All that had wearied Lee considerably, and
his leg had ached as badly as his bruised back
ever since.

"Now if you're as neat with a pistol as with
that knife of yours," the trapper had recovered
both, and brought them in with the stew, "if
you're as neat with a revolver, why, I don't
believe I've seen many men who could stand
against you. Daley and Pruitt were no daisies,
I can tell you."

Lee lay back, the stew untasted, trying to
ease the pain in his back. He had thought for
sure that something was broken in there—hurt
too badly not to be so. But the nurse, a big-
boned woman with improbable red hair, had
rolled him over without ceremony, having
finished her stitching on the back of his leg,
and, pressing hard here and there along his
spine, had ordered him to stop cursing and to
wiggle first these toes, then those. That done,
she pronounced him uninjured except in the
muscle—and a baby for complaining.

Since that examination, Lee had slept a
little, spent more time awake and hurting. Supposed the woman must know what she was
about—damned well better had, since

according to Tatum the town's doctor was usually drunk, and always dirty as a toad.

Toward the morning, more to get his mind off his injuries than to effect, Lee thought some on George Petroff. Fellow had stolen a march on him; that was clear enough. Had returned to his home, heard Nancy Parker out, and had sent to Daley and the Irishman's small friend and advised or ordered them to find Lee and kill him.

Supposed he could deal with the legalisms, after. With Lee dead, it wouldn't be difficult to force Nancy Parker to say it had been Lee, that rough drifter, who'd taken advantage of a confidence to abuse and threaten her into signing the sale. The deed then, would be worth nothing at all. No Territorial court would allow an instrument signed under threat of force.

And now what?

This whole day in bed, for a start—it had taken only a try to get up for the chamber pot, early this morning, to teach a little lesson about hatchet slashes to a man's calf and about bruised back muscles as well. He was out of the game for another day and a night and would be tender a few days thereafter. No more rough-housing; that was certain.

Next time, he'd have to hold onto the Bisley Colt's.

Next time . . .

Peabody woke him in the afternoon, and Lee was not sorry for it.

He'd been dreaming about his father—about the Rifle River place, really. Had dreamt he was riding the tough little paint up the long rise along the river, up through the willows toward the house. It was odd, but he knew his mother was alive and would be waiting for him, yet knew at the same time that he was all of twenty-nine, a man grown. His mother would be alive, and still young . . .

He spurred the paint up past the north pasture, thought sure he smelled the grass crushed under the animal's hooves, heard distant thunder rumble past the mountains to the east.

A cool day, and cloudy. Cloud shadow scudding past printing mile-long patterns on wind-blown grass.

A gusty day. Cool rain would be marching down the river soon enough . . .

He dreamed he saw the house, standing where it had always stood, and bed sheets and such billowing along the line behind it. Wash day, and cold beef sandwiches for dinner.

Then somehow Lee was at the house without riding the rest of the way to it. He saw mares out in the corral field but recognized none of them.

His mother came out onto the front porch, wiping her hands with a scrap of cloth. She looked pleased but tired, and smiled at him and said, "*Your father's home.*" Her voice sounded strange to Lee; he had remembered her voice as deeper, sadder sounding . . .

"When did he come?" Lee asked in his dream and his voice sounded as strange to him as his mother's had. He must have climbed down from the paint, because he was standing, looking up at her on the front porch.

His father came out then, and stood in the doorway behind her. "I rode in last night," his father said. His father was in his shirt-sleeves, and had traces of shaving lather on his throat. His razor was in his hand. "How have you been, son? How's your schooling?"

Lee was surprised how lean and young his father looked. There was no grey in his hair at all. His eyes were grey, though. Silver grey . . . Except for his eyes, Lee would hardly have known him.

"All right in mathematics . . . not so good in Latin."

"Learn it," his father said. "That sort of knowledge bespeaks an educated man. It's an enrichment to your life."

"I will," Lee said, in his dream. "I'll learn it . . ."

"It's good to be home," his father said, and came out on the porch and put his arm around Lee's mother. It was shameful, but Lee imagined them for a moment, naked in her bed the night before. Wondered what his father had done with her . . . had her do . . .

"I'm making money," Lee said, to be thinking of something else.

His father kept his arm around his mother, looked hard at Lee, and said, "Using a man's

157

gift to his woman against him?"

Lee had nothing to say to that, and noticed that his father was wearing his revolver, another Bisley Colt's . . .

"A damn poor doings," Lee's father said to him. "A man should think of a better way to make money than to be sticking his nose into another's man's bedsheets, taking a woman's side against her man."

"I suppose," Lee said, though he didn't feel angry, and noticed the fineness of his father's hair, dark brown, cut long, and clean as a child's. "I suppose you would be faster than me in a fight."

His father just smiled and said nothing at all. But Lee's mother looked down at him like a stranger, and said, "Don't you make my Frank kill you. My Frank don't fight with dwarfs!"

"Then God damn you!" Lee called out as he woke—and lay still in late afternoon sunlight, trying at the same time to forget what his father had said and what his mother had said to him, and to remember what they both looked like, as if he had been on the rarest of visits to beloved people, and this had been marred at the end by a quarrel.

He lay still, his eyes closed, trying to remember what the ranch had looked like . . . what they'd looked like, standing together on the porch.

"I'm sorry," he said out loud, as if those ghosts could hear him. "I suppose I spoiled it."

"Spoiled what?" said Mister Peabody,

walking in and closing the door behind him.

It occurred to Lee that anyone could walk in on him now, while he slept, stove and crippled.

"Startled you?" Peabody asked. "Well, don't be scared. Billy was down the hall in a chair all morning." He'd brought up a bowl of what smelled very much like the stew Lee's had that morning. Peabody saw Lee's glance, grinned and said, "You bet—it's Columbia's special. Man can't get enough of good cooking."

"I appreciate it," Lee said, "but what's Tatum's put in?"

"Don't get all hot," Peabody said and handed Lee the bowl of stew as he sat up against his pillows. "Bill ain't that crazy about your hide." He stood, his face half concealed behind those enormous mustachios, and watched Lee taste the stew. "Put more pepper in it," Peabody said. "Stew gets tastier in the pot—gets weaker, too. Seems like that pepper just floats up in the air and out of it."

"Tatum."

"Well, now, I'll tell you about that. Has nothing to do with you, personal, at all." Peabody remembered the bar towel he'd carried in over his arm and handed it to Lee, who'd just dribbled gravy down his chest. "A resort," Peabody said, "even in this sort of a town, has got what you might call a ration of trouble allowed it—not so much by the law, Garrison don't, by an' large, give a shit about anything. It's the regular folks in the town don't like it.

159

Don't like a lot of wildness goin' right out of hand, lots of killin's, that sort of thing . . ."

"You're saying I tipped the sack?"

"You got it. That's exactly the truth of it! Not so much that big Irishman—nobody would have minded him goin' under. Little fella sort of sticks in folks' craws, though."

"Shit—he was in it all the way. He wasn't picking his teeth with that hand-ax!"

"I know that," Peabody said, and bent over to look into the stew bowl. "I see you're avoidin' that big piece of turnip. Well, more the fool you! Turnip's about the best vegetable there is—ten times better for your guts than any potato could ever be!"

Lee spooned up the piece of turnip, and ate it. There was nothing like pain and a bed to make a man a child to others.

"You were saying about the Columbia?"

"Yes, I was," Peabody said. "Truth is, I put old Bill out in that hall because the jacks and other folks like him wouldn't want to see him get hurt, should they come for you."

"There would be more than Tatum hurt."

"I dare say," Peabody said. "I dare say . . ." and stood watching Lee finish the bowl of stew. Peabody had milky blue eyes, very mild, humorous as placed above that bristling mustache, a dragoon's handle if ever there was one.

Lee scraped the bowl clean, burped a good, round, thumping burp, and handed up the empty. "Tell Tatum I'm much obliged for his courtesy. Should I offer to pay him?"

"Jesus, no," Peabody said. "He knows damn well he'll get a balance in breakfasts and free beers. Be sure and don't offer the old man money—he'd take that real hard."

"All right, I won't. But I am obliged to you, and to him, for seeing I was left alone." He wiped his mouth with the bar towel, scrubbed at his chest where he'd spilled the gravy. "I believe that I do owe that nursing woman some cash money . . ."

"You owe her four dollars and fifty cents," Peabody said. "You can leave that with me when you go—I'll see she gets it."

Lee slid down in the bed. His back felt better lying level. "And I will get on out of here without delay, Mister Peabody, if you can give me another day or two."

The saloon keeper seemed quite relieved at that, apparently having had some worries of Lee being a hard-case pleased with trouble. "There you are, now," he said. "I pegged you for a right one all along, Mister Morgan! You just stay cosy for another day or so and then be on your way." He reached down and retrieved his bar towel. "Damn sure wouldn't do to stay till Saturday night. Every jack in the world comes in to run mad drunk on Saturdays."

"I'll be gone from the Columbia before then," Lee said, "one way or another."

* * *

For the rest of the afternoon, Lee dozed and drifted, and received two or three short visits from Billy Tatum, the old man tiring, it seemed, of his peaceful vigil in the hall. The first visit had occasioned the sharing with Lee of reminiscenses of the "Old West" (that was the west before the war—before the country was flooded with half-mad veterans and land-hungry farmers.)

Lee had, of course, heard such tales before—of giant grizzlies twice the size of any seen today, of the great buffalo herds (taking a week to pass any particular spot), of truly lovely Indian girls, all expiring for the pleasures of a white man's embraces. Above all, of the emptiness of the country, the stretch and ease and beauty of endless, vacant country.

"Full of mountains, full of giant God-damned trees, full of buffler—and too God-damned full of Blackfeet!"

"I'll believe it, every bit, except for the grizzlies. I've had to do with a grizzly and never saw a giant one. Big, I found, was big enough."

"Shit . . . I've seen a grizz pick a bull buff up in his jaw an' carry that son-of-a-bitch away!"

"Over his shoulder, maybe—and that not far."

"You're lucky you're sick, boy, 'cause you're perilous close to calling Bill Tatum a liar!" This while the old trapper was perched on the washstand (lamp and bowl and pitcher having been set on the floor).

"Never do that," Lee said, and tried sitting up on the side of the cot. It was creaky doings, sitting up, his back giving him more fits than the leg.

"Need some bear grease on that," Tatum said, "speakin' of bears."

Lee got to sitting but it had been no joy. He stretched out the cut leg, foot to the floor. There was a catch to it, running pain down the back, but nothing he couldn't do with.

"You thinkin' of walking out tomorrow?"

"Have to," Lee said, and put more weight on the leg. Didn't think it would do to stand on, though. Not tonight.

"Try again in the mornin'," Tatum said. "Hurts is always easier in the mornin's."

"Yes," Lee said. "I'll try again in the morning." He hitched himself back onto the bed, leaned back into the pillows.

"Smarts a bit, do it?"

"More than a bit."

"Well," the old man said, "if you plan more mischief, it better not be rough-housin'."

"I know that." Lee said. "Would there be a walking stick of some sort in the place?"

"Hell, yes—a passel. Drunks come in here an' get carried out at a fine rate—leave more'n their sticks behind, sometimes! Peabody's got a raft of 'em."

"I may need one. Suppose Peabody's sell one off?"

"Sell—shit," Tatum said, and straightened up off the washstand to go. "He'll *give* you one

—give you a July rocket up your butt would it get you out of the Columbia quicker."

The old man had gone then, at least to down the hall, where as evening came on and Lee tried first to stand, then to hobble (hanging on to cot-post, chair-back, then doorknob) out into the hall, he saw the guardian, chin on chest and snoring, his cane-bottom leaning at a hard slant against the wall.

Lee was left alone that night except when the big-nose whore came bustling in with his supper and a line of chatter about another whore named Beulah Patch who'd had a medical sort of an emergency early that very morning, having lodged a beer bottle where she oughtn't, then needing the assistance of nurse Gaines in its removal. Nurse Gaines was doing very well for herself in the medical line, these days, what with one thing and another.

After that visit which apparently failed to wake old Tatum, Lee was left to himself and the company of yet another bowl of Peabody's stew. It seemed that Peabody had put whiskey into this bowl, to no benefit whatsoever. But Lee ate it—there was strength in the stuff, if no savor.

He finished the stew, and lay stretched, considering in the darkness, listening to the night-sounds of the town. Lively shouts . . . a child crying somewhere, likely not caring to be put to bed. A wagon of some sort going down the alley into the stable . . . He'd need to look in on the tough little paint in the morning; didn't do to leave a horse too much alone, especially such a rank little barb as that one. Though if he had some luck with that son-of-a-bitch tomorrow, he might well be trading for a thoroughbred . . .

Might be . . . Maybe. Sending that damn Irishman with his broken arm—that sad little wart of a midget or whatever—Mister Petroff had a bit to answer for, his property and that to one side. Of course, a man might say he was only defending his own. A man might say that, if he hadn't been at digging ditches, carrying crates like a nigger. Hadn't, one day, picked up another man's cigar stub out of the dirt in Sacramento, California.

Tomorrow would tell it—had better tell it. The two men last night were just for starters. There'd be another to face, perhaps by tomorrow, and if Petroff wasn't brought to some agreement, or to death, another after that.

Tomorrow would have to tell it; for if Petroff was clever, he'd soon pay the Federal Marshal in Seattle (that fellow that cared so much for money) to come out and do his duty for the Territory's peace.

Lee had no notion he could stand against a Federal marshal and his men unless he cared to be running for the rest of his life.

Sleep then . . . sleep again. Let the leg, let the sore back ease as they would. The injuries would have had their rest and all the good a night, a day, and a night would do them.

Lee wondered if Petroff had abused the albino woman when she'd faced him, told him what she'd done with her birthday present. How she'd cozened him, rung a hungry drifter in on the deal. Lee's father, in the dream, had all but called him a thief; Lee supposed that that had been his way of calling himself one, to dream it in that fashion.

Well, he'd come into this northwest country to steal if he must. This, at least, had the color of honest business to it—and Petroff ripe to be stolen from, if the word must be used. Shrewd business is what it was, on the woman's part, and on Lee's, and any banker would say so. If that meant moving to the banker's side of the table, then more the fool Lee if he didn't. It was the side with the money stacked on it.

Lee hauled out of the cot one last time to stand at the small window, pissing in the chamber pot, looking out at the moonlight patterning the stable roof. No drunk was visible on the sawdust pile tonight—must have danced his way into a warmer bed. Lee stood peeing, smelling the pinewood odors of the town drifting on the cool night air.

He supposed that odor was a smell of money, too.

Lee woke late the next morning. Sunlight already fell smoky with dust motes through the small window. He stretched gingerly under the covers, found his back much better, hardly stiff all, and when he sat up, then carefully

166

climbed out of bed, discovered his leg wound was better, too—but not quite better enough for much unsupported walking on it. There was a sharp, painful catch at the wound when he tried to pick up his leg at the finish of a step—some torn muscle there, tugging at the stitches.

Getting dressed was fairly easy; getting his boots on was not. His left boot slipped on over the bandage reluctant, and flashed a jolt of pain through the injury that made Lee grunt. But when that boot was on, Lee thankfully noted that the pressure of the leather boot top appeared to support the bandage in some way so that the pain was less when he walked.

Lee was in his boots, trousers, and undervest when a pale little whore with a cast in her right eye brought in his breakfast. She was the girl had been dancing with the dwarf two nights before—hard to forget that wandering right eye; it appeared to gaze shifting and occasionally, toward distant regions, unexplored. It gave the little whore's flat face a look of constant surprise.

She brought Lee a plate of eggs, ham, and sourdough biscuits, with a thick china mug of coffee to wash it down. It was a dandy of a breakfast, especially following all that beef stew, and Lee assumed Peabody had had some woman cook it up.

"You cook this breakfast, honey?"

"Nossir—Miz Peabody cooked it."

"Well, thanks for bringing it up . . . What's

167

your name, honey?"

"Beulah."

Lee found he had nothing more to say—kept his face pretty much in his breakfast, after that. The girl waited for him to finish, apparently under orders concerning the plate, which was a fine one with flowers painted on it—waited placid as a heifer in a spring field, staring vacantly at Lee with her good eye, wildly, yearningly, at the room's ceiling with the other.

The girl and the breakfast plate gone (with Lee's compliments to Mrs. Peabody) he finished his dressing, strapped on the Bisley Colt's, and tried a draw.

It surprised him. Lee had supposed his injuries, particularly the stiffness in his back, must slow his draw, make him awkward at it. But, not so.

Only his leg hurt. He shifted his weight, he supposed, as the revolver came level.

"You damn sure will need this! Look like a ruptured hound scratchin' his ear." Tatum in the doorway, and in his hand, a heavy, curved-handle Malacca cane. Handsome piece of wood. "Saw Masterson once clip a drunk 'breed acrost the snout with one of these—hickory, though, I think it was. That asshole's teeth went flyin', I can tell you that!" Tatum had apparently been appraising Lee's draw. It occurred to Lee again that he'd gotten sloppy about watching his back, his room door. Every creature in the Columbia seemed content to stroll in and start peeping. He'd never liked to be watched, practicing—made him feel a childish fool, playing bad-man.

"Knock on the God-damn door, why don't you?" he said to the old man.

Tatum was not abashed. "I surely will from now on, now I've seen you produce that Colt's! Son, you are very, very quick with that piece. Can you shoot that thing and hit?"

Lee said nothing, but reached out and took the Malacca to try it.

"I suppose you can," Tatum said. "Well, you are a wildcat and no mistake. I don't suppose Daley and that shorty ever had a chance down there, to speak of . . ."

Lee couldn't see himself shoving the old man out. To hell with it. He steadied himself a bit with the cane, held it in his left hand. Then he drew the Colt's again.

"Holy Moses! Damn if I ever saw faster than that! Well, maybe one. Maybe once. But son, you are *fast* with that iron! You're a damned dangerous man, aren't you?" This last said too reverently.

"Only to old farts who are always funning," Lee said, and turned on the old man in mock anger. Tatum threw up his hands in feigned terror, backed out the room door and strolled off down the hall, whistling "What Mary Showed Him" as he went.

But the trapper had been right about the walking stick. It took weight off that left leg and turned a deep, lurching limp into a slight one. Supported him nicely for a draw.

Not so bad. Lee posed before the washstand mirror, the Malacca at a jaunty angle. Not so bad. And might, after all, come in handy to strike someone about the head with. If Masterson could do it, then why the hell not he?

Not, as it proved, quite so jaunty on the stairs. The stairway to the ground floor tired Lee to descend. Without the cane it would have wearied him more. His back felt better and better as he walked it out but the wound in his leg objected. Lee stiff-kneed it down the two flights, planting the cane hard to support himself. Just a notion, he supposed, of what it might be like to be old. A damned tedious notion, too.

Peabody was out, it appeared, or back in his apartments with the breakfast-cooker, so only three bar-flies turned from their morning beers to watch Lee's stilty come-down. They looked, then shifted their eyes and looked away— mindful, Lee supposed, of the stains still showing through drifts of sawdust along the saloon's floor.

The glances and frightened looks away annoyed him.

"Morning!"

Mumbles. Each peering down into his beer, as if he might have lost something there.

"I said, 'Good morning,' damn it! I won't eat you!"

They looked at him directly then, produced hurried smiles, and said softly that they knew he wouldn't. And it *was* a fine morning . . .

Lee limped across the floor, swinging the cane alongside his left leg, and felt their glances on his back as he went.

If Lee hadn't known better, he would have thought the small paint was somewhat glad to see him. It nickered and nosed eagerly enough at the handful of oats he held out to it. Dead bored from two days and nights in a closed stall, was the truth of the matter.

The dancing Irishman looked on, seemed fresh wakened from some feed sack bed in the back of the stable. Fellow appeared mighty ragged and hung over.

"He's a little sturdy thing, ain't he?"

"I believe he's a goer," Lee said. "For distance, anyway." He palmed another handful of oats for the paint, and felt the animal's soft nose work against it, snuffling and munching at the grain.

"Could do with a curryin', though." The Irishman shuffled his feet, looking expectant as a fice dog at Lee. Rheumy blue eyes peered through a hedge of tangled black whiskers.

Lee had considered riding the horse—had asked this sad Hibernian the location of Mister George Petroff's offices of business, and been given an address on Third Street, not seven corners away. Close enough to be walking, no more than good exercise for the leg if he stepped carefully and used the cane. And then there would be the difficulty of mounting the damn animal, then dismounting; have to bear

171

hard on his left leg, either way. And the paint was not a horse a man mounted from the right side, not unless he wanted to part company right smart. That was the last thing Lee wanted, to be dumped down hard with this leg . . . the back, too.

He'd walk. And if that cost him what S'eon had been used to call "face," then so be it.

"I'll be footing it," he said to the Irishman, dug into his vest pocket and produced two bits. "Pull him out, clean his hooves, water and curry him down." The Irishman held out a grimy paw, and Lee dropped the coin into it.

"If I come back and find you've scamped it—chased off for a beer instead, I'll take a crop to you."

"No fear of that, your honor," the Irishman said, ducked his head and grinned like a monkey. The man was a better than fair dancer, and jolly enough, but Lee almost found himself preferring big Daley's honest hate. What an odd folk these people were . . .

"One thing. Watch his heels—he's a dangerous kicker."

"Oh, I will that. The darlin'll miss me a mile!"

On his way out of the alley, swinging the Malacca between steps like a swell down Fifth Avenue in New York City, Lee made a stop at the back-house, limped in, sat down, and got rid of considerable of Peabody's beef stew. Damned if he'd ever known a less inspired dish. Man couldn't produce a decent stew, ought not to cook at all . . . leave it to his wife. McCorkle, now—*there* had been a ranch cook could make with the best. McCorkle couldn't be brought to shame by any French chef ever was. There was a man, untutored, had cooking in his blood, could make a rag-out from old boots would make a society woman smile.

He wiped himself with several leaves of last year's Sears and Roebuck's catalogue— damned harsh wiping they were, too—stood up, pulled up his trousers, fastened his galluses, slipped on his vest and buckskin jacket, then lifted his gun-belt off a nail and buckled that on, seeing to it the revolver rode comfortably at his right side. Adjusted his Stetson to a finer angle, picked up the Malacca from the near corner, opened the door and stepped back out into the alley fresh as paint and equally ready for the stroll, some business, or trouble, of Petroff chose.

Lee took one wrong turn—he stayed walking in the streets, stayed off the boardwalks where he could (too damn close and troublesome to climb the steps) took one wrong turn at the corner of Second and Pine Cone, but caught his error by himself, turned about, and went limping back.

The leg was doing quite well—only a catch now and again, when he failed to support it properly with the cane. Would have hated to be hobbling without the stick. Would have been a chore . . .

Two small boys had trailed along for a street

or so, having him spotted as the desperate character of the Columbia, no doubt. And Lee'd noticed a man or two staring as he limped by, but nothing much more than that. He supposed that most of the townspeople had no notion what he looked like—had only heard garbled tales of the fight, if they'd cared to listen to them. Those sort of saloon brawls were not of universal interest in any case. Some citizens preferred minding their own business and getting on with money-making. . .

Petroff Land and Timber.

Lee saw the spanking yellow painted sign nailed across the front of a narrow two-story building. Place was spruced more like some set of offices in Philadelphia than a deep-woods doings. Sign bright yellow, building clean white (painted, too, not white-washed) and a window box with petunias in it at every window, ground floor and second story. Front door was painted yellow to match the sign.

Fancy makings, suitable to a prosperous firm. A firm that might well afford a payment of some three hundred thousand dollars for necessary right-of-way. Might well, and would, perhaps, if the matter were not too personal. That last, unfortunately, a serious "if."

Lee felt his heart thumping as he stood out in the street.

Not all so calm and confident, then, after all. Not so wonderfully in the right, either.

But needing that money and determined to get it.

Lee thought again of that morning in Sacramento. He'd just come off three days' labor digging a sewer trench along a street of fine big homes. The wealthy people there having had enough of back-houses, enough of walking out in the rain to do the necessary. Three day's of digging—work hard enough to tear a loop of a man's guts out, to pop that gut right down into his ball-sack.

He'd made one dollar and sixty-two cents for those three days and had been given the right to sleep down in the ditch under a scrap of canvas. The children of those comfortable people had often come rolling their hoops down the walk, and paused to see him and several others emerging from their dens to get back to work after a ten-minute break to eat windfall crab apples and stale bread.

That last morning, the sewer-ditch dug, Lee'd walked downtown, looking for some penny-chore loading fruit, or stacking lumber, had seen a police-officer, ducked down an alley behind a restaurant, and found a cigar stub there, its end still wet from some fellow's mouth, and had picked it up to smoke.

Better to be safely dead than shamed in such a way as that again!

A clerk came forward as Lee walked through the yellow-painted door, a spring-bell jingling above him.

"Good morning," the clerk said. A decent looking young man—didn't appear to have spent his whole life behind a counter. "Can I be

175

of assistance?"

There was a note of style, and not chewing-and-spitting, either.

"You can assist me to Mister Petroff, if he's in," Lee said. "You can tell him that Lee Morgan's come to see him."

The clerk nodded, and two others (not such notable specimens) looked up from their ledgers at the back of the long room. Place was as filled and filed as the land office had been, but was neater. This room had been painted, too. It was the first inside room Lee had seen painted in a business building in some time. The lawyers in Boise had had their offices painted, but that was city doings.

"If you will follow me, Mister Morgan," the nice-looking young clerk said, "Mister Petroff is expecting you." He led the way to a glass paned door, and a narrow staircase beyond that. The other two clerks watched as they went—Lee saw their reflections in the glass of the door. There were two who were not too pre-occupied to know what had happened at the Columbia. Knew more than that, too, as did the decent looking young fellow.

Must be as hard to keep business secrets from your clerks as to keep secrets of the bed from the maid that changed the sheets.

Lee followed the young clerk up the narrow staircase, letting the Malacca take the weight from his left leg as he climbed. For some reason, it was easier going up then coming down.

176

At the landing—it had been a steep flight of stairs—there were two doors; the nearest was half open, and revealed a little water-closet, with washstand, flush-pitcher, and double bottom shit-pot. Petroff apparently did himself proud even here, for this little closet was also painted, and had a coal oil lamp lit and hanging on the wall. So, Lee supposed, a person could read the catalogue before he used it.

The second door was the raspberry—a thick oak number, carved to a fare-thee-well, fine brass knob.

The young clerk rapped and tapped, then opened it up and politely gestured Lee on through.

No Petroff in here. It looked a sort of ante-room, another filing office. And there was a woman sitting at a desk right in the middle of it. A young woman, pleasant looking. School-teacherish look about her, and pretty enough. Dark brown hair knotted up fairly severe.

Lee thought for an instant this girl was some customer or client of the business, or a wife waiting for her husband to attend to his affairs. There was another door, to an inner office, he supposed. He thought that about her, but she looked up at his entrance, bright as a button, and said, "You are . . . ?"

"Morgan," Lee said, and realized she was employed here. A confidential secretary, it appeared. He'd heard of such, and talked to one man who'd seen an office woman in Denver, but this was the first example of the species that he had met for himself.

She nodded brisk as an auctioneer, said "Mister Petroff is expecting you, Mister Morgan," picked a speaking tube off a hook on her desk, uncapped it, whistled gently into it (first time Lee had ever known a lady to whistle, and was interested how delicately she did it. Nothing a like a rude boy's doings, or a drunk whore's either) whistled her slight, decorous whistle, spoke softly into the small brass trumpet, listened, and hung it on its hook again.

"Would you go straight in, please, Mister Morgan?"

Indeed he would. Hard to think such a thing was becoming popular . . . having a decent woman, as this one appeared to be, in the company of a man in his office all day long. Didn't seem to Lee that the men's wives would be standing for that sort of a situation.

He shut the office door behind him.

A richly paneled room, more like a wealthy man's library than an office for business. Back-lit by sunlight streaming in from three tall windows, two men in their shirt-sleeves were playing pocket billiards at a carved oak table in the middle of the room.

Lee saw a glint of light off the steel of one of the revolvers the taller of the men wore, with another tucked down into a brown silk sash. Remington .44 conversions, the weapons looked like. Lee'd known some men who wore their pistols in that style, often to copy Bill Hickok.

The man with pistols was tall—looked to be very strong in a long-boned way. A big head, black hair parted in the middle and cut quite short. Cheekbones. More than a little Indian in that face—at least an eighth, maybe as much as a quarter blood. This man had dark eyes, and a hard, forward stare to go with them. He looked more than a little tough.

Big hands on his cue stick as nicely manicured as a gambler's.

The other man's hands were smaller . . . nervous. Nail-bitten.

"Do you play this game, Morgan?" A light, dry, professor's voice. And a professor the man —George Petroff for certain—looked. Medium height, a bit thin, short, goatee-cut red beard . . . losing his hair up top. Red hair, with a dusting of grey to it at the sides.

"I have," Lee said. He took an easy, limping step to one side of the doorway and stood in front of the bookcase there. The room was full of books. Books and the trophy-heads of animals.

"Care to play a stick?" Petroff had hazel eyes—now grey, now amber. His eyes had small sparks of intelligence flickering in them; self-knowledge . . . self-mocking. Very quick. He reminded Lee strongly of Professor Riles.

"I think not," Lee said. "I've come on business."

"Damn shame you've come at all," Petroff said, and bent over the table to take a shot.

"Could go just as quick, G.P.," the tall man said, and stood powdering his cue stick, staring at Lee.

Petroff missed.

"No man can concentrate on two things at once," Lee said.

Petroff straightened up, smiling. "Bonaparte was able to do so, I believe."

"Wellington didn't," Lee said. "And I have come to talk business."

"Now, you . . ." the tall man began, and set his pool cue down on the table.

"*Charles,*" Petroff said, and the tall man paused, then picked up his cue again.

Petroff turned fully to face Lee, and Lee noticed he wore no vest. No vest, and a shirt with a soft collar. A modern man, then, with a female clerk, and an albino woman to toy with in his home.

"This is Mister Charles Quaid, Mister Morgan," Petroff said. "Mister Quaid is from Portland . . . used to be with the Pinkertons, as an agent and detective."

Quaid said nothing. He stood, his cue stick in his hand, watching Lee as a dangerous dog might do.

"Mister Quaid has agreed to . . . support my interests, should that be necessary," Petroff said. "I hope that it will *not* be necessary."

"Daley and that little dwarf," Lee said.

"Were they to support your interests?"

Petroff looked Lee up and down as if he was interested in the work of his tailor, but not very. "That was no affair of mine," he said. "You beat Daley, I understand. Micky was not a forgiving man."

"Daley or the dwarf—this Quaid or some other," Lee said, "it makes no difference at all to me." He didn't look at the tall man with the Remington. "I will sell you that river strip for three hundred thousand dollars in gold. And if you send your jacks to cross it in a crowd and armed, I'll find you and kill you for it."

Lee saw some movement where the tall man stood, but he didn't turn to face him. And he kept his hand clear of the Bisley Colt's.

"Hard talk," Petroff said, and did not appear alarmed by it. "And surprising, since you are obviously not a fool." He turned his back and walked to a rolltop desk against the wall. "Finish our game another time, Charles," he said to the hard-case, and stood for a moment, absently turning the pages of some document on the cluttered desk top. "Murder aside, young man," he said, "if I do not pay that amount—and you may be assured that I will not—not that amount nor any other in these circumstances, what in the world do you intend to do about it?"

"I will go to Seattle," Lee said, "and find if there are any men there who will pay perhaps half that sum to control the timber shed off the

181

Cascades for one hundred miles and more. I will be some startled if I can't find a few such men."

Petroff smiled and nodded, looking down at the paper on his desk. "Yes," he said. "I also would be 'some startled' if you couldn't find at least two or three men out there would be glad of that chance." He stood silent, considering something.

Then he said, "Shrewd business—and, I suppose, not undeserved . . ." He reached down to turn another page in the document, and appeared to peruse that for a few moments. "Do you hunt for sport, Mister Morgan?"

"I have," Lee said.

"Seen a weapon like this, have you?" Petroff said. Reaching up to the wall above the desk, he lifted a slender bolt-actioned rifle down from an antler rack. "This is a German gun—a Mannlicher."

"I've heard of those sort of weapons," Lee said. "Never seen one."

"It's new—quite superior." He hefted the rifle. "Now, say that a man is like this rifle . . ." He worked the bolt. "And this bolt, the part of the piece that makes it effective . . ." Petroff eased some sort of catch, and the rifle bolt slid free into his hand. "Let us call this bolt the rifle's . . . honor. As essential to the weapon as honor is essential to a man. Without it, a man is a lump of meat, walking and nothing more."

Petroff re-assembled the rifle, reached to put

it back up on the antler rack.

"Mister Morgan," he said. "You are no mystery to me." He glanced at the tall man standing staring at Lee. "Mister Quaid's friends at the Pinkerton office in Saint Louis were quite forthcoming. A telegraphed report came in on you yesterday evening. I know your petty history pretty well, I believe." Petroff picked up a pair of *pince nez* spectacles from the desk top, fitted them to his nose. The lenses magnified his eyes as he looked at Lee. "I know of your brawls, your petty shootings, your failure in the more grown-up world of business." Petroff smiled. "I have seen your type all over this frontier—and seen them, every one, end in the gutter, or under earth." A ray of sunlight sparkled on the left lens of the spectacles. "I, you see, am *not* the son of a murderer and pimp. I am a man of honor, and I have never, *will* never, submit to any compulsion whatsoever."

"Pretty speaking," Lee said, noticing the tall breed shift restlessly by the billiard table. "But a professor once told me that rhetoric devoid of factual foundation is horseshit pure and simple. And the cold fact is that I have you gripped hard by the nuts, and I intend to squeeze them till you yell." The tall breed shifted his stance again. "So it's deal with me, or deal with some men from Seattle in the weeks to come. Deal—or try the gutter for yourself."

Lee reached behind him for the knob to the

office door, turned it, swung the door open, and stepped back through it. Petroff hadn't moved . . . stood watching him, no sign of anger on his face. The tall man, his eyes darker than before, was leaning a little forward, the fingers of his big left hand brown, smooth, hairless as a glove, still resting lightly on the edge of the billiard table. The sunlight was very bright behind them both.

Lee, being careful not to tangle his left leg with the cane, stepped back clear of the door frame into the outer office. Stepped back again, saw out of the corner of his eye, the woman clerk getting up from her desk, and closed the door behind him, then turned, opened the door to the hall, stepped through.

He went down the stairs in a rush—*careful . . . careful with the cane,* and was only four or five steps from the bottom landing when he heard the office door bang open, turned to look up, and saw the tall man, looking at this angle big as a thunderhead, walk out onto the landing above. He had the Remingtons in his hands.

Lee turned a bit more, tried to plant the cane tip to steady himself, and drew the Bisley as the breed took his first shot. The tall man, looking furious, fired his left-hand gun. The round smashed the plaster by Lee's head. Lee fired up into the smoke but saw no effect, didn't know if he'd hit the son-of-a-bitch or not. The noise of gunfire in this narrow place was terrific. Lee swung up to sight for a second try,

184

slipped, the damn cane kicking out, and fell against the stairway wall as Quaid's second shot tugged the right side hem of his jacket. Quaid, cool as Christmas, stood up there four-square, and sighted his right hand gun for a hit.

Lee, glad for the wall to steady him, shot the man through the head just as the fellow's revolver fired, that bullet cracking past Lee to snap into the landing floor below him.

Through the head—but low. Quaid stood up straighter; the Remington in his left hand fired frivolously to the side, and the tall man shook his head and sneezed a spray of blood and bits of bone. He made a loud crowing sound, still shaking his head, still sending red spatters to the walls, and raised his right hand revolver for another shot.

Lee fired up the smoky ladder of stairs into the man's chest, and saw his vest front jump as the slug went in. Quaid fired his pistol as he was struck, staggering back, still crowing that gargling cry, still spurting bright blood from his smashed face. He stumbled back, both Remingtons still gripped tight, then fell out of Lee's sight with a slamming sound that jarred the staircase.

Lee, half standing, half propped up on that blessed wall, his leg hurting like sixty, peered up through a haze of drifting powder smoke and saw the bottom of one of the big breed's boots just showing over the top step. There was no sound from up there now.

Lee waited, the Bisley cocked, waited for Petroff to show, to come out onto the landing where his ex-Pinkerton lay bleeding out and dead.

But no sign of any such.

The building now seemed quiet as a summer afternoon, though perhaps the woman clerk was sobbing, or crying out in fear behind her business desk. Lee might not have heard that soft sort of sound, for the dull ringing in his ears the gun blasts had left.

Powder smoke stung his eyes, hung in the air up and down the stairs, eddying slowly this way and that.

It occurred to Lee to climb the stairs again, to reload and finish the matter. But the difficulty of the climb appeared suddenly enormous, as if it would wear him to death to mount those steps again. Then the woman would be staring at him, perhaps screaming as he limped by . . .

He decided not. He decided to let that go for now.

CHAPTER SEVEN

The air in the street was like iced water—wonderfully refreshing to him.

Lee paid no heed to the crowd gathered at the building door, pushed his way through them, used the cane to make his way, anxious for a clear, open breath of air. He wanted no one near him at all, and struck out for the middle of the street to get as far from people as he could. Men looked after him as he limped away—he knew they were doing that. But none approached him, or tried to stay him in any way.

He limped down the rutted street, taking in great gasping breaths of air—so cool, and rich, perfumed with hemlock and pine. It was fair enough, he felt, just to be alive, and wondered as he went why a man would want anything more.

After a while, he began to feel not so well. His leg pained him more than a little as he walked. The cane tip sank into the street dirt.

Lee felt as he sometimes did on waking from a pleasant dream. The sounds . . . voices, all much too loud. He paused at the corner of Second Street, remembering his way. Then he turned left, climbed the boardwalk steps, stopped at a confectioner's just there, and dug in his vest pocket for two cents for taffy. Paid the little girl and walked on, chewing at the sweet stuff, getting his fingers sticky . . .

Remarkably single-minded, that half—or quarter—breed had been. A hard man, and more than willing. Had made a business of his courage, no doubt. Informed and peached on men in labor unions; broke their heads also when required.

Two revolvers in a sash—old fashioned, in that way. And might have gotten lucky, too, if Lee hadn't lost his balance, fallen to the side. Hard to know if he would have been hit but for that, or not. Not much sense ducking a bullet—just as likely to duck into it . . .

Terrible noise he'd made. Bullet should have struck him through the brain. Hard to imagine what that must feel like, having a heavy revolver bullet smash into your jaw, your face. Surely a man would hardly feel anything at all, only an extraordinary impact, as if God Almighty had reached out to strike you with his fist . . .

The shot through the chest had been a good one, though. Had put paid to him smartly. Stopped that noise . . .

The taffy was really very good. Lee saw the Columbia's sign two corners down. Damned if he remembered the last time he'd had a sweet. But this was exceptionally good stuff, lot of molasses in it.

Lee heard some shouting behind him. He assumed it concerned the shooting. He stopped walking and stood still on the south side of the street, chewing a bite of taffy and listening.

Sounded like the news being shouted out—considerable excitement. News, gossip, event. But no hunting cry. No wolf-pack sound to that.

He threw the taffy away (damn stuff was sticking up his fingers) and started walking again, leaning hard on the cane. *Lucky.* Lucky the leg had held up to get him almost down the stairs; lucky it had given way to throw him to the side. How in God's name had his father survived all those shootings? How had simple luck not turned on him?

A man called something across the street and Lee turned that way, but the man was already joking and joshing with his responding friend. Lee stopped walking again, stood propped on the cane, drew the Bisley Colt's, the steel still warm from firing, dumped the three empties out the gate, and reloaded. Must have been flustered and then some, not to have done that before.

He holstered the Colt's again, and went on his way, looking forward to Peabody's free lunch. Surely no beef stew this time . . . Lee felt hungry enough for two sandwiches, hard-boiled eggs, pigs' feet, the works. Hungry enough for a three beer lunch. Damned if he could remember getting out of that building, though. Couldn't remember those clerks downstairs as he left the place . . .

The food, when he'd piled a plate with it, taken it to a table near the front windows, suddenly seemed poor stuff. A ham sandwich, the pigs' feet he'd wanted, didn't appeal somehow.

He sat sipping his beer, leaving the lunch things alone. Lost his appetite, that was all. Still not well from that injury to his leg, was the truth of the matter.

No one standing at the Columbia's bar had come near him. They stood in a row like blackbirds on a fence over there, muttering, exchanging pleased, excited glances in the bar mirror.

Peabody had not been happy to see Lee again, had already had his war-bag brought down and tucked behind the bar so there'd be nothing to hinder Lee's going, or to delay it. Lee'd asked for the bill of charges, heard the sum—a little low, if anything—and paid up right there. Then he'd taken a beer and gone to the lunch table for his food.

Now he had it he didn't want it.

Was getting to be a warm day; the sunlight was coming down from those second story windows pretty strong. Turned the beer in the mug bright as molten gold when Lee shifted the handle this way and that . . .

"Killed him, by God! Son, I thought you had some sense!" Tatum, apparently somewhat drunk (and this early in the afternoon), stood by Lee's table, swaying ever so slightly as he stood. "Killed a damn *Pink*? Boy, those assholes'll chase you from here to breakfast, killing one of their own!"

"Fellow had left the Agency," Lee said.

Tatum snorted through his nose, a loud, farting snort, like a horse's. "You better hope that makes a difference. I sure as shit wouldn't want to be standin' in your boots! I hear you went to George Petroff's place to kill him!"

"No. Business."

"Shit," Tatum said, and pulled up a chair to sit opposite. "Some business!" He picked up one of Lee's pigs' feet and went to munching it, using as much gum as tooth. "I suppose," he said around the pig's foot, "I suppose old George had hired that hard-case to ward you off?"

"I wouldn't know," Lee said. "I had some business with him, and that fellow came after me, shooting."

"That sounds unlikely as the second coming of Mister Jesus H. Christ."

"Then how's about minding your own business, Tatum?"

The old trapper nodded briskly at that, took another pig's foot, shoved his chair back, and got up to go. "Now there," he said, "is the sort of talk I understand. Sorry I couldn't stay and visit longer. Give you a free piece of advice, though, boy; I was you, I'd get the hell out of this town!''

"I intend to do just that," Lee said. "And I want to thank you for watching out in that hallway for me when I was down sick.''

"No skin off my ass," Tatum said. "I got some breakfasts out of it!" He lifted a hand, turned and sauntered off a way, then turned again. "You pick up, now, and get out of here, boy! I can't tell you plainer than that. Old George is not the man to let a grudge lie.''

Not the man to let a grudge lie . . .

Lee didn't suppose that Petroff was. Still, grudge or not, the man had to pay or go under, and Lee doubted that all the talk of honor would prevail—though what sort of honor a man could have who purchased curious, deficient girls, who bought other odd women and took them into bed—what sort of honor such a man might have somewhat escaped him. Doubtless, though, Petroff *thought* of himself as a gentleman.

That might drive him to something surprising.

But not to poverty, long-term. Few men could comfortably bear that. Not Petroff—not Lee, either. Petroff would not be ruined for his honor's sake, however dear he held it. That was certain sure.

And time now, to follow Tatum's advice and clear the town.

194

He'd ride out past Petroff's house, see that he'd treated Nancy Parker gently, tell her what had happened. Perhaps she'd care to go to Seattle with him. One way or another, the business would take time to settle, now. Time to find a buyer (alas, likely for a good deal less than three hundred thousand dollars), time to get a new deal done.

Lee got up, leaving the food untouched, went to the bar ignoring the looks and look-aways to thank Peabody for his hospitality. Peabody nodded and nodded, hurried the handshake, and slid Lee's war-bag over the bar.

"Keep that cane," he said. "And Mister Morgan—I hope it brings you luck."

"Meaning that I'll need it?"

Peabody looked mournful behind his great mustachios. "I mean exactly that," he said. "And I'm sure sorry for it."

The paint once more seemed pleased to greet Lee and take a handful of oats from him. Whatever the animal's faults, he had some memory of his owner. Lee had known horses so stupid they could recognize no particular human being, years of riding and good treatment not withstanding.

The dancing Irishman was nowhere in evidence this afternoon. Probably gone drunk and to sleep in some hay loft or other.

Lee bridled the paint in his stall, then led him out to saddle him. Be trouble to mount, but pleasant to be mounted on a horse again—and off the new boots. His leg was sore as a carbuncle boil. Be pleasing, riding out into the country . . .

"Only a fool, after all."

Lee heard a small machine go *"click-clack."* He stood stock still, the saddle in his hands, the tangle of stirrup leathers and cinch straps against his legs.

George Petroff, looking even more the professor than Lee remembered from his offices, stepped out of the next stall down, the beautiful German rifle in his hands. He came edging past the paint's haunches, smiling a dry academic smile.

"For simple men, all men are simple," he said. "A quotation. *Pascal.*" The rifle-muzzle was a circle of silver, perfect and pretty. Lee had a vision of his head stuck on Petroff's office wall along with elk and moose and bear. He almost smiled at it.

"I have never asked a man to do," Petroff said, his spectacles reflecting the open stable door in twin round miniatures, "I have never asked a man to do anything I might not do better myself, if I cared to take the trouble. *Pace* poor Quaid—I am perfectly capable of killing my own game."

Petroff moved slightly nearer, almost past the paint's haunches, and lowered the rifle's muzzle to shoot Lee through the chest.

The horse's kick nearly missed him.

But not quite.

The right hoof flailing, just caught Petroff at the shoulder and spun him around with a smack. He held on to the rifle, but all awry, the muzzle cracking into the stall partition behind him, the piece somehow not going off.

As the paint shied away, Lee dropped the saddle, saw Petroff staring over his shoulder at him, an odd expression in his eyes (his spectacles gone flying) as if to ask for an instant to compose himself, as if to share with Lee the comedy of the moment.

Lee dropped the saddle, drew the Colt's, and shot Petroff in the right side as the man struggled to turn back from the force of the kick to face him.

The slug struck the slight man hard. Lee thought it a killing shot.

Petroff gasped in a breath of air—Lee heard him quite clearly over the revolver-shot's close echo—then stumbled away over the muck and straw, teetering, still trying to turn full toward Lee. Lee fired into him again, lower, heard the round go thumping in, and Petroff screamed and knelt, then sat down. He dropped the rifle as he was sitting there, put his hand to his wounded side, and screamed again, staring at Lee as if Lee were a nightmare he was attempting to wake from.

Lee was exasperated by the man's noise—it was frightening the paint—and he stepped over to Petroff, presented the Bisley to the man's head, and shot him through the temple.

A small piece of stuff like pudding spattered the toe of Lee's right boot.

* * *

197

At first, it had been her colors—for colors she had, delicate, deep, and various. There, tucked beneath the silver floss that hardly concealed her, was a narrow, rich world of nacreous pinks, pale purple, and blood-gorged crimson. Here, the interior of a woman otherwise unremarkable save for her pallor, was as extravagant as a carnival in color. Every shade of red was there.

And wet.

And odorous as fresh-boiled glue.

Nancy Parker, without her clothes, was straight-limbed and skinny, her thin legs and arms covered with the finest silver down, her small breasts already sagging slightly, drooping like snowdrops in warm weather, the nipples nearly as white as the blue-veined skin around them.

Skinny, and awkward as she walked naked in the upstairs suite of rooms that Petroff had occupied. Frail white feet. A child's white toes sinking into the blue-green Turkey carpet.

Lee had come into her bedroom the second night—had ignored her talking, the snap of temper, had commenced to strip her off *boudoir* gown, and then had spanked her when she'd struck at him.

She'd wrestled with him finely, after that—spanked him in return, her thin hands pattering on his buttocks as he rode her, her long, nervous, slender legs stretched straining wide.

Lee could feel her every rib, feel even the divisions of the fine bones of her arms. Could, if he held her hand to a strong lamplight, see the neat bones that built her wrists and fingers. Delicate doings . . .

She had a smell to her, and not only to her privates. A smell as fine and sharp and rank as a fox's. This lingered in the silks and laces she wore next to her thin body. At times, when he was alone in her rooms, Lee would go to the wardrobe, open it, and bury his nose in that fine stuff, breathe in the scent of bitch foxes.

Five days of this, and nights. The breed, Lucy, attended them, self-effacing, silent, never smiling. It occurred to Lee that the Indian was mourning Petroff in some way. If the woman was, it was a mourning Nancy Parker never shared.

"Tell me how you killed him," she commanded Lee once, and he did. This seemed to satisfy her—nor did the prospect now of waiting for some time to realize any cash money from their jointly owned strip of river land seem to trouble her.

"We'll make our profit," was all she said, and Lee, resting, using her as gently or as roughly as he chose, his leg stronger every day, his back bothering him not at all, was content to drift and to waken, when he had to, to avoid dreams. Dreams of the tall breed, Quaid. Strange that it was Quaid whom Lee shot to death over and again. Quaid—not Petroff. It was the tall man's crowing cry that woke Lee in the early morning well before dawn, as he lay restless in satin sheets the color of peach flesh, a silver lady still beside him.

On one of those occasions, Lee had wakened her, led her protesting from the bed and out onto the balcony in late moonlight, and moonlight flooding down like rain, as polished and pale, soaking the lawn, the trees below in light looking brighter than it was.

Here, on the white boards of the balcony, Lee made Nancy Parker kneel, thin and naked, her long hair flowing down, so that she took him into her mouth and suckled at him, he standing before her, his hands buried in the snowdrift of her hair.

No word, no trouble came to them from Berrytown, only the single visit of George Petroff's woman office clerk on business. This woman, dressed in Sunday best, and appearing proud to be out on business of importance, had come to see Nancy on the mechanics of Petroff's death; Nancy being, Lee supposed, the only person who might claim any immediate interest at all.

When Lee'd asked her, Nancy had laughed and said Miss Lattimer was concerned about submission of deeds and such for the building in town, for the timber land, to the Territorial Commission. Was afraid she wouldn't be paid for that work.

Five days of this, and very fine days they'd been, some of the nights having been even better . . . Decisions to be made, of course. A ride out to Seattle pretty soon . . . they'd need a buyer for that strip. Have to get money sometime. Sooner or later, some heirs or other—or men from the Territorial tax office—would come to take the house and everything in it.

A ride to Seattle. If they'd enough cash, she might come with him, make a vacation of it. She was fond of him, Lee thought—and he, in a way, fond of her. An odd woman. He had never seen her out of control, never seen her wild, except when he had his hands on her, had her grappled close. His hands seemed to provide a freedom for her; by holding her, he seemed to set her free.

An odd woman—odder than her pale skin, so intricately traced with thread-thin veins of the lightest possible blue.

At breakfast, on the morning of his sixth day since shooting Petroff's hireling, then Petroff himself, Lee sat alone (Nancy still asleep upstairs) and spread English orange jam onto a piece of toast. Lucy had just brought the toast-rack, the toast still baking hot, cut thick.

He'd started his eggs before, turned over light on a warming pan, impatient of waiting for the toast. Now, having taken a bite of the toast, the orange jam rich and bitter-sweet in his mouth, he heard a tapping at the house's front door. He chewed while Lucy came gliding out from the back hall to the foyer, then heard her voice, a man's voice answering.

"*Yew just sit right there, Bub.*" A backwoodsman's voice.

Lee turned slowly in the dining chair, kept his hands on the table.

A lanky man in a grey Derby hat was standing at the window about fifteen feet behind him, his head, chest, and double muzzle of a shotgun showing above the sill. The fellow was wearing a yellow checked vest. There was a deputy's star pinned to the right lapel.

"Don't move them hands or I'll cut loose on yew."

Lee thought he might kick his chair over backwards—might draw and shoot and kill the fellow . . .

Lucy came into the dining room. A large, rumpled man with a big belly strolled in behind her. He had a small revolver poking out the side of his coat, and a very relaxed air. Well dressed, though not well pressed. A round Federal Marshal's star was pinned to the lapel of his black claw-hammer coat.

Lee decided to kill them both, the deputy and his boss, if some sort of an arrest was what was planned. He put down the piece of toast. (That English orange jam was something special.)

"I got him from here!" a man called, and Lee looked across the room and saw a stocky fellow in a wide-awake hat pointing a revolver at him from the library doorway.

Covered cold. And dead, if that was what they wanted.

"Thank you, Miss," the Marshal said to Lucy, and bestowed a politician's smile on her. He had perfect white teeth, false teeth, for sure.

"Mister Lee Morgan," the marshal said, sighed, and sat down in a chair across the table. He had not sat in anyone's line of fire.

"What can I do you for, Marshal?" Lee said.

"Good question, Mister Morgan! And I have a straight answer for you. What I want you to do for me is to get your hard-cased ass out of this whole northwestern territory." This was said with no heat, pleasantly.

"And why in the world should I do that, Marshal?"

"Why, for the very good reason—that toast hot?"

"It is."

The marshal helped himself to a piece.

"What's this?"

"Orange jam. It's damn good."

The marshal spread some, bit into the toast, and nodded, chewing. "I'll say," he said. "That's prime!"

"You were saying . . . ?"

"I was saying that we want you out of here—way out, and out for good. If you don't go, if you want to give us some trouble . . . Well, that would be unfortunate."

"I'd just as soon not kill lawmen if I can help it."

"Sentiments do you credit," the marshal said, and took another bite of toast.

"Who asked you people in on this?" Lee said, and knew the answer as he asked.

"Why, the lady, Mrs. Petroff. Sent quite a

note up to my office . . . said you'd killed her husband, had her living in a state of merest terror."

Wife. The man's wife.

Petroff had fallen in love with his oddity.

"Nancy Parker . . ."

"Nancy Parker Petroff," the marshal said. "I checked up on that. Folks were married in Portland before Mister Grant—Justice of the Peace."

"Holding her in a state of 'merest terror'?"

The marshal smiled. "Some exaggeration is always permitted to a lady," he said.

This was the marshal, Lee recalled, who was very fond of money. Nancy had told him that when they'd first met. And now, of course, she was acting on it. No use sharing, no use having a partner at all if one was no longer needed.

Lee realized he'd acted fool enough to play it on the New York stage. Daley and Pruitt had been *her* men, of course—Daley easy to persuade after that beating—and had been sent by *her* to kill him—rather *try* to kill him. That had been her only risk; that they might succeed. She had apparently been sure enough they wouldn't. A shrewd judge of men.

And the attempt, of course, had set Lee against Petroff as set in stone.

Fool!

And the man had *said* he hadn't sent those two . . .

Leave or get shot. And this easy-going lawman and his deputies just the law-birds to get it done. To win a shoot-out with them was to lose everything but a lifetime spent running from the federal law. Days were over a man could kill such police officers then fade into badlands. The telegraph, and telegraph posses, had seen to that.

"I suppose," he said, "the lady won't be coming down."

The rumpled marshal shook his head. "Nooo, I should think not," he said, and winked. "Would you?"

Lee sat for a moment, thinking. He found his own anger humorous. *Taken*, by God! Taken to the cleaning-shed, plunged, scrubbed, wrung, hung, dried and folded.

"I suppose," Lee said, "a sensible man knows when to raise and when to fold." He pushed his chair back.

"*Marshal?!*"

"Leave be, Tod," the marshal called to the deputy in the window. "Everything's just fine."

"My horse?"

"Saddled and waitin'," the marshal said. "Saddled and waitin'."

Lee got up slowly. It might occur to them— to Nancy Parker, Nancy Parker Petroff, rather —that Lee might be more convenient dead.

A third deputy was waiting in the foyer, a double-barrel Greener very steady in his hands; must picture Lee a fearful ogre.

"Out the back," the rumpled marshal said, walking well behind. "Straight on out the back . . ."

The breed woman, Lucy, was standing by the back door, her eyes as dark and deep as lake water. She handed Lee his hat and didn't ask his hurry.

It seemed to Lee he was getting clear with it, if they let him clear at all. Just to get to that small paint, mount it, and ride off down the drive . . .

"Mind now," the marshal said when they got to the horse, "we don't expect to see you again in this Territory. Not for the longest while."

"I get the point," Lee said, and climbed aboard the paint. His heart was pumping hard. *Damn near clear with it . . .*

"Now, before you get to ridin'," the marshal said, smiling up at Lee in a friendly way, "there's this paper, belongs to Mrs. Petroff. She's most anxious to have it returned."

All three deputies were out now, standing spaced in the carriage drive as if they knew their business. Shooting was still possible. The marshal, yes, and one or two of the others. Then the fastest, longest ride the paint could support. It might be done—and to no purpose at all.

Lee reached into his jacket pocket, took out his snap-open purse, tugged out his folded copy of the land deed and handed it down.

Then he lifted the reins, nodded to the marshal, and booted the paint off down the drive. The small horse was happy to be going, happy to be moving along; it danced as lively as maybe down the gravel, sidling left as it went.

Lee looked up to her windows as he rode past and after a moment saw her standing in the far one on the right, half hidden by the curtain there.

He lifted his Stetson, stood tall in the stirrups (his leg paining him for it) and swept her a most courteous bow as the paint trotted past.

Might as well go out in style . . .

Miles out on the track south, lounging in the saddle, Lee found himself commencing to laugh. He laughed until his belly ached, the small paint shifting uneasily beneath him, its ears rowing forward and back.

When he finished laughing, Lee began to consider whether, further south, there might be some reasonable town containing a freight office, or stage station or some such. Some establishment down there, surely, where cash might be gotten by a young, enterprising, hard-working, intelligent fellow with a cocked revolver in his hand.

Surely in this lovely rich, and various country such an opportunity must present itself. . . .

TRIGGER GUARD

Chapter 1

Juan Soto, as a child in the mountain *pueblo* of San Hermin, had dreamed of being a bandit.

It had seemed to him of all lives the most perfect, the most romantic, the most comfortable. To be always on horseback, to be always fed (and well fed), to have a fine pistol, to have all the prettiest girls staring after him in admiration . . .

So much for the dreams of youth.

The dreams had not encompassed the *Rurales* and their ready nooses or the brutality of his companions, the filth, the desperate need for warmth in bitter mountain winters. The scratching, scrabbling, the murdering for a pitcher of stolen goat's milk, a few *tortillas* wrapped in some peasant's shirt-tail.

7

A foul business, and too seldon rewarded by the likes of a prize such as this, this treasure on horseback which now rode down the *arroyo* toward them.

The *gringo* rode a small and undistinguished paint, an *Indio* horse, it appeared. But the *norte-americano* was dressed in fine wool and leather, and wore such boots—Juan had seen them clearly when the Yankee stopped for a cup of *mescal* at Las Rosas. Fine tall leather boots. And a superb pistol—a Colt's, of the type called "Bisley."

All this was too much wealth for any one man to possess, wealth sufficient to earn him a cut throat. It was unChristian wealth!

More than sufficient, even without the saddle-bags, those fine tooled-leather bags in which two much smaller leather bags were stuffed. A thousand silver pesos. Perhaps a *thousand* . . .

For this, it was true, they had only the word of Severio's sister, whose husband labored at Don Luis' mine. And this information appeared correct, for since when did the Don's Yankee ride the mountains to no purpose? Never.

And the purpose now? *Banco National* at Paso Robles.

But he would never reach it—nor should he, being not only a *gringo* dog, but an accursed Protestant as well. Let him die here, then, well served for being what he was . . .

It would have been more pleasant to have a larger number of men—these affairs were sometimes surprising—but these three would have to do. Severio, who had the crack-stocked Spenser rifle and kept it to himself as if it were a child (not even allowing Juan to test it with a shot or two); Manuel No-name, a brute from the coast, an Indio who barely understood Spanish; and Mercurio Fuentes, a slender, evil man with unnatural tastes.

These three and no more. A poor following for a man who had, only two years before, robbed the Sinaloa Express train with a band of fifteeen men. True, that deed had not ended well, but at least it had been a deed of significance.

This now, compared to that, was nothing.

It was also a day like a furnace. In this gullied *barranca*, the sun came hammering down hard enough to beat a man into the earth, turning all of Jesus's blessed natural colors on the earth to the harsh tints of hell. The air quivered with the heat, but sent sound only slowly.

Juan could barely hear the hoofbeats of the *gringo's* horse. That doomed one was well in sight now, riding his ugly little *pinto* as if he and all *norte-americanos* owned the very dirt they rode upon.

9

Coming at a walk, ignorant as a child toddling into a next of *tarantula*.

A fair-enough looking man, it must be admitted. And close enough, too. If the Yankee only turned a little in his saddle, looked up over his right shoulder, then perhaps he would see Juan Soto in the rocks, ready to whistle death down upon him. Young—or almost young, his face clean-shaven as a boy's. He had taken his jacket off—a fine buckskin jacket it was—and rolled it at his saddle cantle with his blanket. A rifle, too. That treasure had been forgotten for a moment; now it was remembered. A shining Winchester rifle. A *General's* weapon. An *Haciendado's* weapon.

And soon to be Juan Soto's weapon. Let Severio brandish his old piece of trash, then!

This *gringo* walking his *pinto* past—and far enough.

Vaya con Dios!

Lee heard the shrill whistle, swung low to the left side of his saddle, and spurred the paint as hard as he could kick. A rifle bullet went droning past, just over his doubled back as the paint, snorting in surprise, bolted to the left, already into a gallop. Down the damn *barranca* he should never have ridden into.

Been riding, day-dreaming like a kid.

10

Thinking of Rosalia . . . Asking for trouble. And now some other fools had surprised *this* fool.

The little pain was flying, hooves rattling on the stones, the gully's sun-packed sand and dirt. Galloping in a haze of heat and light and dust. The paint canted to the right, leaning as it ran, and Lee swung down further off the saddle, left hand hooked about the horn, ducked lower still, under the racing horse's neck, drew the Bisley from that position, and fired a shot into a huge Mexican lumbering at them from the canyon wall, reaching out for the paint's bridle.

The shot had no effect that Lee could see in that instant and, in the rolling, jolting commotion of his hanging ride, he stretched the Colt's out under the horse's neck again and fired another shot, this directly into the reaching giant's chest as he put out his arm to grip the paint's leathers.

That shot surely must have killed the big man, because he did not grasp the paint's bridle and haul him to a stop. The *cabron* is a dead one, Lee thought, and was just hauling himself back up into the saddle (had spurred the pinto hard as he did to keep it galloping full out), was just barely set up in the saddle, when a rifle shot came cracking across the gully floor, struck the little paint, and killed it in mid-stride.

Lee stood, shaking out of the stirrups as

the paint folded under him, its legs still pumping, hooves ringing on stone, its powerful, slab-sided muscles still racking in its run. Doing all this, though, it still folded, sank, collapsed, and finally struck the streaking dirt with its nose, its neck and chest and slid, already dead, a long, rough, noisy slide along the stones.

Lee parted company, and went sailing quite a way beyond.

He tried to stay upright, windmilling through the air, feet running on nothing, but could not do so. The moment one boot sole struck the earth, so did he, and very hard, was rolled and beaten and skinned along the ground.

He kept the Colt's in his hand, and was saved by doing it, because a thin man came running up the *arroyo* toward him as he lay in a heap, frosted with yellow dust, small bright purple dots revolving and revolving in his sight. He could see the canyon dirt and rock beyond them, but the purple dots continued to revolve, though they grew small as Lee managed to sit up.

He saw the thin man—dark skinned, heavily oiled black hair worn long as a woman's . . . a handsome, clever face. Or would have been handsome with the addition of a few of his previous teeth. Fellow was grinning, happy as a hog at trough, coming at Lee with a single-barreled shotgun and now just stopping his run to catch his breath and aim it.

Lee lifted his right hand and fired before he thought to do it, before he'd noticed he still had the hand-gun in his grasp. The Colt's might have done his thinking for him.

That shot missed, but made the thin man wince before he set himself again to level on Lee and kill him. This flinching cost the man his life.

Lee rose up onto his right elbow, stared hard at the fellow's belly covered in torn, stained-cotton trousers and shot him there.

At first, Lee thought the man'd exploded from the injury; then he realized it had been the shotgun going off wild. The bits of shot went humming off across the gulch in a quick sort of swarming. Lee thumbed the hammer on the Bisley Colt's, and shot the thin man again. The fellow was staggering this way and that, crooning, gripping his red-soaked trousers with red and delicate hands.

This second shot knocked the man off his feet and he lay in the bright yellow dust on his side, his legs making slow walking motions.

As that thin bandit went down, Lee got up, stood still for a moment, testing whether he had broken any bones—and ducked as another rifle shot came buzzing past him to smack into the gully wall a dozen yards past. The round had missed Lee by very little.

The new Winchester was still in its scabbard with the pinto.

Lee lit out running, heading back to the heap of dead horse—that nasty little paint, that sturdy, vicious kicker. It had carried him down out of the Oregon Territory, out of a certain small town up there where two men had been shot to death. Had carried him, later, out of an even smaller town in northern California, where a sawmill payroll had been looted at gunpoint, a constable killed.

Lee lowered his head as though he were running in a rain, and galloping along for his life. Knew he must look ridiculous to the man or men who watched him from the *barranca's* other side. He had seen men run for their lives. No dignity. No dignity in that.

The few yards to the horse's body seemed a British mile. Lee was almost there when he felt he was sighted down. He *knew* it.

He fell flat as though shot already and the round came clipping through the air above him, snapping past with a personal sound.

Lee twisted up, hoping for a glimpse—the son-of-a-bitch must be up high—and caught more than that, saw the man as big as life standing at the gully's opposite rim, some thirty or more feet up outlined in a blaze of sunlight, aiming his rifle again.

Lee raised the Colt's and fired at the fellow. No effect at that range, of course, near two-hundred yards. He heaved up onto his feet again, fired another shot for theatrics, and dove for the paint and his rifle.

The little horse had fallen and rolled to his right side. Inconvenient. Lee, feeling skinned knees and an aching elbow—hurt enough to be near busted—for the first time since his fall, scooted around to that side of the animal and commenced to wrench at the rifle stock protruding from under the dead beast's shoulder.

Hard tugging.

The man on the rim fired again. Lee didn't know where the bullet went, but not into him, thank God. No question, though, that he was a dead *gringo* if he didn't get the Winchester clear and working. Such a fine piece, too. Beat the old Henry all hollow . . .

Lee sat down in the dirt as another rifle slug came at him—knew where *that* one went; it slammed into the dead pinto's haunch. Didn't shift him but might as well have, since it gave Lee sufficient encouragement to grip the end of the Winchester's stock near hard enough to dent the walnut, set his boots up against the horse's body, and heave for all he was worth and then some. Would be surprised if the rifleman (and friend or friends) weren't laughing hard enough at this spectacle (Don Luis' ferocious Yankee *pistolero* trying to pry his rifle from under a dead horse) to spoil their aim.

Lee devoutly hoped so, anticipated the next rifle round and pulled even harder at the Winchester's stock. The rifle came suddenly sliding free from under the pinto's bulk and Lee threw himself back and away as the next rifle shot popped past his ear.

He rolled onto his belly—no time to scramble around to the horse's lee side—levered the Winchester (difficult to imagine a sweeter sound in a tight) and leveled it at the *barranca's* rim.

The fellow there was something of a slow-top, it appeared. He must have seen Lee haul his rifle free but he seemed to pay no heed to it. Still stood upright as a lead soldier, and as Lee brought the Winchester's sights down upon him, stepped from the gully rim and commenced a slow, awkward, sliding descent, his rifle held in one hand as he did it.

Hard to say why a man will do such a foolish thing in a fight. The constable at Russian River had done just such a foolish thing as Lee came walking out of the sawmill shed on a pitch black night, leaving three men (two guards and a clerk) hog-tied and gagged behind him. The gagging and tying of one had been superfluous—a gunman and guard named Ike Perry had objected to the robbery, and Lee had had to beat him unconscious. The constable, a young man named McManus, had surprised Lee there in the dark, and had thrown the light of a lantern upon him, while naming him arrested. Some stray mill-hand must have seen or heard the action in the office, and run to fetch this young law-bird.

McManus had accosted Lee, called him to account and thrown the light of a lantern on him. Lee had instantly fired into that light and struck McManus in his chest and killed him. The foolish man had been holding the lantern directly in front of him.

So, a first-time robber—a sort of romantic highwayman he might be regarded, if one were not too particular—had become a law-shooter. A police-killer.

A fugitive into this warm land of Mexico.

Lee got his bead . . . held it—what in hell was the man climbing down for?—then squeezed off his round.

No puff of rock dust anywhere around the fellow. A certain hit, though the man didn't show it. Kept that awkward slow scramble down the *barranca* wall, rifle still held up and out of the way of stone-scrapes or scratches . . .

Lee levered and shot the man again.

This round, at least, made a considerable impression. The bandit, who appeared to be a tall, well set-up fellow, a *serape* still neatly draped across one shoulder, suddenly threw up his hands, as if Lee's rifle had called for such a surrender, threw them up and commenced a slow turn, like a show-off at a *baile*, then slowly toppled forward off the wall's low face. He fell past twenty feet of rock wall and landed, as near as Lee could tell, directly on his head. Man had held his rifle all the way down.

There, by God! Pack of damned greasers, to run an attempt on Don Luis' Yankee!

Lee looked over his shoulder to see if the other two were still down. Further along the *arroyo*, the thin one with oiled hair had stopped his walking lying down. Looked dead as mutton.

Back a ways, Lee saw that the big one who'd tried for the paint's reins was not down and dead.

That fellow, a first bullet in him somewhere, a second surely in his chest, was up and about after a fashion. Crawling up the gulch as if going for help . . . as if help might be found out there, in the fry-pan heat, the nests of scorpions, rattlesnakes, cactus spines.

Lee had an opportunity then, for one of those cruely comic shots that will occur in a long and complicated fight. The big man's large buttocks presented themselves as he crawled slowly away, each cheek shifting massively under its trouser seat of dirty white cotton. A bull's eye for sure.

Plenty of men would have taken that shot, laughing.

Lee shot the big man through his left thigh and, as he toppled and rolled half over, levered again and took him very neatly with a second, just over his crotch and belly, and through his head.

Crisp shooting, and satisfactory.

Lee levered the Winchester again for fresh—and the weapon jammed.

No surprise—Mexican re-loads into used brass. Had sworn he'd go to Del Suberio for *Yanqui* ammunition, and had not troubled to do so. No surprise and his fault, not the Winchester's. Lee knelt up to clear it—the cartridge had caught half-ejected—and a man came running at him from near where the fool with the rifle had fallen. This man was short, and thick through the shoulders, but he seemed at the distance to have a face at odds with his body, a thin, big-nosed bird's face. He wore crossed bandoliers—a sign of leadership among bandits—and he fired a large revolver at Lee, once, and then again as he came running. He also shouted something but Lee couldn't make it out.

Lee didn't think. He dropped the jammed Winchester, drew his Colt's, flipped the gate, dropped one empty out into the sand, pulled a fresh round from his belt, thumbed it into the cylinder, eased the hammer, spun the cylinder, pulled the hammer back, swung the piece up and aiming, and slipped the hammer to fire. The live cartridge had spun to where it should be. The Colt's went off.

The slug struck the shouting man in his chest, broke his shout off in a grunt, and a bone there in a quick crack as the lead went through.

The bandit leader glared at Lee as if he could, by staring dreadfully enough, kill him. He stumbled to a stop no more than ten feet away and carefully lifted his revolver—an old Smith and Wesson Russian .44, Lee saw—to put this bullet where he wished it. And looked steady enough to get it done.

Lee scrambled to his feet like a kicked dog. He took a great stomping leap to the left, spun on his heel, and dove to the right, reaching down into his right boot-top as he did. He rolled, and came to his feet just as the Smith and Wesson went off with a considerable bang. Lee felt a sting at the inside of his left knee—could still stand—palmed the broad-blade dagger in his right hand, drew that hand back like a baseball pitcher, and threw the knife spinning.

The bandit saw it coming. Lee saw the flicker of his eyes, but the man was too badly hurt to go tumbling over the countryside as Lee had for the dodge. He stood stock still (dying, no doubt, from that shot to his chest) and fired the Smith and Wesson as the dagger whacked into his belly—nine inches of broad, double-edge steel—and left him doubled over on his knees, his big revolver fallen into the sand beside him, of no use at all.

Lee stood beside the dead paint, and his hands trembled for a moment as though he had a chill . . . as though he were in the mountains to the east on one of the cold nights there . . .

This weakness in his hands had happened before a time or two, and always after a serious fight. There was no difficulty about it. The fight was always over when the trembling came and it didn't last long.

He walked over to the kneeling man. The bandit *jefe*—a small chieftain, surely, to command only three men—was doubled over hard, his bloody hands clenched on the dagger handle almost concealed in the billow of his dirty shirt. The leather bandoliers looked too heavy for the man as he crouched there.

"*¿Que tal, hombre?*"

But the kneeling man had no answer to make, except to slowly shake his head as if in comment on Lee's stupidity in asking. The man shook his head and gripped the handle of Lee's knife as if he were afraid the blade would slide out and escape him. Surprising the fellow was still alive, with a bullet through his chest as well. Perhaps not so surprising. In his year and a half in Mexico, besides finding himself oddly adept at learning Spanish (Lee'd been all the more startled by this knack since he'd had no call even to try another tongue, unless Professor Riles' Latin could be counted) Lee had also learned that the Mexican people possessed a particular toughness, a bitter sort of endurance that had little to do with what an *Americano* regarded as hardihood. They were an enduring people, silent, merry, and cruel. Lee had grown very fond of them and had learned from them.

It seemed to him now that it would be unpleasant, for some reason, to go about the business of reloading his revolver in order to fire it into this *bandito's* head. No more pleasant to reach under him and wrench the knife handle from his grip so that Lee might cut his throat.

Simplest was best, it seemed.

Lee looked about him, saw and dismissed a small rounded stone, then saw a larger one, a rock with an angle to it. He walked over, picked it up, walked back.

"*Vaya con Dios,*" he said, raised the rock in both hands, and brought it smartly down onto the back of the fellow's head. The blow made a dull cracking sound, not as loud as Lee expected, and laid the man out flat. Lee stood over him, his hands stinging from the force of the first blow, and struck at the fallen man's head again.

This time the bone broke thoroughly, and as if in approbation the corpse loosed a long tootling fart.

Chapter 2

Lee found their horses, four dreary little saddle-galled scrubs, at the far south end of the *barranca* rim. His little paint would have made two of any of them. A horse to be missed, that nasty little kicker. Had saved Lee's life, once, kicking.

Lee unhobbled two of the scrubs and let them drift away. The better two he led back down into the arroyo. No one of the animals would be able to carry him, his stock saddle, his war-bag and rifle, his *Saltillo* blanket roll, and the saddle-bags with the silver.

Have to be ride one, pack the other.

And so he did.

The land rising up into the *Porcupinos* was dry as a dead cow's skull, dotted with *maguey* and cactus. It humped itself slowly up in broad shelf after shelf, ridge after ridge, like a great brown beast rising from a long sleep under the broiling sun.

It was big country, and beautiful in its way, but there was no shade, no ease at all in it. It was country indifferent to what human or horse might come crawling over it. It cared nothing for them.

Four kites were circling high, tiny black crucifixes swinging against an endless blue-white bowl of sky. And even here in the wilderness, Lee could faintly smell the scents of Mexico drifting in the breathless, baking air. Human shit was there . . . always present, even in the corridors of Don Luis' great *hacienda,* even in the governor's palace at *Hermosillo;* the scent of dung, if not its actuality. That, then, and half-tanned leather, and sugar cane drinks all the colors of the rainbow. Spilled beer, and marijuana smoke.

All the stinks of greaserdom, a North American might say, and be dead right.

Lee had grown to enjoy them. They spoke of life, stubborn and quarrelsome, still at its work in this fierce country. He had ridden down across the *Bravo* nearly two years before, had stopped at *Renosa* to drink and whore and rest and to take the measure of this Mexico. He'd liked it from the first and had not been troubled by the hatred many of these brown men felt for the white men of the north who had whipped them in two hard wars.

Lee had pretended to be nothing but what he was—a horse-raiser, a gunman, and now, a thief with a price on his head. He had also, much more important, swiftly learned Spanish (or at least a fluent sort of border variety of the language) and so had pleased many Mexicans who were too used to being shouted at by Americans who refused to try any language but their own.

In that way and not, for the time being, being handicapped by poverty, Lee had gotten on well enough, staying clear, when he could, of the other Yankee roughs who'd drifted south in preference to a sheriff's noose.

Had gotten on well, had enjoyed himself, had minded his own business . . . until a visit from an agent of the local *policia*. This small man, named Rosario y Vega, had come to the Florita one morning; found Lee in his room, and sat down on Lee's only chair for a small conversation.

It appeared that the Federal marshal of the Territory of Northern California had made certain approaches to the Captain— one Edgar Swaine—of the Texas Ranger Post in McAllen, concerning a fugitive wanted in connection with the slaying of an officer of the law . . . a certain constable.

This same Captain Swaine, a fierce man,

very bold, and not particularly a respecter of borders and boundaries, had made peremptory demands of the police in Renosa to produce this fugitive.

So, Rosario y Vega, *agento,* had come to the Florita on this cool, rainy morning— "And haven't we needed this rain? And who but the Sweet Virgin, and of course, his Excellency the Governor, could be praised for providing it."

Brought gently to the point (Lee had no wish at all to murder this little man, then to flee the Florita in a hustle and bustle headed God knew where) *Senor* y Vega, by and by, reckoned that a sturdy tale of death in the back country, supported by a very ripe corpse (there were, as it happened, two appropriate Yankees currently sick to death with the tar shits in the wards of the convent clinic even as he spoke) allowed perhaps to ripen for some days . . . properly clothed . . . found by the nuns to have this and that about him . . . a proper watch . . . proper papers . . .

Senor y Vega reckoned that such an exhibit might persuade even the Protestant Swaine that a bad man had gone to his certain punishment in Hell.

"It sounds an expensive exhibit," Lee had said in very creditable Spanish, and *Senor* y Vega had agreed sadly that that was so. A wonderful arrangement and an expensive one.

It cost Lee every penny he had taken out of the sawmill office safe, except for the sum of one hundred dollars. This last was allowed him because, as the chief of the Renosa police said, "Without it he will surely rob Mexicans, as he has already robbed his own."

This incident, which made armed stealing seem like a losing game indeed to Lee—though he wouldn't, it was true, have been harrassed over the border had not McManus been such a fool with that lantern—confirmed for him the necessity of finding some more acceptable employment, even if only slightly more acceptable.

"We would also desire you, at your convenience, to depart . . . to ride away from Renosa, if you could bring yourself to do so . . ."

"Much as that will pain me," Lee had answered the Chief of Police in his improving Spanish, "much as I will sorrow to be parted from such municipal loveliness . . . such civilization, I realize the necessity of doing so."

"Tomorrow?"

"My plan exactly."

"At least, a gentleman," the Chief said to *agento* Rosario y Vega, after Lee had bowed, shaking hands, and left the offices. "A cut above the usual Yankee *pistolero.*"

"A dog of breeding," said y Vega, and both men laughed and then went out to lunch, though usually they did not lunch together.

Thereafter, Lee, trusting that he was dead as possible to the American authorities—but not trusting that completely enough to wish an interview with Captain Swaine of the Texas Rangers—traveled west a long way, into Sonora. And was mighty pleased by it.

He rode there through a mountain range of stacked boulders, stones, pebbles, the like of which he'd never seen—and saw besides, huddled in each narrow mountain valley, a small *rancho* carpeted with grass as green as ever grew in Idaho Territory. That sweet grass . . . a small, sturdy *adobe* ranch house . . . running water (always a good year-round creek draining from the odd mountains rising at either side) and small herds of very respectable stock. Long-horned cattle . . . very good horses.

At these *ranchos,* he had stopped, not missing one, and had accepted his meal and night of hospitality, and asked for work in the morning.

Struck, perhaps, by the oddity of a *gringo* and a *malo,* obviously, requesting honest work, many of the *rancheros* had taken Lee on for a few days' work or a few weeks' work. They had, most of them, no more work than that to give, since their own people, living in tiny cabins on their land, had an hereditary right to what stock-chivvying or haying had to be done.

Still Lee worked and kept most of his hundred dollars safe in his purse.

He had serious trouble only once and that came from taking sides at a country *baille* against two brothers who threatened his *patron* of the week, a gentle work-worn man who leased his land and ran only seventy head of scrub cows on it.

This man, named Gaspar Molina, had offered Lee shelter and two meals of tortillas and beans a day to hold that small herd still on the banks of a creek called Chabectli, while Molina and his son went up into the mountains to round strays, there being no more than seven or eight of those.

Doing this small duty, Lee had held the cattle by the water—no difficult feat, since cinch grass was also growing just that high through the whole stretch of grazing—had held them for six days until Molina and his boy rode in happy with five of their strays.

Pitiful doings, this would have been called in the north . . . in the States. But Lee enjoyed it and liked both Molina and his boy, Toribio.

It was this man Molina that the two brothers Sanchez attempted to bully. Some question of winter graze back in the hills.

The Sanchez brothers—Lee never knew their Christian names—approached Molina as he and his boy were watching the dancing, and commenced to insult the man

30

right there publicly, insulting the memory of Molina's wife, who had been from all Lee had heard a decent woman, though sickly.

Molina was no coward, but he was slow-witted and gentle; his boy like him as two peas. They weren't up to disputing.

The Sanchez brothers were odd bullies to see, being middle-aged with white in their hair, one shorter than the other with a sharper face. They were well dressed in wool and leather, had spent money on their clothes, and on hair oils and perfume. They each wore revolvers in *buscadero* holsters at their hips.

Lee had gone to get a sweet roll from a woman selling some, and was considering the courtesies of asking one of the Mexican girls to dance—he had his eye on a tall girl, very handsome, with a faint wine-colored birthmark at the corner of her lips. Looked as though she'd been eating strawberries.

He'd noticed the crowd gathered to listen to the baiting of the Molinas, and walked over there, munching the sweet roll.

Heard what one of the brothers was saying, over the heads of the crowd, and then pushed his way through to the front. Ordinarily, Lee would have stood wide of such a show, the Molinas' business being, after all, their business. Ordinarily, but not now.

He was a Molina hand, though for only tortillas and beans. A Molina hand, and would be till the hour he quit or was sent off. Lee behaved as he would have expected any of *his* hands to have behaved on Spade Bit. When you worked a place you were *of* the place or you weren't worth much.

". . . A fine pair," the taller of the Sanchez brothers was saying. "Thieves of grazing land today—who can say what will find its way into their pockets tomorrow! Perhaps some of your pigs, Olivero? We wouldn't be surprised by that. A family of pigs . . . what could be more natural than their gathering more pigs to themselves?"

Some awkward laughter at that sally.

"The mother of this Molina son . . ." the other brother chimed in like a hallway clock.

"Silencio! With your permission, Patron." Lee stepped clear of a man beside him, crowding his gun arm. "I say, be silent," Lee said to the Sanchez brothers. "The only pigs I see here are imitating human speech, and poorly."

"By the Saints! This damn *gringo* barks like the Molinas' dog!" The taller Sanchez put his hand on the butt of his revolver. "You Texas thing," he said to Lee, and started to say something more, but Lee had no intention of letting him run on, of letting this matter come to shooting.

Lee stepped one step forward and kicked the taller Sanchez in the stones.

That man, very badly hurt, stood frozen,

still gripping the butt of his holstered revolver but apparently in no condition to use the weapon.

Lee shoved the injured man aside so hard that he staggered and fell down and drew, cocked, and leveled the Bisley Colt's while the other Sanchez, barely decided, had his revolver only half out of the leather.

"Don't force me to kill you," Lee said, proud to have remembered his Spanish in such a pass.

Neither Sanchez looked to be forcing him to do any such thing, though the crowd about them seemed something disappointed at their tameness.

"Protestant!" the taller Sanchez said, sitting on the ground. His face was very pale from the pain of being kicked. He was keeping his right hand away from the butt of his revolver.

The other brother stood staring at Lee's Colt's as if the pistol had sprung into Lee's hand by witchcraft. This brother had nothing to say. He watched the muzzle of the Colt's.

"Please . . . please," Molina said, and put a worn and calloused hand on Lee's gun arm. "There is no need to harm them . . ."

"As you order, *Patron*," Lee said, glad to be so easily out of it. "Should they insult the Molina land and the Molina name further however, it will be my pleasure, if you send for me, to return."

"No, no . . ." Molina said, as the shorter Sanchez, still keeping a wary eye on Lee's revolver muzzle, helped his wincing brother to his feet. "No, no . . . we have no need of violence here," the worn brown hand patting at Lee's arm as if Lee were some wild young stallion to be quieted.

There was considerable murmuring around them; an event of the first importance had apparently occurred in the pueblo with this fracas. A stranger *gringo* had, in Molina's name, humbled *both* of the Sanchez brothers. "Pride goeth before a fall" indeed. And this North American, with eyes the color of amber and a pistol so quickly obedient—there even seemed a possibility he was *El Cabrito*, Billy the Kid!

So that story began its silly round. The elder Molina inquired of him the next day as he was saddling the little paint. "If I am being rude, I beg you will tell me, *Senor*. Is it that you are Billy the Kid?"

"I am not," Lee told him, and saw that the *ranchero* was somewhat disappointed. "I have met him, however. He is bigger than ordinary men, and fierce as a puma."

"Truly? You met him?"

"Only once. A noble fellow, for all his fierceness."

With this lie, Molina was well pleased—to have met a man who had met that legendary defender and friend to the Mexican people in distant *Nuevo Mexico*.

Lee had had no heart to tell him that the Kid, a small Brooklyn hoodlum with buck teeth, and by all accounts mean as a snake, had been shot to death in a dark room by a panicked Patrick Garrett.

Lee'd bade the pleased Molina farewell, leaned down to shake Molina's boy by the hand, and spurred the little paint on out to start the long switch-back climb up the next narrow range of pebbly mountains. Was a hot day, but with a breeze—not bad for riding.

That was the only trouble he'd seen so far in Mexico—and had, after all, been nothing for a man to preen himself on—to have cowed two blustering old *rancheros*. Not precisely a hero's deed . . .

A month or a little more later, Lee had ridden down into the valley of the Rio Matape, and seen La Colorado. The pueblo stretched along the river bank for a quarter of a mile, white-walled, red-roofed in the dazzling sunlight. A light green haze of cottonwoods ran along the river's course, and backed the town like a curtain, cool and verdant.

It was a small settlement . . . peaceful.

Lee had ridden into La Colorado's cobble-stoned streets at *siesta* time, the paint's hooves ringing on the rock. There was otherwise no sound at all about the town except for a woman singing far down the street and a distant noise of crows in the fields beyond.

The town was asleep and Lee, deciding to join it, rode down a jacaranda-blossomed alley to the grassy river bank, pulled the pinto up, unsaddled him, hobbled him, and left him, ass high, sucking water from a glassy, shallowy eddy of the stream. Lee walked back up higher on the bank, found a deep shifting patch of shade beneath a very old cottonwood, lay down, hitched his gunbelt more comfortable, tucked his crumpled Stetson beneath his head, and drifted to sleep as if he drifted on the waters of the Metape.

Lee lived in La Colorado for three months, made some money working for Geronimo Gayana, the smith in the town, and made some friends as well.

Then one morning, on the fourth of August, two deserters from the *Rurale* station at Empalme rode drunk up the river and, stopping at La Colorado to refresh themselves, broke into the back of Pedro Alvarado's dry goods store to rob it. While there, they stabbed Alvarado and his wife to death; then, apparently repenting of their haste, stripped the woman's corpse and raped it.

The whole street had of course heard the Alvarados' screams, but they had also seen that the men who were the occasion of that noise and who had kicked the store's door off its hinges to enter, were dressed in the grey-blue jackets, the silver buttons and facings of the *Rurales*. So the people of that street had listened to the screams but had left their own weapons, their *machetes,* their hoes, their ancient muskets, undisturbed. They had gone to their houses and stayed there.

When those two men came out of the Alvarados' store, one still fastening up his trousers, and both spattered here and there with blood, Lee had been standing by the town fountain—a very handsome fountain, with a carving of an eagle on top of the stone—with his Winchester rifle in his hands.

It was a puzzle to the townspeople afterward why he had interfered at all, the Alvarados not being special friends of his. It was thought possible that *Senora* Alvarado's screams had worked to irritate nerves unaccustomed to such sounds. It was well known that Yankees of all sorts were somewhat spoiled with soft living, and had no notion of fate at all . . .

The two men, owlish drunk, had barely time to recognize that some difficulty impended before one was shot through the head like a duck. The other, he who was buttoning his clothes, was shot thereafter through the body, fired back with his revolver, and then was shot again, the bullet carrying a piece of his intestine away.

And no sooner had the gunsmoke drifted off than, just as in a play at the theater in Hermosillo, a troop of *Rurales*, hanging ropes at their saddle cantles, came galloping into the square, searching for their deserters. The *Rurales* had a short way with deserters.

A North American might have expected the Lieutenant of *Rurales* to be pleased that his business had been done for him, even if by a *gringo*. A citizen of Mexico would have known better.

It took some talk by the *Alcalde* and other men of the town to prevent the Lieutenant from ordering Lee strung up in the deserters' place.

It took some talk, but the talk had prevailed.

A week later, a *vaquero* rode into town. He was a rider from Las Sabrinas, and Las Sabrinas was the land, the country, the hills, the great Rancho to the north. All— and much more than that—was the property, the kingdom, of Don Luis Arturo Ortiz-Cordoba de Spania.

It was this kingly man, as powerful, almost, as the Governer himself, who wished to see the *norteamericano*, Lee McCann. (Lee had felt "McCann" to be a reasonable substitute for a name Captain Swaine of the Texas Rangers would be almost certain to notice, should it accidently be brought to his attention north of the border. "Lee Morgan" was a bit too famous a fellow.)

Lee, on the advice of the townspeople, had packed up his war-bag, saddled the paint, and followed after the *vaquero*, meek as a sheep, to go and kow-tow before this Mexican Grandee. It had seemed a wise vacation in any case, as long as the troop of *Rurales* stayed quartered in the town. Their Lieutenant gave Lee hard looks every time their paths crossed, and their paths looked to cross often if Lee remained for the while in La Colorado.

The *vaquero*—his only given name Vincente, as far as Lee could tell—was an elderly man, gnarled and dark and twisted as a root. He was silent as a root, too, and occasionally reminded Lee of his foreman, Ford. Ford was something younger, of course, and white. But there was the same reclusive toughness, silence, about both men. And for all his age and the age of his horse, a long-toothed grey named *Rosinante*, the old man kept the lead with no apparent effort in the five long days it took them to arrive at Las Sabrinas.

They rode the ridges of the hills bordering the Matape, rode them the hot days through. Then, in the evenings, they walked their horses down the slopes to the river . . . camped there, fished (the old man an expert with hook and line) cooked the fish over mesquite twigs, smoked vile corn-husk cigarettes, looked at each other occasionally, went off into the brush to do their individual necessities, returned to the fire, smoked other cigarettes, and went to sleep to the music of the river and the soft, murderous, high-pitched cries of the owls that flew through the cottonwoods, hunting.

Lee woke in the middle of the first night, saw that the old man was not in his blankets, picked up his Winchester and walked out to find him.

Vincente was standing by a lightning-killed water oak, on watch, his old Spenser cradled in his arms. Lee came up to him, motioned with his thumb for the old man to return to his blankets, and took his place.

In that way, the two of them came to their agreements about standing guard. Over the next few days of traveling, their agreements grew to cover all trailing matters. Still, the old man hardly spoke at all, and whenever Lee essayed his not-too-awkward Spanish, would look at him in apparent astonishment, as if he expected that *gringos* had hardly been gifted with speech at all—much as if Lee had been a cattle-dog, and had suddenly remarked upon the weather.

In this fashion they traveled, and did well enough, and rode always higher along the river's course, higher into ever greener country. It was cattle country, now, or horse-raising country. The grass, when Lee leaned from the saddle to pluck up a long yellow-green leaf of it to chew, had the salt-stone taste of fine grazing. Sure enough, on the morning of the fourth day, he saw the first herd. Long-horned cattle, as Molina's had been, but bigger, fine, and fat, and branded with a large and simple "S." *Sabrinas.* It appeared to Lee an easy brand to imitate, and he wondered how this rich Don kept his beeves from being stolen from him. Any Idaho rustler—even any Texican rustler—would have made the finest "S" seen with a few strokes of a running iron, and been a small rancher in a jiffy.

The costs of this sort of enterprise, however, Lee saw to be high on midday next.

He and Vincente were riding a track—very nearly a road, it was, well carved by wagon wheels—when they came upon a large sign erected on two strong, tall poles. LAS SABRINAS. The letters had been burned deep into the wood.

At either end of the long sign, a naked man hung by his heels, swollen and dead—dead, evidently, simply from hanging for a considerable time upside town. The great Sabrinas "S" had been branded deep in each man's bare belly.

Perhaps not so easy and safe to use a

running iron in this country after all. Likely not.

Lee had no notion that this sign represented the beginning marker of Don Luis Arturo Ortiz-Cordoba de Spania's ranchland. He knew, had known from the way the old vaquero sat his saddle, that Vincente had been riding home grass for two days. This marker simply stated the commencement of a yard or perhaps, a lawn leading to the man's home itself.

Lee guessed that home to be another day's ride to go.

He was right.

Chapter 3

At dawn of the sixth day, Vincente had risen, gone to piss, come back to camp—they'd slept under chaparral along the brow of a hill—and had announced simply, "Las Sabrinas."

There was no second gateway . . . no sign or cairn or marker of any sort. Only the track grew more traveled, deeper scarred by wagons and horses' hooves.

Lee and the old man rode the track all the morning, over slowly rising hills and breaks thick with sedge and broom-grass. Birds flew up beside their horses, and cloud shadows flowed over the hills like floods of shade, and drifted on.

It was handsome country, and it made Lee ache to ride over it. He felt at times that he might lift his head to see the Rocky

Mountains rising to the west . . . to hear the shouts of his men chivvying horses down the hills . . .

They saw only two other riders that morning. Two *vaqueros* sat their mounts on a distant rise, watching them, and did not move to answer old Vincente's wave. The two horsemen watched Lee and the old man for a few minutes, then turned their horses' heads and rode away.

Just before noon, by Lee's fine silver-backed repeater watch won in a poker game in Amarillo, they came upon the house . . . not a house, really, rather a collection of dazzling white adobe buildings, several two stories tall, that clustered around a central walled yard big enough to play a game of baseball in.

More like a village than ranch-house.

And it grew bigger as Lee and the old man rode toward it.

The old man left Lee at a black wrought iron gate, then led the horses away. The gate was let into a low snow white adobe wall compassing a wide yard of combed and raked yellow gravel. Eight lemon trees, equally spaced, fronted the house beyond.

Lee looked at the house for a while—looked as much like one of the Spanish mission churches as a house—then leaned at his ease against the gate, lit one of the dreadful corn-husk cigarettes (longing considerably for a Havana cigar, rum-dipped), and baking like a lizard in the heat.

After a while, a big woman dressed in black came waddling down the walk, opened the gate, and motioned Lee to follow.

The house was cool as the day was hot. Cool, and very large, with glistening black hardwood floors, black oak and leather furnishings looking old as sin . . . high walls white as laundered sheets, and hung with paintings too old to read as to detail, or tell the original colors of.

Lee waited for some time in the entrance hall. Then a fat old man in black trousers and a long white shirt came slippering along to beckon him to follow. Lee trailed this fat old fellow through other hallways and waiting-rooms as well until led to tall double doors, black as the polished floor.

The servant tapped on one of these, and a young voice called in English, *"Come in!"*

Don Luis de Spania was unexpected. Lee had anticipated some tall hawk-nosed old hidalgo, proud as Lucifer and as grasping.

"Come in, please, Mister McCann—it is 'McCann,' is it not?"

Don Luis de Spania was Lee's age, or a little older, short, broad-shouldered and broad-faced as a peasant, with teeth discolored from smoking and eyes as round, sharp, merciless and black as a magpie's.

Lee suspected he had been right, at least as concerned the "grasping."

"It's McCann at present, *Senor.*" Only after he'd spoken did Lee realize he'd spoken in Spanish. That habit had grown on him.

The Don threw back his head and laughed. "At present! I do like a man with a sense of humor! And a man so quick to learn a civilized language—and not too badly, though your accent smacks of Texas." The broad-shouldered man opened a small silver box on his desk, reached in, took out a cigar, and stood to walk around the desk to offer it to Lee. The Don limped, and very badly.

"A fall from a horse some years ago," he said, seeing Lee's glance at his legs. "Entirely my fault. The horse, an animal named Lagrimas, was perfectly splendid. I was an . . . imperfect rider."

Lee had been impressed by the days of land he had ridden to get here and impressed by the house and its compound, the power and wealth both represented. But he had seen fine houses before and great stretches of country owned by one man (had, in fact, owned a great deal of that commodity himself), and nothing of Las Sabrinas so impressed him as the Don's admission of poor horsemanship. He had known few men who would concede to that, and none of them had been rich and powerful.

There was more to Don Luis than his acreage.

He had another trick, too. The knack of knowing what a man wanted.

Lee took the cigar—a Jamaican and a beauty—pulled a Lucifer from his jacket pocket, and set the cigar tip to glowing.

The Mexican returned to his desk chair, limping deep as a woman with an aching hip. He sat down with a sigh, leaning back into fine Cordovan leather . . . carved walnut. He was dressed like a gentleman of the town in a dark gray suit. No putting on the *charro*, it seemed.

"Don't credit me with second sight in seeing you needed some good tobacco, Mister McCann. I watched you from this window . . . saw the face you made, puffing on your cigarette. Our Mexican tobacco is, I believe, second only to the French in vileness."

Lee drew on the cigar, saw an armchair near the Don's desk, and went and sat down in it without being asked. He felt he had stood and been impressed long enough. And as he sat, he was interested to see the slightest flicker of displeasure in the Don's bright black eyes.

"You're quite right," the Mexican said, and reached to take a cigar of his own from the silver box, "I am not really used to Republican ways . . . Too accustomed to the more punctilious manners of my countrymen." He lit his cigar, leaned back again to puff upon it and look carefully at Lee. "Please do have a seat."

They smoked their cigars at each other for a little while.

"I am considering," the Don said, after this while, "I am considering employing you—or asking if you *wish* to be employed, as a general factotum, an *executor* . . . an iron fist, you might say, in my velvet glove."

Lee took a bit of tobacco off the tip of his tongue. "Why choose me for such an offer?"

"For two reasons. First, as a stranger in this country . . ." He smiled. "Though one who speaks our language quite well—you would have few allegiances and would be allowed few, except to whichever considerable man employed you. And second, because you, far more than most fugitive North Americans, bring some special qualities to your employment."

"The shooting of *Rurales*?"

"Oh, that skill is the least of those qualities. Mind you, Mister McCann—or is "Morgan" more comfortable?—mind you, I don't make light of your abilities with that revolver, nor, I understand, your abilities with any weapon. You, Lee—may I call you

Lee?—are the rarest of commodities, a killer born (and that, with your parentage, is hardly surprising). I'll be blunt and say I'd have hired your father, if time and fate had not prevented it. I always hire the best."

"And those are your 'special qualities?' "

Don Luis de Spania must have spent a busy week telegraphing or having an agent telegraph from Hermosillo to the States and must have very efficient people up there as well, to have learned so much in so short a time.

"Not at all," the broad-shouldered man said. "Nor do I mean to boast of my information, which can be bought by anyone who wishes so to spend money. The qualities I spoke of are those that come with the owning of great lands and the managing of those lands, and the livestock and the people concerned with them. I wish, in other words, to hire a *man*, (he used the Spanish *hombre)* and not a hoodlum, or a vicious boy who enjoys injuring."

"I doubt I wish to be hired," Lee said.

"Oh, I believe you will." The Mexican's cigar had gone out and he paused to re-light it. "I believe you will, out of sheer boredom if nothing else. Assisting a village blacksmith is well enough if you are a man without sense or without balls. I might also, if I thought it necesary, point out that a man who has killed three law officers— even if, in the case of those two at La

Colorado, quite justifiably—is likely to stand in need of a friend with influence. You are, after all, a guest in my country . . ."

Lee appreciated that Don Luis did not trouble to state the obverse: that a man in Lee's position, who had an influential enemy, would be in perilous case.

"Do you care to speak of wages?" he said, and Don Luis smiled.

"Ordinarily my man of business would deal with business," he said, "but in this matter, I will relieve *Senor* Obregon of the necessity. You will be paid two hundred and fifty silver pesos each month you remain in my service."

Lee was startled by the amount; it was twice the wages a top foreman would command—more than twice the wages. It meant that the Don expected no naysaying. It meant he expected results . . . however.

Lee sat still, thinking about it. He might, he supposed, ride out of Sonora Province, ride far away, perhaps further south, to the jungle country, and let this pleasant, rich, and powerful Don find another man to do his shadow work. Lee might do that. And would surely find another such person in a few weeks . . . or months. It would not be possible to spend years assisting blacksmiths in the pueblos of Mexico. And even if it were possible to drown his life in such a way, he would end with nothing for it, not even the hope of getting back to the States again, back to the high country.

Don Luis was waiting patiently, sitting back at ease, watching the light blue smoke from his cigar coil slowly toward the room's vaulted ceiling.

"I'll take the job," Lee said. "And I'll do it for a year."

"Done!" said the Don, and he sat up straight, and held his hand out for Lee to shake. "You are of Las Sabrinas now!"

"Of Las Sabrinas . . ."

True enough.

Lee left Don Luis' study and entered a world all its own, a place separate from the common usages of men and women, a place where the Don, the Don's property, the Don's people all formed a community as richly self-involved as any bee-hive in mid-summer.

This was not perfectly strange to Lee. Any rancher, any great proprieter knew something of that working, living, breathing creature formed by any great single enterprise, any grand business upon the land.

Las Sabrinas enveloped him, took him to its bosom, made him its child.

Lee was led to the ranch store, where his worn trousers, ragged shirts, battered Stetson, cracked boots all disappeared and were replaced, for nothing but his initials on a paper chit, with fine grey wool charro trousers (two pairs), flannel shirts in grey, light blue, and dun, underthings of white cotton, wool socks, a Vera Cruz *sombrero*, dark grey, with a high, creased crown and wide, deep-curled brim. The new boots were a lengthier matter. The store keeper, a lively young sissy with oiled Burnsides, informed him that once his measurements were taken, it would be a matter of overnight before delivery of the new boots.

"Then I'll take the old ones back, until."

Impossible. Absolutely impossible. New men were given new clothes.

This was, Lee assumed, something like enlistment in an army, and he resigned himself to whatever foolishness Las Sabrinas required in order to make him one of its children. Better a few hours barefoot—a Mexican habit in any case—than to set about beating a sissy and searching the store for his old boots.

It was barefoot, then, but otherwise splendidly clothed (the ranch seamstresses did work above the ordinary) that Lee sallied out of the store room to the bathhouse, where two dull-faced *mojos* stripped and plunged him, soaped and scrubbed him. Then toweled him dry. Glad enough, after all, to be shut of a week's trail dirt.

Old Vincente was waiting for him at the bath-house door, nodding something more familiar than he had in all those days of riding—apparently considering Lee more of the family—and took him away out of the stable building where the bath-house and laundry were located and off across another wide, gravelled yard to what seemed a bunkhouse row, and more particularly, to the last section of that row, a low-ceilinged room, puncheon floored, holding a wide bedstead, a dresser of drawers, a mirror and washstand, and (an oddity) a small bookcase with, it proved, copies of Fenimore Cooper, Shakespeare, Hawthorne and Charles Dickens—all, Lee was relieved to discover, in English editions. A neat enough courtesy, and the Don's doing, no doubt. Speaking a fair Spanish was one thing, reading it another.

Vincente, from the doorway, crooked a gnarled thumb into this chamber, stepped back, inclined his head the slightest bit, turned and walked away.

Lee was home.

For now.

The two little nags were near foundered before Lee was half the distance to Paso Robles.

Whatever the bandits had been, they had not been two things—good shots, and wise about horses. These saddle-galled little beasts weren't fit to carry a child, let alone a grown man, baggage, and silver.

Lee, at the base of a lengthy rise with yet another rise beyond, pulled his horse up, heard the led beast shuffle to a stop, and swung down out of the saddle. Walking time, unless he cared to end up carrying all his goods afoot. Once on the ground, though, he had another of those attacks of the trembles, as if the fight had been but minutes ago, rather than two and more hours past.

Hands trembled, skin started sweating up a cold rain of salt water, and something seemed stuck in his throat. He walked a little way off, to be more by himself, away from the shifting horses. Walked over there, near a stunted *cholla*, bent, his hands on his knees, retched, and vomited nothing much at considerable cost of discomfort.

Spat that out, drew a deep breath, went back to the horses and picked up the reins to lead. It would be a long climb to the top of the pass. He missed the small paint already, had missed him from the instant he died. Lost a friend there—a stupid one, perhaps, but a friend nevertheless. Animal had tried to kick him only once, had never tried to bite him at all; more than could be said for the mule Lee had given in partial trade. That creature would have bitten the balls off Jesus Christ.

The nags balked at the slope, though it was slight enough, and Lee, a foul taste of nerves or cowardice or whatever still in his mouth despite three long pulls at the canteen, had to lean down nearly to the ground to haul the lead along. Early evening, and the sand and rock under his boots still glowed with heat, the air still shimmered with it.

A long haul. Several times before he reached the crest of the pass Lee was tempted to swing up into the saddle and let the damn rack-of-bones founder, stagger, and die, just to teach him a lesson. As it was, in the considerable climb Lee was afforded the opportunity of stomping on two scorpions, an opportunity he took advantage of, and another of doing some harm to a small, sand-colored rattlesnake, an opportunity he let pass.

At the crest there was at last some sort of breeze, and Lee seemed to have sweated out the last of the four *banditos*. No question they had asked for killing as persistently as men could—had asked for it, and gotten it. It was also true that those men had known about the silver and shouldn't have. Some Las Sabrinas hand, or his woman, had talked when they ought to have kept their mouths shut.

And this had had to happen when Lee was making the run, not when the treasure cart and ten outriders was rolling on delivery every third week.

A special delivery for the Don. And, to be fair, more fighting than Lee usually saw in the Mexican's service. Don Luis hadn't lied when he'd said he wanted more than a killer. Delicate chores was what he'd had in mind. Delicate chores . . . and only a little bit of murder, here and there.

On the down-slope now, Lee hauled the lead nag in and swung up onto him. The little beast grunted and sagged at the weight, but Lee didn't give a damn; a three-mile uphill climb was walking enough!

Paso Robles was just visible far, far down the pass, guarding, as it had been sited to guard by the *conquistadors,* the entrance pass to the whole of northern Sonora.

Not much of a town, for all that. The *Banco National,* three *cantinas,* a few shops, numerous cattle-pens, and a railroad station visited once every two days by the *Especial* on its way to the coast. First class on that train was wood-slat benches stinking of piss and chicken feathers. Second class was for the cattle.

Delicate duties . . .

The first had been the persuading of Martin Torres.

Senor Torres was a decent fellow and a stubborn one. It was, the Don had explained, a matter of winter graze and water. There had been numerous attempts to point out to *Senor* Torres the foolishness of a small ranch owner being so greedy and unChristian as to deny his grass to those great proprieters, such as Don Luis himself, who had need of it during long drives to the north.

It was this stubborn and foolish man whom Lee was sent to reason with.

Lee rode north on the small paint—rode only at night, and rode fast. Torres had two strong sons, and Lee considered this as he rode. A man's sons were often the key to his purse as well as his heart.

Torres was a decent man and lived as a man, and not, as did many small ranchers, rather like an animal with cattle. He had a decent house rather than a wattle shed to live in, and had, besides, an out-house behind it. An amenity.

Lee arrived at *hacienda* Torres at dawn on the fifth day of riding and went to earth as deep as a fox. The paint was left up on the mountainside.

Lee lay in a ditch past the rancho's west pastures. Lay there through the day, the evening, and lay there still longer.

At moon-rise, other members of the Torres family having gone from their home out to the necessary house and then returned, *Senor* Torres himself, eschewing a latern, depending upon the moonlight, came out to relieve himself.

Lee met this decent man upon the path, struck him from behind, and dragged him away from his house, his loved ones, away from safety. Dragged the gasping man by moonlight out into the brush, and there woke the man, saw him recovered, and spoke to him.

"*Senor* Torres, are you well enough to listen to me?"

Torres had nodded, looking furious as a goaded bull through the mask of blood that striped his face. The blood was black in the moonlight.

"*Senor* Torres, I have been sent to murder your sons."

Not such a furious bull now. Beginning, perhaps, to be a frightened bull, and not for himself.

"I should prefer not to do so. My . . . employer . . . also hopes such measure will be unnecessary."

"I will not sell my land." The bull had found a source of courage. His land.

"But what is land without a son to leave it to?" Lee said. "It is only stones and dirt and empty of any other value to a man. Believe me when I say I'll kill your sons. Believe me also when I say I would regret it." Having said that, Lee struck Torres again, harder than he had before.

When Torres woke, his face bone-white here, blood-black there, Lee gently mopped at his injury with a bandanna.

"I struck you," Lee said, "so that you would listen more carefully to what I say to you. It is not, as it happens, a matter of *selling*. It might be a matter only . . . of *leasing* your land, say for ninety-nine years?"

Torres had begun to weep . . . possibly

from pain, possibly from a greater discomfort.

"Lease it, *Senor. Lease it.* You will not possess it then. Your sons will not possess it. But *their* sons will. Their sons' sons will possess the land again. Lease your land, *Senor,* and I will speak to my . . . employer. And then I will not have to kill your boys."

Lee had gotten up from the ground then, and left *Senor* Torres, a brave and decent man, sitting in the dirt. Lee left his bandanna with that *ranchero.* The cloth was caked with blood, and not worth taking away.

The Don had, at first, been less than pleased, but Lee had persuaded him that nearly a century's lease on that land was more wholesome for Las Sabrinas than a slaughtered *ranchero,* his slaughtered sons, and a daughter and widow still to be slaughtered.

"Very North American," said Don Luis later. "Very practical. I am not certain, however, that this sort of 'practicality' is most effective in dealing with our people. In future," he said, "do not substitute your judgment for mine, particularly if you are right."

The Don had not been joking. Lee had not thought for an instant that he was.

Chapter 4

Paso Robles was chilling now in the morning air, chilling with the approach of night after a day of frying. The bank would not be open till morning. Time now for a stable for the nags, a meal and a bed for Lee.

Perhaps, if the memory of four fools did not interfere, a girl at *Mamacita's*.

Lee didn't trouble to spur the bandit's horse down the cobbled strets of Paso Robles; he was content if the poor thing would keep staggering on to its stable. Have to sell the beast and its friend tomorrow. . . .

Tomorrow would also mark the last day of the year he had agreed to serve Don Luis. Something to think about. A man could play dog for only so long, then he stood in danger of becoming one . . .

Two small boys stood at the side of the steep street to watch Lee pass. He saw them staring at the worn little nag he was riding—staring at him, as well.

No people like the Mexicans for a nose for trouble. Well before Lee could have the bandit's horse stabled, well before he could have his first glass of *aguardiente*, Paso Robles would know that Don Luis' gringo *pistolero* had found trouble in bringing *something* (perhaps a sack of the Don's silver pesos) . . . had had trouble carrying some small cargo in his saddlebags.

And it was so.

Lee stood at the long bar in Mamacita's, content in a roar of noise, guitar music (which he had learned to care for; piano playing now sounded harsh and pounding to him, particularly when he had been drinking) the cracking sounds of boot-heels on the splintered flooring as vaqueros from two of the local ranches danced with the whores, told lies in loud voices, and occasionally glowered at their opposites from other brands, threatening knife-work if insulted.

It was a pleasant resort and not particularly a violent one. Lee had never seen a man killed at Mamacita's, though he had seen a fellow too drunk to defend himself have his eyes cut out by two bullies.

There were other *Norte Americanos* in the place. A drummer for some American barbed-wire company (Lee had seen him passing through before) and two roughs in Texican hats sitting in a corner, grinning at the whores and talking smut to any that passed their table.

As to the long bar, it was comfortably lined along both sides of him with serious drinkers, talkers, and thinkers, all with their drooping wide-brim sombreros pushed well back so as not to interfere with the lifting of glasses.

Beer was the tipple at Mamacita's for thirst, aquardiente and tequila for the rest. Lee had opted for beer and aquardiente, a large and very dirty glass of each—served to him, as it happened, by the owner of the joint—unless a short, sour man named Urube, who visited occasionally and was treated with considerable ceremony, was a part owner as well.

Mamacita (Luz Obregon) rarely worked the bar; that tall, dark brown, stork-like lady (her left eye white as milk) was usually found perched by her cash-box near the door. Her name, or nickname, was ironic, since anyone less the plump, amiable, motherly figure of Mexican womanhood would have been difficult to imagine. This "Mamacita" had no comfortable looks at all, no generosity whatsoever, and a tongue so poisonous the town priest crossed himself when they met.

Luz Obregon had asked Lee—had told him, in fact, when he first began riding to Paso Robles—that she would prefer he *not* make Mamacita's a regular watering hole. One-eyed Luz did not care for Yankees, even temporarily, and had no intention of having one as a regular customer.

This had all been said to him publicly—at the bar, in fact, and to a very interested audience. Lee had heard her out, agreed in his then still improving Spanish that she was quite right, and was showing the sort of social discrimination expected of the descendant of generations of Castillian ladies. Having said that, he had leaned far across the bar, and kissed the astonished (and very ugly) woman on the lips, declaring that unfortunately he was in love, and could not long bear to be away from her.

This event became a legendary one in the town, at least for a time, and Lee was regarded as a considerable curiosity, even for a gringo gunman.

It was felt at first that he was mad.

Later, it was decided that he was humorous—though perhaps mad as well.

At any event, The Kiss, as it became known, had had its effect, and though her manner to Lee did not change—still an elaborate demonstration of contempt

—there were those who claimed to see some rusty coquetry in it. And Lee was never denied entrance to Mamacita's.

It was this rail-thin woman, her good eye dark and constantly furious as a summer storm, who now slid another beer over the chipped cottonwood bar to Lee. She paused for a moment while he sipped it and smiled at her, then, with a disgusted snort, spun away to see to what degree the chuck-a-luck spinner was cheating the house.

Home.

Or, at least, a place as near a home as the bunkhouse room at Las Sabrinas . . . And other camps and shacks and whores' chambers.

Likely some sound along the bar, some voice raised toward the back of the room, reminded Lee of his men. Strange, with no folks alive at all—with Catherine Dowd dead, his father dead, his mother long since dead and gone. With Dowd, the little rich man, dead as well . . .

S'ien dead . . .

Strange that now, and more and more, it should be the faces of his men that haunted him, chased him through his dreams. Strange, since these not-much-more-than-ordinary cowpokers were certainly still alive and, if golden references could help them, had as good jobs in cattle and horse management as could be got. Strange that

that small bunch of horn-handed drovers, a bit handier with weapons than most of their kind, should stand so firmly in his memories.

Unfinished business, was what they seemed. Appeared to still be standing on the porch steps of headquarters house at Spade Bit, hearing him say the place was bust, hearing him say he was selling out to pay his debts.

"Hoof-and-mouth"—a nasty name for a nasty sickness. And the ruin of his horse herds, and their ruin the ruin of his land holdings, and their ruin, his. The men had stood, hats in hands, and listened to his talking. Ford ... Sefton ... Charlie Potts. ... Bud Bent, and two new-signed men who hardly counted.

They'd stood patiently on the porch steps and listened to him, listened to Lee trying on his dignity, trying to make the matter seem simply business. Simply business— and him dying of shame as he spoke to them.

Did die, he supposed, in a way. Certainly left a piece of himself fallen away on that porch, or in the lawyer's offices in Boise and Denver.

Somewhere along there, he had certainly lost a piece of himself. As if there was a chain hooked through his flesh, linked in some way, buried in, knotted to the land, the high mountain country at Spade Bit ...

at Rifle River. The country his father and mother lay rotting in . . . the country S'ien lay rotting in.

Lee Morgan had ridden then, to anywhere, having left something behind him. His try in the Northwest, then a damned bungled robbery, then, Mexico.

How was he different from those two roughs at the corner table? He'd bathed more recently, was better dressed, had a master to serve. In these slight ways, and no others, was he different.

If his men had dreams of their own, of riding Spade Bit again, of riding Dowd-Leslie-Morgan land, they had better do as Lee had better do and boot those dreams out of their beds. There was no money to buy back two mountain ranches. Likely there would never be such money.

Lee finished his second beer, considered the bar—and felt the men on either side of him move slightly away.

It was a subtle thing. One moment, these two strangers had been siding him, drinking their drinks, talking with friends perhaps, perhaps only brooding on some woman, some luck, or some misfortune, and then they were gone. Oh, still standing at his side, but not so close.

The noise in Mamacita's had changed as well. Not quite as strident—slightly more subdued.

Lee eased back from the edge of the bar-counter, put down his beer, and looked up into Luz Obregon's cracked and fly-specked bar mirror.

Past his reflected shoulder, he saw a man standing facing him. Sergeant's stripes on a light blue uniform jacket.

Lee turned from the bar—not quickly—and noticed the men on either side of him stepping away, crowding back and no subtlety to it.

"You are wanted, gringo. Most immediately. Why he wishes to speak to such refuse is a question that only Capitan Gonsalves might answer."

This was said to Lee by a short, barrel-chested trooper of *Rurales*, a sergeant. A man Lee had seen before in Paso Robles but whose name he did not know. The sergeant had a strong Indian accent; Lee found it difficult for a moment to understand that last phrase about "refuse." Then he did. This sergeant was no charmer; he was one of those powerful, stocky men with a misleadingly fat face. Seeing only the face, a man might suppose the fellow to be no great shakes in a pickle. And would suppose wrong. Man looked like an overfed fighting dog, with a shade too much bull, a shade too little terrier in the breeding. He had clever eyes—very clever, for a sergeant.

Many of the *Rurales* had been recruited—as had, to be fair, many American lawmen—

from the general body of thugs, road-agents, and owlhooters whose tendency to violence made them so useful for that work. Lee sized the sergeant as just one such and clever enough to realize the *Rurales* made a more comfortable berth than a Mexican penitentiary or a hasty ditch beside a bullet-pocked wall.

"It is surely not that you are fool enough to be being rude to me, *Sergeanto!* Even though your low-born looks, so very Indian, would indicate it."

Spanish was a wonderful language of insult, particularly in its more intricate forms.

The sergeant flushed a darker brown, and one thick hand spidered slowly along his uniform belt toward his holstered pistol—a converted cap-and-ball, it looked, and slow as molasses in a high-fit holster.

Another trooper stood behind the sergeant. This one was taller, with that dreamy, introspective air so common in these people. Lee had decided long ago that Mexicans spent only a portion of their time considering the actual. They were dreamers to a man, though when they acted, they *acted.*

Lee didn't doubt the trooper with the carbine would be more trouble than the sergeant if it came to shooting.

Those neighboring had heard what the

sergeant had said, had heard what Lee had replied. This part of the room was very quiet now, though in the back they'd scarcely noticed. It took trouble indeed to silence all of Mamacita's.

Lee stood easy, his hands at his side, and waited for the sergeant's hand to stop moving along his belt. If it continued to move, Lee would draw and shoot the man, try for the trooper with the second, then back to the sergeant for a finisher . . . then back to the trooper for his. It was, once the fear of death or injury was out of it, much like juggling some noisy, barking indian club in a gentlemen's gynmasium. It was a hand-skill, quick and alternate shooting, only a hand-skill.

The consequences, of course, could be grave—certainly would be, here. With these two dead, providing Lee achieved his four shots very quickly and accurately, the squad-rooms of the *Rurales* and the police would empty like wasps' nests, and those hard-bitten men come to kill him. Even Don Luis would not be able (and would likely not try) to help him out of this. Lee had already killed his allotment of Mexican mounted police.

It would be a long ride out of Sonora. And a long ride thereafter.

The sergeant's hand still moved . . . seconds, and few of those, had passed since Lee answered him. It moved—Lee noticing the sergeant's nails were clean—and then it ceased to move. The hand rested quiet, still two inches from that converted cap-and-ball.

"I will," Lee said, "take your shame-faced silence for all the apology of which a sad animal such as yourself is capable and will be certain to convey my regrets to your captain, that he, a Mexican officer, should be burdened with such an inferior."

The thick brown hand slowly clenched but moved no further along the sergeant's belt.

"Go along," Lee said, "if you can remember where you came from, and I will follow."

"A pregnant pause," play-actors called it.

Then the sergeant shrugged, turned, and marched out. The trooper, however, did not. This fellow indicated that Lee should precede him. A slight and gentle inclination of the carbine's barrel.

Lee, feeling he had pushed his luck quite far enough and weary from a long ride and a hard fight, went before, docile as a Saltillo sheep.

Outside in the street, ill lit by a few smoky pitch-pine flares, the sergeant stolidly marched away, the trooper as dutifully marched behind, and Lee strolled along between them, keeping a casual eye on the sergeant as they walked and looking out as well for horse turds, dog turds, and human turds, too, come to that. Lee still noticed after a moment or two that the sergeant's broad shoulders were shaking.

Lee assumed the fellow was not in tears. Which meant that the sergeant was laughing.

Nothing proves a man a fool more thoroughly than mistaking another man for one.

"My apologies, sergeant. I enjoy my Spanish, poor though it is, perhaps more than I ought."

The stocky man turned as he walked; his face was red with suppressed laughter. "To hear a *gringo . . .*" he said in his strong Indian accent . . . "to hear a gringo such as you trying to talk like a *caballero!*" This was too much for the sergeant, and he chuckled with pleasure, shaking his head at such a marvel, such an absurdity. "I assure you," he said to Lee, walking backward as he talked—and quite lightly on his feet, Lee noticed—"I assure you that you were funnier than the Don himself!" More chuckles. A considerable demonstration for a man with so much Indian blood.

For an instant, Lee thought the sergeant meant Don Luis de Spania. Then, with a painful jolt of embarrassment, realized that this unprepossessing policeman was referring to Don Quixote. It was a book Lee had tried to read in Spanish and had read enough of to realize this copper had pegged him to a "T." *The man who imagined himself more than he was.* In this case, a border ruffian with pretensions.

This sergeant, if a brute, was a brute who read. Another reminder not to underestimate these people. Not to over-estimate Lee McCann, either. It might be, for example, that this sergeant and his trooper had had orders . . . orders not to use violence unless it was necessary. Possibly, otherwise—maybe more than possible—that the sergeant and his man might have made a try, and to hell with Lee's fast gun.

Live a little, learn a little.

Two lessons learned today, or learned again. First—when carrying silver, don't ride into canyon passages, no matter how much they cut the journey. And second, never sell a stranger short.

Two lessons . . . and now, a talk with the Captain.

The Captain was a larger man than the sergeant had been—perhaps a bank robber in his salad days, before he'd taken the government's wage, the light blue coat and silver facings. A big, lazy looking man with small black eyes and a considerable nose. His hands were big as garden spades, and not well cared-for, nails bitten to the quick.

A big man, and sensitive, and looked to be very powerful physically. He wore no weapons, and sat behind his small splintered-top desk, at the back of his small whitewashed office, like a brown bear packed comfortably into its den. He was losing hair at the top of his head and where that was occurring, the local barber (no doubt a sissy Lee knew, named Mercurio Sanchez) had carefully trimmed and oiled and plastered each long black hair across the Captain's head.

Lee had been walked past the *Rurale* squadron's guard-room to reach the Captain's office, and had no notion that the Captain needed to be wearing weapons in his lair. An even dozen very rough cobs had been lounging along the corridor as Lee was shepherded past that guard-room and into Captain Gonsalves' small den.

"Sit," said the bear, and indicated a busted-bottom chair. Lee sat and was glad to do it. His bones hurt. Odd how a fight could bruise a man, and those not even smart or ache till long past the fight being done.

"There has, I understand, been some difficulty," the Captain said and didn't appear likely to say any more. Lee'd learned his lesson; there'd be no showing off his fancy Spanish grammar with this man. He answered the Captain in plain straightforward.

"I was sent here on a mission of business by Don Luis. Four men attempted to rob me at Canyon Rojo. I killed them."

The Captain swallowed that with no sign of indigestion. Thought about it for a moment.

"The horse you brought to this city . . ." (it seemed to Lee that "city" was stretching it for Paso Robles) "the horse you brought to this city is not your horse, then?"

A year before, and a stranger to Mexico, Lee would have thought that an irrelevent question, considering that four men had been shot to death attempting an armed robbery. But that was a year ago. Now he knew better.

"No, sir, it is not my horse. Since my horse was killed in the fighting, I used the animal, which belonged to one of the deceased bandits, to transport the Don's . . . business, and to bring me here to report the attempted robbery."

"You go to cantinas to report attempted robberies?"

"I was foolish not to go to the authorities at once. I also felt the need for a drink."

The Captain, apparently not satisfied with that, sat looking at Lee exactly as a bear might have . . . considering him. Considering the influence of Don Luis, also, Lee supposed . . . the usefulness of four dead bandits to an overworked squadron of police with a hundred thousand square miles to partrol . . . the annoyance of it being a Yankee hoodlum who had killed these four bandits . . . the discomfort of an armed and arrogant *pistolero*, and a gringo at that, who thought nothing of riding into Paso Robles on an animal in no wise his own, whatever his excuse.

The Captain, Lee supposed, was considering all these matters as well as the tried and true police tactic north and south, of beating and jailing anyone seriously brought to their attention. An object lesson —always useful.

Lee, a fighting cock only a few minutes before, was now reluctantly ready to be beaten (if only moderately) and was more than ready to be jailed if that meant a decent night's sleep on a corn shuck mattress, or a wooden bench. He was suddenly tired right down to his toes.

This indifference perhaps made some slight impression on Captain Gonsalves, who, after a minute or two, grunted, told Lee to go and get the horse he did not own, bring it to the military corral, and then to get out of the Captain's sight and to stay out of the Captain's sight.

Lee was happy to do that.

Lee slept.

He slept a long, long, sweet sleep, drugged only slightly by a pipe of marijuana hemp and two or three glasses of mescal.

He slept out the rest of the night and slept through the morning as well—all the going and coming, the to'ing and fro'ing, the clatter and chatter, singing and what-not that saloons and whore-houses produce in midmorning, with the sun well up and bean pot put to boil. The women made enough noise for a wedding, but they never woke him. Two girls even came into the room to sweep it out, saw him on the bed, giggled and retreated. He didn't wake for that, either.

It was the smell of food that finally roused him—pinto beans, and chilies, and roast pork. That, and the coffee. Those odors woke him and woke him nicely, slowly, his dreams accommodating to those rich smells of food, so that he was sitting in a fine restaurant in the Palmer House in Chicago. He had ordered a huge dinner and was smelling it being cooked . . . was some-how also in the kitchens, watching the beans being cooked, the women sitting in a row along the black Garland stoves, patting tortillas while the *Maitre de* tried to hurry them. The Chicago wind, icy off the lake, whined past the kitchen windows . . .

He woke, reached for the Bisley Colt's, and felt the curved butt snug in his hand (the holstered revolver hanging from the bed-post) before he was certain where he was. He had taken to touching the weapon in that way whenever he woke. A nervous habit, Lee thought, and unpleasant.

He sat up in the bed, the worn springs

sighing musically, and noticed he was naked. Had not slept in his boots, then. Some sort of civilized going to bed.

Lee recalled his interview with Captain Gonsalves. It might be just as well to get about his business and get out of Paso Robles. He had never known just how far Don Luis' influence, his political power with the revolutionary government, stretched. Likely that waxed and waned depending on which general was appointed where, which governor was in well with Mexico City, which not.

These were matters that Mexicans knew in their bones. And Lee did not.

The *Rurale* Captain—who must be very efficient or very well connected to be posted in Paso Robles rather than some God-forsaken little hole in the desert—might have to take Don Luis' wishes seriously to account. Also, he might not. In fact, he might have some obscure reason to please some obscure person by having Don Luis' gringo pistolero taken out to a corral and whipped, or out to a wall and shot.

Might be waiting for instruction on just such an action.

And Lee had killed two blue-jackets already.

All in all, time to buy another horse (being very careful about the bill of sale), time to get Don Luis' silver out from behind

Mamacita's bar (where it was probably safer) and to the Banco National. And then, time to get the hell out of Paso Robles.

Chapter 5

But now he was hungry as a lobo wolf in midwinter.

He swung his feet to the floor and was just standing when he heard the room door swing open behind him. It was a hard, quick stretch to reach back for the Colt's, to turn to the door with the piece cocked and coming up.

The girl stood pop-eyed—assuming, Lee supposed, that she was about to be shot to rags. A new maid, Lee saw, and raw as could be. A small, stocky country girl. Not too much breast on her, a big head, strong-boned face, brown-black eyes and midnight hair, coarse as a horse's and chopped short. Perhaps fifteen years old . . . more likely a year or two younger.

She had a rough straw broom, was clutch-

ing the handle as it might save her from
gunfire. Had dropped a wad of rags when
Lee'd turned to her.

Lee stepped back to the bed to slide the
Colt's into its holster. "Don't be frightened.
I don't make a habit of shooting girls."

The girl said nothing. Lee saw her glance
flick to his groin, then away. Likely a virgin
bought by Luz or her silent partner from
some *campeseno* family poor as dirt.
They'd have promised the father not to
whore the girl, but would nonetheless, soon
enough.

"Go on, do your work," Lee said, speaking slow Spanish to her, and turned to pick
his clothes off a chair-back beside the bed.
Some of these people spoke no Spanish at
all . . . talked one of any dozen of Indian
dialects instead.

He put on his shirt, then stepped into his
long john pants, turned again to find his
socks and boots, and saw the girl glance
over at him over her shoulder, then recom-
mence dusting down a walnut wardrobe
with enough carving on it to be in the
Viceroy's bedroom, as the local saying had
it for any fancy-work.

Perhaps it was that glance, perhaps the
bowed bare nape, brown as sugar, that
showed beneath the weight of her hair as
she bent her head to her work, perhaps only
the blind hornyness of morning.

Lee, still barefooted, walked round the

bed to her. She stood still as he came close
—probably too scared or shy to look around
again.

He walked up close enough to touch her
. . . stood looking down at that dense black
hair—clean enough; Luz or her girls must
have scrubbed this one with carbolic soap
when she came into the place. The girl
smelled of that strong soap . . . smelled
some of sweat, too, and wood smoke from
the kitchen fire. She was a small girl—came
barely to his chest. Barefoot, her brown feet
square-toed and sturdy. Probably never
had a pair of shoes. Likely only red-painted
huraches to wear to mass. Carry them to
the church, put them on, then carry them
again on the walk home.

No breasts to speak of—the Indian blood
—but looked to have a solid ass on her.

The girl stood quiet before him, frightened even to turn round and look at this
strange gringo *pistolero*. There was a sweet
smell to her, too. Smelled of girl, was the
truth of the matter. That odd, sweet smell
that most women had. You could catch it on
the street sometimes. Just walking past
one or two women walking the other way,
you could smell that faint odor. Nothing of
made-and-sold perfume about it, either.

This peasant girl had never got within a
country smile of store-bought perfume.

Lee saw her small, strong brown hand
clutching the broom handle—she'd been

doing her dusting left-handed, appeared to think the broom some protection against this strange man—had likely seen her mama dust some drunk drifter off with one, send strange dogs flying out of their mean yard.

The girl's hand was trembling.

Lee heard the voices of other women downstairs . . . heard Pablo Cienfuegos joking with them. Pablo was Luz's bully—a big, fat, strong fellow, as likely to jape a man out of pulling a knife as to crack the fellow's head to prevent it.

"Don't be afraid of me," Lee said. He put his hand on the back of the girl's neck.

It was like touching a frightened horse or laying a hand on the side of the locomotive engine at a railroad station. Same subtle, continuous trembling.

The skin at her nape was smooth as pressed cotton. He slowly slid his fingers up into her hair and she started and made a sound in her throat.

Lee squeezed gently at the back of her neck, not near hard enough to hurt her. Then he spread his fingers down across her cheek and gently pressed there, to turn her head toward him.

She looked up at him from under a coal black fall of hair. Wide eyes full of fear. Her wide mouth fallen half open, lower lip trembling.

Small teeth were even . . . white enough. . .

"I said I wasn't going to hurt you. Now come here." He guided her as much as forced her, keeping his grip on her nape, squeezing gently if she seemed to hold back, drawing her along with him step by step back to the bed.

She was dragging the broom with her, betrayed of any help it might have been. Whatever—it was only straw and stick, now.

Lee reached out with his other hand and gently pulled it from her grip. She clung, and then let it go. She bowed her dark-haired head under his grip as if he were exerting all his power, as if he were crushing her there, squeezing all the strength from her. As if this firm hold was the most dreadful of all grips.

"Come here, now—you do what I tell you. I won't hurt you. You're a decent girl. I would never hurt you . . ."

He drew her to the bed and made her sit down there beside him. She resisted sitting down, and Lee did grip her harder. Then she sat down beside him in a rustle of black cotton cloth, the cloth of her white apron.

"What is your name?" Lee said. "Is it as pretty as you are?" He stroked her neck gently, stroking her lightly under her ears, over the smooth skin just sheltered by her hair.

The girl was weeping, but silently, a few, slow, gleaming tears coursing delicate down the strong planes of her face, shining wet on her cheekbones. One tear had reached her mouth; it glittered in the sunlight, trembling at her upper lip.

Her eyes were tight shut as if what she could not see, would not happen to her.

She began to gasp for breath, at first quietly, then louder. Lee judged she was working up crying out.

He put his hand on the back of her neck again, forced her head down so she sat beside him bowed over. "Don't be noisy, now," he said. "There's no need for it."

Gone wrong here, no doubt of that. Doing a wrong piece of work, no doubt of it at all. A cruel piece of work . . .

His cock was standing up in his underwear, hard enough to hurt him.

Tears were dropping on her little white apron. Some fancy of Luz's—to have her maids decked out like French girls in service. Duds had probably cost more than buying the girl to wear them.

"You cut that out, now," he said, and shook her a little, from side to side. She was pliant as a reed, felt close to fainting. "You dry those tears and cut that crying out."

Obedient as a nigger in Mississippi, the Indian girl picked up a corner of her apron in a shaking hand and daubed at her face with it. When she was finished, she sat still beside him, head bowed beneath his hand.

"Look at this, now," Lee said, and unbuttoned the flies of his underpants so that his cock was out. "Look at that, now." He turned her head with his hand, so that she was looking at it. She was panting softly, like a caught rabbit.

Lee reached over, took one of her hands from her lap, and put it on him. The palm of her hand was wet with sweat. Her hand was shaking as she gripped him. She was looking up at the room door now as if someone—her father, her mother, perhaps, might come by magic from their distant village, might see what she was being required to do . . . might storm into the room by magic or the priest's prayers, with *machetes* and rocks, to destroy this strange and terrible man and save her.

Lee held her by the back of her neck very hard now—he thought he might be hurting her—he pulled the girl half over against him. Then he shoved her head down hard.

She strained back, trying to sit up, her eyes rolling like a terrified animal's. She was a strong little girl. Lee did have to hurt her then; he gripped her so hard that her mouth opened with the pain of it. He put his other hand in her thick black hair, and so forced her head down until her face was pressed awkwardly against his cock . . . her clenching hand.

"You put that in your mouth, now. You do that, or by Jesus Christ . . . !" Truth was, he didn't know what he'd do, except have her do as he wished by any way at all. But the words did his business for him.

Terrified, shaking under his weighting arm, the girl clumsily kissed at the purple, swollen head of the thing she held, then tried to sit up again, to twist free of Lee's grip, as if that single unspeakable thing she had done were more than enough.

But Lee wouldn't let her up.

He pressed her head down again—guiding her, gripping the nape of her neck hard enough to make her gasp with pain. That small desperate Indian face, boned for dignity, was forced slowly down, trembling in resistance, until her soft cheek, then her mouth were held against it.

The girl made a sound, and kissed at Lee's cock again, and he held her to it, managed and maneuvered her head to keep her mouth there and raised his hips to thrust his cock up against her lips, her mouth.

The girl moaned as he gripped her neck still harder and her mouth slowly opened, and his cock slid into her. Lee felt the last resistance, then the rough edges of her parting teeth. Then wet, and heat, and softness . . . the struggle of her tongue as his meat drove up into her mouth.

She moaned and gagged, her throat convulsing. The swollen head of his cock was in her and a few inches more than that. The girl's cheeks were bloated with him.

She gagged again—tried once more to wrench away, to sit up from what she was doing, but Lee wouldn't let her go. He did not, then, care if he killed her.

He shoved her head down hard, seeing her mouth stretched so wide it seemed her jaw must break from it. He held her there, held her head still, his fingers clamped at the back of her neck. Lee's heart was thumping; he was wonderfully excited . . . oddest damn thing, in this small, sunny room . . . like a dream lasting past sleep.

The girl kept her eyes closed, as if what she couldn't see couldn't be happening. She was snorting softly, breathing through her nose, trying not to gag at the size and length of him thrust up into her mouth. Lee could feel the back of her throat at the tip of his cock, feel it gently convulse from time to time against him as the girl tried to keep from retching.

Lee slowly took his hand from the back of her neck, slid his fingers up into her thick, soft hair. Stroked her hair gently for a moment. She didn't try to raise her head from him. Sat quietly, head bent to his lap, the thick, pale, purple-veined cock forcing her jaw wide, thinning her lips as they strained around it.

The girl's brown-skinned throat moved as she gulped to keep from vomiting. Spittle was running in glistening strands from her mouth, running down the length of him, small drops of it clustered in the hair there.

The girl still kept her eyes tight closed.

Lee gathered a handful of her hair . . . slowly lifted her head, just a little . . . then slowly pushed it down again.

Her mouth made a wet noise on his cock as he did that.

He did it again. Lifted her head a little, then slowly thrust her down on the stake of his cock again. The girl snorted, breathing noisily through her nose.

Up—then slowly down again.

Lee felt something seem to soften in her mouth, to stretch deeper.

He let her rest for a moment. Sat feeling almost like a fool for his roughness, his frowardness. Sitting here in a down whores-house with his dingus up a maid's mouth. He looked down at the girl's shining black hair, at his fingers tangled in it. Tugged gently . . . felt the hot wet moving slowly up him—the cool of the room air where her mouth was leaving him soaked with her saliva. Felt the slightest touch of her teeth there . . . Then pushed her head down again, a little faster this time.

The girl gulped and gagged—tried feebly to resist him—and Lee pushed down harder. Shoved her head down on him till she heaved and bucked under his hands, retching, strangling on it.

Damndest wish to jam it up all the way. Up into her throat.

Hard to see why she should live, when the four yesterday had died shot to rags ... Not much to death, when you looked at it close. Just like breaking wet clocks, was what it was, and waiting for someone to break yours.

Hard to see why he shouldn't choke this greaser bitch with it.

He had both his hands on her—used one to brush the hair away from her face ... hair as black and coarse as a Chinese girl's. Riles had said the Indians came from China or thereabouts. Hair was surely the same sort ...

He brushed the girl's hair back, ducked his own head to look at her. Damned if women didn't look odd with cocks in their mouths. Odd expressions on their faces ... The girl's eyes were open now, wide, expressionless. Truth was, the poor thing looked dead already. He felt her tongue moving against him. Not so dead then ...

Lee slowly began to move her head again, raising it ... letting it fall. The girl seemed to have given something up—perhaps had given everything up. Her mouth was slack as an old whore's privates. She slobbered on him as Lee moved her head up and down to his pleasure. Made a wet, pumping, sucking noise. Damned it she wasn't near to taking it all.

He took his hands from her hair. For a few moments, like a steam machine slowly running down, the girl continued to suck at him . . . lifting her head, then letting it fall, her mouth as soft and accommodating as if he'd smashed her jaw. She did that for a little while . . . then slowed . . . then stopped, her head poised above him, the fine double tendons on her nape prominent with strain. She still held the head of his cock in her mouth. Held it there in warmth and wet . . . moved her tongue slightly against it. For whatever reason (fear, or some odd surrendering fondness) she suckled it softly.

"That's a honey . . ." Lee said to her in Spanish. "That's my honey . . ." Crooned to her like a lover as she crouched over, the gleaming black helmet of hair almost concealing what she was doing.

Lee reached down and pulled her head back and off him. She left his soaked cock with a damp kissing sound. The thinnest bright thread of saliva ran from her lower lip to the tip of it for an instant, then broke and vanished.

The girl sat supported by Lee's arm, leaning against him as if she were injured or sick. Her soft mouth hung slack as if it could never close. Her chin ran with spit. She looked at him as he'd seen men look that he had shot. Reproachful . . . mildly surprised that such a thing could have happened to them . . . happened to her.

"I was too rough," Lee said. "Wasn't I too rough for such a sweet girl?" He eased her gently back and down, and she lay back obediently across the bed, legs hanging down, small bare brown feet just clear of the floor.

Someone was walking down the hall, a woman by her light step. Down the hall and past the room door. Down to the far end of the corridor. And called out: *"Florenca!"*

Called the name once, then came back down the hall, and on down the stairs. Lee heard music from down there. Someone playing *La Paloma.* Not playing well . . . Playing the song badly on the guitar.

"There," he said to the girl, who was lying staring straight up into the ceiling . . . who did not turn her eyes to look at him, even when he leaned down to kiss her on her bruised, wet mouth. "There," Lee said. "Is that your name—Florenca? It's a very lovely name. It suits you . . ." And kissed her again, gently enough, he hoped, to heal some small part of her hurt.

Chapter 6

Suddenly—and to Lee's great surprise—
the girl turned as she lay, and struck at him
with one small fist. It was an awkward blow
that barely touched him, but it startled him
some.

He gripped her wrists and held her still,
feeling a brute and a fool in equal measure.
"Now, now . . . dammit!" he said, and she
hissed and spat up at him like a kitten.

"Be still, now!" Lee said, "and cut that
out!"

The girl lay panting. Her long black
dress, her apron had flounced up as she'd
struggled. Her brown calves and knees
were bare. Her calves, though round and
smooth, were sturdy as a boy's from
climbing the hills in the back country. Her
knees were scarred from the scrubbing

work she did, kneeling on brick and board and tile.

Having rested for a breath or two, staring up at him, her eyes round and black as California olives, the girl suddenly tried to draw one of his prisoning hands close enough to her mouth to bite it. Lee wrenched his hand away, and stretching her wrists out wide, pinned her to the crumpled bed sheets, bearing down with his weight to hold her there.

His naked cock, still wet from her mouth, still stiff as a wooden billet, rubbed for an instant against the stuff of her dress. That small touch alone sent a jolt of pleasure through him.

"You dumb little bitch," he said to her in English, "you wouldn't know beans if the bag was open!"

Leaned down like the damndest of idiots, and kissed her.

And got the fiercest bite for doing it. The girl caught his lower lip in those small white teeth and bit it almost through.

It hurt like fury but Lee didn't try to pull away. Didn't try to strike her, to force her mouth apart. He just kept on kissing—and tasted blood. He murmured something to her—didn't know what it was, himself. Damn fool . . . Felt like she was chewing that lip right off him . . .

Lay half on her, but as lightly as he could,

kissing . . . kissing her. Felt blood running down his chin. Whispering to her . . . to this ignorant peasant girl. Damn ignorant Indian. Telling her all sorts of things—as well as a man could tell with his lip near riven in two. Stroking her hair . . . must have hurt her, tugging at her hair like that. He stroked it as lightly as he could.

Suddenly felt her sharp teeth ease up. Hurt near as much when she let go as when she'd bit. He was kissing her in a welter of blood. Saying some foolish thing to her about how startled . . . well, how suddenly scared he'd been in Canyon Rojo. Scared shit-loose when those bandit mutts had cut down on him. What that sort of stuff had to do with fucking, damned if he could see. Made him feel better . . . less of a jackass, in some way.

Kissing her . . . tasting blood. Tasting the sweetness of her with the blood.

And she kissed him back.

Soft . . . hesitant, little pecking kisses. More like a child's than a woman's. She put up a hand to touch his face . . . touch his lips where she'd bitten him. She said something, softly.

"Honey . . ." Lee said. "My little honeycomb." He turned half on his side, gathered her up into his arms, and she came to him soft as feathers. "Little honeycomb . . ."

He stroked her hair as if he could caress

away the roughness he had used with her. What a fool, to take anything so pretty, and to hurt it . . .

Her big, dark Indian eyes were open, looking into his own odd amber ones as if she could see straight through him. Faces were close enough for Lee to feel the light touch of her breath on his mouth, the side of his cheek. Her breath smelled of sweet milk and wood smoke.

"Are you a good man or a bad man?" she asked him in Indian-accented Spanish. And waited in his arms, watching his eyes, to hear what he would say. It was a child's question.

"I am sometimes bad and sometimes good. I try not to be too bad a man." Sounded to him like a child's answer, as well, but it appeared to satisfy her. *Florenca.* An unusual name. Something half Spanish, half *Indio*, likely, but it suited well enough.

Startled him as much then as she had by striking at him. She reached down between them and directly took his cock into her hand. She held it for a moment, then commenced to stroke and pet at it, looking all the while into Lee's eyes, and apparently well enough pleased by what she saw there.

Lee was seized by such a pleasure that he felt the jissom rising in him in a terribly sweet pain, and almost let loose of it over her small hand, her stroking fingers. He rose up over her instead, and kissed her hard, driving her head back down into the bedding, and she bucked up against him, her mouth loose and wet under his. The taste of blood was like the taste of a camp knife blade red with the blood gravy of a roast. Lee sucked on the girl's tongue, drew it up out of her mouth to suck and lick at it.

She let him do what he wished.

He kissed her for a long while, finding something new with her mouth somehow through all the kisses. Her slight body seemed to grow under him . . . to become more and more defined the longer he kissed her . . . licking along those small even teeth, touching the slickness and perfection of her inner mouth, her gums, the slippery insides of her cheeks, the neat ridges at the top of her mouth.

He took his time . . . and he learned it all. He gathered in her saliva, and sipped it, little by little. He kissed and worried at her lips, not minding the pain from her bite. Kissed her so hard she gasped for breath, murmured to him to let her breathe.

Then, bit by bit, he forgot all the gentleness that he'd intended and hugged her to him hard—squeezing her, crushing her to him as if he could weld her to him as a smith hammered hot iron to iron.

She groaned, and licked at his throat.

Lee reached down with one hand to gather up the girl's skirts—tugged the cloth up to her thighs—then lifted her to him and pulled her dress and apron to her waist.

She made no move to hinder him.

Lee pulled a little away from her, braced up on his elbow, and looked at her. She lay beside him, wide-eyed, panting like a doe that had been dog-run—her black hair tangled, the plain bosom of her dress rising and falling with her breathing. Below the ruck of black cloth and white apron at her waist, Lee saw she wore little pantelettes of white cotton—looked to be cut from some flour sack, then carefully resewn along the seams. The soft, burnished brown skin of her thighs looked very dark, rich as fine ground coffee against the whiteness of that cloth.

"There, now . . ." Lee said. "There, now . . ." He couldn't take his eyes off that place. Such ordinary stuff, a woman's privates. Not many men who hadn't seen a number of such. Certainly he had seen a passel of such splits . . . shouldn't be in such a sweat, now, about seeing another. Shouldn't be.

He reached down, and gently put his hand on her. Resting it lightly on her thigh. Smooth. Smooth. Glossy smooth. And warm as toast.

She made no move at that, only looked down to watch what he was doing.

Lee slowly slid his hand up to her fork. Slowly . . . slowly, he lifted it . . . then put it gently down on the ·small mound, still covered in white cotton. It felt like a slight, soft heart, stirring under his palm.

He squeezed at it lightly, and the girl said something in Indian, and put her slender arms up to cover her face.

Lee slid his arm under her waist, lifted a little, and with his other hand, tugged her cotton pantelettes down her thighs to her knees, down her legs and off of her.

Naked. She lay naked for him.

Lee bent over the girl . . . drifted over her, breathed her in. Her naked legs, her groin, the plump little mound of her sex—only sparsely furred—all seemed to glow in the sunlight, gave off a richness of heat and sweet odor (a sharper gluey smell at her crotch) that seemed to Lee finer than a treasure of gold.

He slid down off the bed, crouched at the girl's knees, put his hands on them, and gently pushed them apart. The girl made no resistance to him at all. She lay still, her arms still crossed over her face. Lay as still as if she were asleep. As if she had no notion what was being done to her.

Lee pushed her knees wide, then half rose to lift them higher, push them farther apart. The girl lay still, legs spraddled wide before him. Letting him see everything of her. The slight notch at her cunt had opened a little with the spreading of her legs. Just the slightest moistness . . . barely visible soft rose-pink in a delicate brush of dark fur. Down in the deeper cleft of her buttocks, only the shadow of the small brown button of her ass.

Lee leaned to her, put his hands on the meat of her thighs, and slowly pushed them wider, shoving them farther apart. Looking up, he saw the girl's mouth open under the shadow of her arms. He saw her breathing as he spread her wider to look at her in the bright morning sunlight.

Her thighs strained far apart now in his grip—the great single tendons that ran up into her groin stood out like India-rubber hose. And this had pulled her private place a little wider . . . stretched it almost open. Damp . . . a patch of wetter red. Her asshole showed now, too, the small wrinkled pucker set in a deep crease of darker brown.

Lee crouched before her, and looked, and saw everything that she had ever hidden since she was a naked child.

Then, still gripping her thighs, he leaned forward to taste it.

He leaned forward, and licked very lightly at the jointure of her thigh, the place where the brown skin stretched tight over that great tendon. Her skin was smooth as powdered ice. It tasted of salt sweat, and some deeper, finer taste, like hotel bread, or some sort of cake. He felt a need to bite into it. Would have been pleased enough, if somehow it would not hurt her, to bite into the skin and break it. Bite deeper into the soft, strong meat beneath it. Bite again—deeper still—bite her down to the white bone. Eat into her there until his teeth clicked on bone . . . Leave nothing left of her in the bed, save blood spots . . . wet, chewed hair.

Could carry her away forever, then. He would have her then for good and all. Would have this girl in his belly, to be made into his bones and blood. A man couldn't be so alone who had done that.

If it wasn't a shame to do—if it wouldn't mean hurting . . . killing her. A thought, that was all—a way to get nearer . . . deeper into her.

He licked her spraddled thigh until the skin there was wet and glistened in the sunlight, until all he could taste was his own spit. All he could smell was his own spit.

He turned to her other, to the thigh ridge of that buried tendon, to the tender hollow beneath it. He licked at her there like a dog, nuzzled his face into her, smelling her, lapping at that sweaty, glossy skin, feeling faintly against his cheek the lightest touch of her crotch hair as he moved against her, nipping gently at her skin. Taking just the littlest bit of her tender skin in his teeth, hardly closing his teeth on that tenderness at all. Just the slightest bit.

With his left hand, he raised her right thigh, lifted it up to make a wonderful roundness where her buttock became that thigh in a sweeping thick curve up and up to the back of the knee. He crouched, looking at that for a while. He stroked that weighty curve with his fingers, but couldn't feel enough; his fingers were too hard, too calloused, too coarsened by reins and rope, by whip-butt and horse-tack, by rifle lever and pistol grip. He couldn't feel enough of her. Saw now what advantage city men had over country men and ranchers. Soft fingers to touch softness with.

He craned his neck and licked at that curve, licked up the hollows of her knee . . . tasted soap there, along with a rich taste of her. All sunny Mexico under his mouth, his tongue. Then he tried all down the curve, kissing and gently biting at her. The girl shifted when he did that. He heard her sigh and murmur something.

He licked down to the fullness of her buttock and held her knee high while he bent further, and ran his tongue down the warm, soft divide of her ass. The girl gasped at that and tried to shift away, but Lee bent his head to her again, and kissed her small rosette, and tongued it. She tried to squirm away again, but Lee put his hand up onto her neat belly, and held her still.

After a while, he leaned back from her . . . looked at her, her damp buttocks, her slack thighs spread wide . . . brown skin shining with wet from his mouth . . . his tongue. He glanced up at her face. She lay looking back at him . . . an odd kindly look, as if he were some sad fellow standing hungry in the street.

He looked up at the girl. She lay watching his hand, that finger touching her there.

"I won't hurt you," Lee said. He said it in English, but the girl smiled up at him as if she understood.

Lee tried to slip his finger up into her— curled the tip of it up to open her little cunt. Did it with all the gentleness, but even so, felt her wince away. Felt her then stop herself from moving away.

She smiled up at him as if he hadn't hurt her.

A virgin. Of course, a virgin.

Lee crouched to her again, put his thumbs to each side of that small, tender, furred place, and tenderly parted it . . . opened it . . . spread it as wide as he could without hurting her.

Saw into her. A complicated little place. Wet . . . red . . . smelling of the glue of life. Fish glue . . . an ocean smell. Smelled like the shore at San Francisco, all those years ago.

He bent his head and kissed it, then he put his tongue into it . . . pushed it far up into her. Began licking at her, pressing his face against that dampness . . . softness. Feeling the wet against his lips . . . the delicate petals, the slippery pink lacework.

He licked it until the girl groaned and moved restlessly under his mouth. Gasped, and shifted her soft thighs slowly this way and that as he worked on her, biting gently at her now. Kissing, sucking at her.

"Ah . . . Madonna . . ."

Lee stood up from her, then leaned forward, reached down to place the swollen, painful head of his cock against the girl's wet cunt. Then, slowly, he thrust into her.

Thrust in . . . felt the heat and squeezing, the soaked, fur-rimmed hole clenched around him. Thrust slowly . . . slowly further, his arms trembling with the strain as he held himself above her. Then felt . . . something. Something . . . and hesitated.

The girl looked up at him then. Looked up into his face. Looked up with dark eyes that saw everything.

And Lee felt her hands, her arms come up to wrap around him, to bind him to her with soft strong bands. Felt her small hips come suddenly thrusting up against him, up around him in one surge as his cock drove through that maidenhead, broke it, and slid into tight and slippery narrowness.

The girl convulsed under him as he fucked full into her. She took the whole length and size of it, gasping, and he drove it in all his strength.

She was stuck on it, impaled, and she kicked out, drew her legs up high at either side of him, grunting, calling out as he pulled it almost out of her, then slowly shoved it all the way into her again. Lee didn't let her rest. He wanted to let her rest, but he couldn't—and couldn't rest himself. His cock slid nearly out of her with a wet, sucking sound, and he drove it in again. Drove it till they came together with a soft smacking sound, she grunting "Oh . . ." as he struck her.

Lee felt her small strong fingers clawing at his back. When his cock was buried in her, felt her sturdy legs come up to circle his waist, to lock around him so that for an instant he couldn't move, couldn't slide his cock back to thrust into her again.

When she had him locked to her in that fashion, the girl writhed and twisted beneath him, driving herself up deeper onto his cock, biting at his neck as she wrestled with him, sobbing, calling out for her mother.

Lee took her in his hands then and pushed her down, held her hard down on the bed and fucked and fucked into her. Willing enough to kill her with it now. His cock, as it pulled almost out of her, was oily with her juices, streaked with the blood of her torn maidenhood. As he wrestled, riding her, Lee reached with one hand beneath them both, searched for her small asshole, found it, and slowly screwed a sweat-wet finger up into her there.

The girl meowed like a cat when he did that, and tried to clench her buttocks against him, but Lee pushed the finger up into her—felt through some wall of flesh there his cock entering her as well, and heard the girl began to scream—saw her head thrown back, the veins standing from her throat—and felt himself begin to go . . . begin to slide away from this to something else. Something that began to tear itself out of him in great throbbing spurts. It swept him away from his life . . . away from everything.

It was more than enough pleasure to die with.

He lay balanced on the girl as if they were floating on the waves of the sea. He dreamed his pleasure, it was so great, and came and came into her . . . felt closer to her than anyone. Felt much closer to her . . . than to anyone . . .

Chapter 7

Lee woke to late afternoon.

He'd slept as if he hadn't slept the night before, and woke feeling wonderful . . . stretched out on the rumpled, stained sheets until his bones cracked . . . drew great breaths of air, smelled the rich stinks of Mexico from the alley outside, the delicate odors the girl had left behind her.

He hadn't known when the girl had left him.

He stretched again, listening to the noises downstairs. Mamacita's was warming to its work. Then he swung his feet to the floor, stood, and went to the chair to get his duds. He'd dress, go down to the kitchen for breakfast (and it would be a considerable breakfast—beans, fried pork, a stack of tortillas, eggs, coffee). Have his breakfast, then go out to the stable yard for a bath and shave. Get a clean shirt on, then, clean underwear as well. Clean socks.

Then to the bank with Don Luis' silver pesos.

And then?

Out of Paso Robles, for certain, once he'd bought a horse. Go to Choo-choo's for the horse. Man was a thief, of course, but sold good stock. Get a big horse perhaps this time. A big gelding with an even temper if the trader had such. An easy-riding horse, too, if possible. Too damn much jolting and jarring, riding these Mexican tracks.

As to the girl . . . As to her, payment for what he owed. Had used her, and used her rough. Needed to pay for that as much as that could be payed for. Luz would likely make a whore out of her now.

Not Lee's fault—well, his fault in a way. No girl could work in such a place for long and not be turned to the life by someone.

Lee pulled on his boots, took his gunbelt from the bed post, looped it over his shoulder, and walked out of the room and down the corridor to the stairs. Looked like a handsome sunny day and not too hot, though Lee had missed the noon of it.

The kitchen at Mamacita's, like most such down here, was half kitchen and half back porch, open to the yard and alley. More chickens running in the kitchen than the yard. A thin old man named Eusebio cooked for the place—was a devil with chilies and chocolate cooking, almost as good with the rest. Eusebio was at his fat black wood-burner this afternoon, minding his business for dinner. Smelled like rabbit stew (and hot enough to burn in the smelling).

Four women were sitting in a row against the side wall, patting tortillas.

The girl was one of them, second from the right.

She looked up when Lee walked in, looked up and smiled at him as bright as the day.

Lee barely nodded to her, then nodded to Eusebio and walked on through. No use making up to her . . . no use playing true love.

He went down the steps into the yard and heard the other women laughing at her. He went to the pump and dragged the big washtub over.

The women would be having a good laugh at her in there.

That foolish smile of hers . . . A smile looked damned odd on an Indian face, anyway. Up to her, did she decide to make an ass of herself . . .

He pumped in a good half tub-full, the water coming up from a way, and cold. Then he went across the yard and into the stable, looking for soap. Found a sliver, dark yellow and hard as stone, on a shelf with toothless curry-combs and a hide brush with pitiful few bristles left to it.

He went back to the yard, and hung his gunbelt on the pump handle. He started to unbutton his shirt—then stopped and buttoned it up again. Walked back to the kitchen steps and up them, saw the row of women still sitting there against the wall, working. The girl had her head down now as she should have had before.

Lee went over to her, waited till she looked up at him, then made her a proper gentleman's bow, reached down to take one small, flour-whitened hand, and bent to kiss it.

Silence in the kitchen.

No noise of patting tortillas, either.

"*Senorita,*" Lee said to her, "I will be having a late breakfast. Would you be kind enough to join me then? For coffee, if you have already eaten?"

The girl stared up at him, tears still in her eyes from the women's laughter. She was, Lee saw, really a handsome girl—not beautiful, to be sure, but pretty enough for a little *mestizo*.

"Until then," Lee said, and leaned down again to brush a strand of that coal black hair from her eyes.

The bathwater had pumped into the washtub cold as cold could be, and would have made for uncomfortable bathing but for the sun. Lee sat up to his belly in the tub

109

—might as well have been sitting naked in snow—but felt at the same time the afternoon sun battering down hot as blazes on his head and shoulders, his arms, stinging his unprotected forehead.

It made for a pleasure of contrasts that even the stone-hard soap couldn't spoil. Always a fine feeling to be getting clean in any case, even if it took harsh scrubbing.

He scrubbed and he soaped and paid no heed to the Mexicans. Give them their due, they were a modest people, and wouldn't stand about (as some Ameerican louts and whores well might) peeping as a fellow bathed. He bent his head and scooped up handfuls of the cold water to soak his hair. Had never cared for lice—saw no need to have the damn things. Scrubbed and lathered, scrubbed again, rubbing his fingertips hard through his hair. This damn soap should kill anything . . . Smelled like a tannery, pulp mill, and kerosene works combined.

Lee could see, just past the side arbor, a space of the street in front, and kept an eye on that as he bathed, looking for light blue jackets in case Captain Gonsalves decided some brusque action was appropriate after all.

Would be the devil to pay, though, rushing about this yard stark naked, scattering chickens and shooting at *Rurales*. Unlikely to end well . . .

110

When he'd finished bathing, Lee whistled for a little boy—called him Charlie, the cook's son (or nephew)—and the boy came running with one of Luz's old sheets, the cotton worn to gauze beneath the haunches of her whores, the materian torn and latticed here and there by the spurs of hasty vaqueros, kicking in their joys.

Lee stood, stepped out gingerly onto hard-pan mud and chicken shit, and toweled well off, some bits of the sheet coming away in his hands at too vigorous rubbing. Finished that and finished fast, the sun doing much of his drying for him. Lee wrapped the frayed sheeting around his waist, bent over his bit of mirror at the pump taking care that the harsh sunlight didn't flash from it into his eyes, shook his razor open, and commenced to scrape his beard away. That completed, and a rub of coarse salt from the kitchen across his teeth with a chewed twig-end, succeeded by a hair combing (and another check for nits) and Lee would be toileted and ready for his late breakfast, a visit to the bank, a stop at the horse-coper's—and a drift out of town.

A woman named Eustacia, wide in the beam as any rowing boat, brought them their breakfast under the trellis arbor. This narrow side porch, dapple shaded from the worst of the sun, was the most pleasant place to eat a meal that Lee had found in

Paso Robles. If Luz had had no girls at all in her establishment, even no bar-room and drinkery, she would still have had Lee's custom for this eating place and its food.

A pot of scalding coffee, oddly cooling in the heat; brown sugar and sweet milk to put into it; syrup rolls, small and sticky; eggs scrambled with chilies and green sweet pepper; a basket of tortillas, piping hot and soft as linen napkins; and a platter of shredded pork *tobasco*. It was—even without the fried chicken skin, the bowl of double-cooked beans—enough of a breakfast for two ordinary hungry men.

Lee cleaned the plates handily all by his lonesome—or nearly, Florenca having only a small cup of the coffee, only one syrup roll to nibble.

Odd, how things—people, and their remembered places—would return to sound in a man's mind as if they were just now fresh minted. Lee, sitting in foliaged sunlight deep in Old Mexico, sitting across from a simple girl he had outraged (no nicer word for it, and plenty uglier) remembered suddenly, as if a person had reached out and struck him, another restaurant . . . a back-yard place, but elegant. A real restaurant, some might say, not just a greaser whore-house with a kitchen, and in that back-yard, a laughing dudish fellow (looked the sissy but was not) in a colorful coat. Ned Bierce in a green velvet coat, smiling, joking . . .

just before, their lunch over, he had made that sad rough go crawling down the street.

Something about this breakfast—a "brunch" as Bierce would have called it—had brought that amusing fellow to mind. Bierce would, Lee supposed, have had something cutting to say about would-be gentlemen who found their level in dining with maids.

Lee regretted some of his killings—regretted them all, at least for a time (had nightmares . . . other manifestations of regret almost every occasion of a killing). But he had never ceased to regret shooting Ned Bierce to death. Seemed to him he'd never been the same man after that. Seemed that he'd killed a friend, though of only short acquaintance and though Bierce gave him no choice about it.

"You don't wish for more of a meal than that, little one?"

The girl, Florenca, smiled at him and shook her head. She seemed pleased enough to sit and watch Lee pig it sturdily through the half-dozen dishes. Seemed to give her some satisfaction to watch him eat. Not the first time Lee had noticed that women enjoyed watching men (those they were pleased with) fill their faces with food. Had something to do with the pleasures of nursing children, Lee supposed.

As to the girl being pleased with *him*, she certainly seemed to be. Though Lee was under no illusion that an Indian girl, having been raped (one of those uglier words) might not smile a considerable while before deciding to try to cut his throat.

Yet there appeared none of that in the air. Whether because he had finally given her pleasure, and a pleasure both great and new to her, or because he had honored her with gentlemanly attention after the other women laughed, or because he was white and a *Norte Americano* (though, of course, Mexicans also, were also *Norte Americanos,* at least by geography)—or simply because he was her first man and had broken into her and forced her close, and had therefore caught some cord to her heart, the girl seemed mighty fond.

Mighty fond.

Of course, he had not ended by forcing her. Had been gentle with her, then.

That might have made some difference to her.

Lee smiled back at the girl, then went to scraping up the last of his eggs. No saying that Eusebio couldn't cook an egg. First trial and test of a stove-man, McCorkle used to say. "They can do a egg simple, or they can't."

There now arose some slight question what he was to do with her. Ordinarily, that wouldn't have arisen—a whore being a whore, and situated where she chose to be. Difficulty here was the girl was no whore, not yet. Difficulty was, she would soon be one, her cherry being busted.

"Tell me, little flower," Lee said, taking the last syrup roll since she refused it. "Tell me—do you wish to stay here? Do you wish the life of the other women here? It is not so unpleasant, you know, though you have to do with rough people, not gentle."

A real choice—and by no means a bad one —for a girl from some desperate peasant family living like pigs in a muddy pueblo in the mountains. For most of these women, whoring was a life of luxury and not work at all, as peasant women counted work. In any case, he had asked, and if she chose to stay and live the life . . . well, it was something he need not concern himself with.

The girl put down her coffee cup (she had been holding it with two hands, like a child) and said, "I would like to go."

Eusebio's eggs suddenly felt a little heavy in Lee's stomach.

"You don't want to stay here?"

"No."

An Indian of few words. Eusebio's eggs had definitely been a little overcooked this afternoon.

"Well—would you prefer to go back to your home?"

"No." An Indian of *very* few words.

"Florenca, tell me where you would like to go."

"I will go where you wish," she said,

115

picked up her coffee cup again in both hands, and took a small sip.

It was near ruining Lee's brunch.

"You can't ride with me, little one."

Nod. Lee was grateful for it. All that was needed was for him to be dogged by some stupid Indian girl. Trailing him in and out of saloons and so forth . . .

"I will go where you tell me . . . *Senor* Lee." The last, the naming of his name, doing mighty quietly.

"Very well then," Lee said, and stood up from the table feeling he'd had his brunch and then some, "I will consider it."

It would cost him money, for the start. It was wonderful, when a man thought of it, how many matters cost money.

Luz Obregon turned her blind eye on Lee, and apparently a deaf ear as well. Showed him her scrawny, dark profile while she counted off a stack of IOU's into her cash box.

"I'll pay the girl's debt off to you and add a gift for the house."

No reaction to "pay"—some reaction to "gift."

"Five pesos for the girl. Two extra for the house."

Fierce Luz appeared to find a particularly rotten IOU. She stared down at it as if the devil had come to Paso Robles to tuck it into her cash drawer. *"Gomez!"* For a thin woman, Luz had a fearsome voice.

116

She only had to call once. Gomez, a very handsome young man and overseer of the chuck-a-luck wheel, came hustling down the bar combing his hair and smiling in a propitiatory sort of way. It was he, apparently, who had accepted the IOU.

Mamacita held the offending paper out to handsome young *Senor* Gomez. When he had examined it carefully, grinned, rolled his eyes, and shrugged a "foolish me" shrug, Luz leaned further forward, tapped at the young man's lips with the folded IOU as if knocking on a door, and when the sad fellow reluctantly opened his mouth, tucked the paper in as if into a letter box.

Then the lady stood back to watch Gomez chew and swallow that particular promise to pay.

Lee stood by till Gomez loped off back up the bar through a heat-struck afternoon crowd, his lesson learned.

"Seven pesos for the girl. Five for the house."

At which, the meager woman cast him a one-eyed glance, and said, "You are a bad man." She made a delicate gesture, thrusting her forefinger through two others, circled.

"Seven, and five."

Luz considered, the lid faintly trembling, half closed, over her blind eye.

"Take it or leave it," Lee said in English. It was a phrase which seemed as understandable to Mexicans as to Americans. No translation needed.

Mamacita appeared to understand it very well. She pursed her narrow lips, ticked her long fingernails on the edge of the cottonwood bar in a hat-dance rhythm for a measure or two. Then she said, "O.K." and held out her hand.

Chapter 8

The *Banco National*, housed in an impressive building—which it should be, having been a small cathedral before the revolution—had nonetheless, Lee suspected, some shortage of ready funds. The echoing, vaulted space (cut red stone, marble facings, the vault set neatly into the place once held by the high altar) was served by only two clerks, neat young men with flat oiled hair and ink-smudged cuffs, and a bank officer, a large soft-bellied fellow with a face like a fish, and wearing a fine English suit.

The bank guard was barefoot and sleeping by the door, a split-stocked breech-loading carbine by his side. Nothing special for protection there; the real protection was lounging in the *Rurale* barracks the other side of town. Men who robbed this bank would have their running cut out for them . . . a long, long run.

There were only two other customers in the place—local merchants, it seemed. Lee supposed that most Mexicans were keeping their cash money under their house floors, at least until it was known that Diaz would be able to stick in Mexico City.

"I will give you a receipt in my own hand," the bank officer said in reassuring style, as if Don Luis might lose all track of his accounts without it.

"That would be very useful, *Senor*," Lee said, hefted the saddlebags and slung them down on the marble counter with a more than sufficient jingle and thump. "You might care to count it . . ."

"No, no, no." The bank officer shook fragrant jowls (Bay Rum and oil of Gardenia, Lee thought). "Not necessary, *Senor* McCann."

Fellow appeared fearful of questioning the Don's honor, even second-hand. An odd way of business the Mexicans had. Who you were was more important, sometimes, than what you had in cash or property. Politics always had to be taken into account, even more than in the States. Family matters were a good deal more important than business matters—in that, not like the States at all.

Did he bring such a sum to an American

bank, there would be receipts signed and cash counted, and no nonsense about it, even for a Vanderbilt—in fact, especially for a Vanderbilt. Well . . . the perfumed bank officer was at least writing out a receipt, though taking Lee's word on the amount. He was writing, Lee could see, with great swoops and scrolls, dashes and darts of India ink. Flourishes. It would be a hell of a receipt.

When Lee left the bank—something relieved, in truth, to be shut of the responsibility for the Don's cash (he had no illusions that Don Luis would ever forgive a loss of cash)—he found Paso Robles in slow, stirring, post-siesta ferment.

In this golden late afternoon light, with shadows stretching long across the cobbled pavements, the citizens of the town had reappeared, refreshed and ready for marketing, for strolling, for preliminary ogling of the few decent women out for a breath of air, for work where essential, for a drink perhaps at the *Tres Toros* or *Casablanca*. Some *very* decent women, and these of the better class, were on their way to church, ensconced in creaky old equipages, driven by men as old and rheumatic as their carriages. These ladies sat wrapped in layers of black bombazine, black lace, black stuff of every sort. Even their necklaces were of jet. Their faces, dead pale, occasionally mustached, were set to the front

(no peeking here or there—certainly no
peeking at a Yankee *pistolero* booting down
the street toward Choo-choo's corral and
horse copery. No peek at such as that.
These ladies went to church every day,
thrice on Sundays, and would have as
happily seen a heretic burned, were such
still possible in these degenerate times, as
seen a horse thief hung or a friend's
daughter disgraced.

Lee thought these proud, stupid ladies
quite formidable, and saw that they stood
like rocks in this town and all others
throughout Mexico, no matter what the
bandits or generals or *politicos* or *social-
istas* were up to in Mexico City.

He enjoyed them, and liked to watch
them ride out to church, occasionally with a
petulant but defeated son or daughter in
convoy.

He had never seen any Mexican—even
drunk, even savage—offer to offend these
pale-faced, black-feathered turkey hens.

So he stood to watch them rattle slowly
by, and swept off his *sombrero* and made
his bow as if he were acquainted. Never, not
once, had any of these ladies deigned to
notice him. Lee would have been disappointed in them if they had.

Choo-choo kept his stable down by the
tracks—had, in fact, won his nickname for
his love of railroad trains; used to go down
to watch the damn engines come in. Still

did, Lee supposed. Hard to see why a man would like railroad trains. Lee hadn't cared for them for many years.

It was a fair walk across town, and Lee enjoyed it, despite the heat. Two or three men nodded to him on the street . . . not many. Others knew him well enough, but didn't nod to him. No women appeared to see him, except one selling oranges.

Two little boys walked after him for a while, strutting and pretending to put their hands on the butts of holstered pistols. Then they walked up alongside him for a stretch, asked him questions . . . asked him how many men he'd killed . . . asked him if he'd ever seen a gasoline machine . . .

A few loafers were hanging in at Choo-choo Morelos'. Town roughs, town philosophers, town tramps. Some boys in love with horses . . .

Choo-choo, a tall, gap-toothed drink of water with a handlebar mustache and skin the color of mud, came out of a holding pen to give Lee a vigorous handshake, a commiserating smile.

"I understand that Captain Gonsalves has left you afoot, Mister McCann. Ah, what troubles the police bring upon us, to take from a man his means of riding . . . to reduce him to a peasant, a foot-stomper."

"Troubles indeed," Lee said. "Though, of course, the good Captain was only doing his duty."

"Certainly," Morelos said. "His duty."

"Trot me out some horse-flesh, Chooey, and don't waste our time with dog food." Under no illusions, of course, that Morelos wouldn't try a stunt or two, regardless.

Choo-choo whistled and a dwarf named Pepito went waddling into the west stable, a long shed with perhaps fifteen stalls. It was this stable, Lee had noticed, that Morelos went to some pains to keep clean. The only one, at least, that had a manure pile in front of it, in preference to a stable floor so paved, as with his shed to the east of the tracks.

The dwarf had hustled and soon enough came flying out of the stable door hanging onto the reins of a slab-sided sorrel with a splint thrown on his left fore.

Lee didn't look further, but waved to the dwarf to lead the animal back inside.

"You're wasting my time."

"You're right," Choo-choo said. "I'm at fault in having such a fool in my employ." He shouted to the dwarf to wake up in there! To be a little less of an ass!

And in a minute or two the dwarf came leading out again, and this a considerable animal. A bay gelding, and big as a house. Good bone. Good conformation. Seemed slightly shy, but that might be from being stall-bound. Mexicans thought exercise was wasted on a horse.

The dwarf held the big bay's head while

Lee checked its teeth . . . its eyes . . . ran his hands down the animal's legs.

This was no stable plug. It looked a formidable horse.

"I regret to tell you," Morelos said, "that this beast is a four-hundred-peso beast."

Lee said nothing to that but took the reins from the dwarf, slung up onto the bay's bare back, and booted him out at a run.

Animal sprang right away and ran like a wolf.

It was a pleasure to be up on him, to feel the great lengths of muscle shift and bunch. Feel the wind of the run come fluttering at your face . . .

Lee galloped the bay out across the flats, listening to the horse's beathing, listening for a lunger's whistle and heave.

Nothing. The animal ran steady as a machine—none of the surge and slacken of an off-center runner. A pleasure to ride and easy on the ass, even bareback.

Lee heard the men shouting to him from the stable, urging the *gringo* to boot the beast up, to make the sluggard fly. He reined to a row of chicken coops behind the Street of the Processions, thundered past a group of children who shouted in excitement at such speed and commotion through a late, hot afternoon, then reined the horse left along a dry wash and down that and out into the flats again, very happy with the animal, and determined to buy it—but not for four-hundred pesos.

It was only with the bay drawn back down to a walk that a notion occurred to Lee—the horse, although high-strung, not having swerved in its run at all when the children had shouted on its right side. The notion occcuring, Lee leaned out to the right and sharply clapped his hands by the bay's right ear.

No notice taken. No notice taken of hand-clapping beside the left ear, either.

Lee drew the Bisley Colt's and fired two fast shots, right and left alongside the horse's head.

No notice taken.

He rode the animal on in, swung down, and handed the dwarf the reins. Didn't have to say anything to Morelos. A deaf horse was, sooner or later, a dangerous horse. Constantly wary of surprise, they sooner or later spooked at the wrong time and broke a man's leg . . . or his neck.

"You're still wasting my time."

Choo-choo Morelos was not a horse-coper for nothing. "You might not have noticed," he said. "Am I to be blamed if a man is ignorant . . . or careless? All honor to you that you were not!" And waved the dwarf back into the stable.

"Now," he said, "no more tricks." He combed his handlebar mustache with his thumb and forefinger. "From now, simply a matter of good judgment."

And out came Pepito, dancing along at the end of the reins of a neat grey—very clean-lined legs, a nice, fine head. Animal was shifting as it trotted—likely stable-bound. Good enough gait to it.

Lee went up carefully, thinking there might be a fault of temper there. But the grey had quiet eyes. Held well to have its mouth, its teeth looked at. A young horse, and lively. It sidled and danced a bit while Lee had hold of the bridle, constantly picking its neat feet up and putting them down. Something like a little boy, held fast in church, and having to pee.

Lively. A handsome horse.

Very lively in the foot.

Lee stooped and picked up the right fore. Nothing appeared to be the matter . . . hoof clean, frog sound enough. Went beside and picked up the hind hoof. Horse stood still very nicely for that; dwarf had no trouble holding the reins.

Nothing wrong to see there, either. Lee bent his head to smell the hoof for rot or pus. Sweet as grass. Nothing there to smell.

He put his thumb to the center of the frog there, pressed gently—and the grey snorted hard and suddenly jerked its hoof free, wrenching Lee's wrist a little. Started away and shied in an uneasy half circle, dragging the dwarf in doing it.

It was unusual to find a sound horse with a case of tenders . . . hoof frogs that bruised at any touch, any punishment on the road. Something a very few horses were born with. It rendered them quite useless for riding, for work of any kind.

Lee had heard of sulphur soaks doing some improvement, or sea-water for a few months. Some horse doctors cut nerves deep in the hooves to stop it. Lee doubted any of those remedies worked well.

Sad horse, so handsome and fine, and must have been traded again and again as its fault was swiftly found out. Some impatient man would sooner or later attempt to beat that fault away. End by shooting the beast that, looking so fine, only made mock of its purchaser.

"I have time for one more horse," Lee said to Morelos. "You might try a sulphur soak on this one's hooves. I've heard that sometimes does."

The roughs and philosophers and tramps meowed a few catcalls at the coper—liking, no doubt, to see the biter bit—but Choo-choo kept his poise. "It is," he said, "completely unnatural for a Texan to so well know horses." Most Americans were Texans as far as most Mexicans were concerned—those violent people, cold and hot at once, that lay above the Rio Bravo, having made over the century an indelible impression.

Choo-choo sighed at the roughage of a businessman's lot and waved the dwarf away with the sore-footed horse.

It began to seem that Lee must buy private in the town. Some individual's horse . . . It would take time, certainly the rest of the day. Perhaps into tomorrow.

Shortly, the dwarf came scrambling out of the west stable again, leading a stocky black with a head like a carpenter's hammer. The beast had a no-nonsense trot —lifted its knees decently high—and had black hooves, not too large, and seeming as dense as stone.

Lee had seen its like a thousand times. A stump-puller, a jolt-trotter with a deep chest and haunches wide enough for a two-hundred-pound whore to ride pillion.

He had a fated feeling, a vision of himself on just this unromantic and ugly engine. A goer for sure, harsh as a hoof rasp and as tough. Not all that young, either.

A horse. A distillation of horse.

He walked up to check the creature anyway. It stood, lower than his shoulder, silent, still, gazing off into the last haze of afternoon light.

Damn thing looked roughly carved of coal.

Lee looked at its teeth. Not all that young

a horse.

Checked its hooves. Just as hard as they looked.

It was an inescapeable horse.

Lee glanced at Choo-choo Morelos. And Choo-choo knew.

"I will pay you one hundred and fifty pesos for this horse. Take it or leave it."

Choo-choo smiled, as pleased as if the *El Presidente* was pulling into the Paso Robles station, whistle blowing, for his delectation alone.

Chapter 9

Lee rode his new horse back to Mamacita's at a hard jog trot. The black would gallop, and fast enough, but evidently considered that gait to be unnecessary, for he slowed from it whenever Lee stopped batting at him with the crop. The jog-trot, however (and a bone-breaker) the black appeared to regard as a horse's most natural and becoming stride, and, to be fair, he gave evidence of being able to keep that pace up for several days, if watered at intervals, like one of Choo-choo's railroad trains.

Lee decided to call the animal "Horse."

And rode this blocky, unlovely, mechanical beast into Mamacita's side alley alongside the trellised arbor to discover he had visitors, unexpected company, sitting at the arbor's back, sipping coffee in a soft, early evening shadow.

Two of them.

One, a vaquero—a gun-handy fellow named Miguel Onofrio, a soft-looking man, continually sighing when one stood near him, who wore two double-action parrot-gripped .38's in fancy Buscadero holsters on his hips. Onofrio was supposed to have done some ten or eleven men to death, and Lee supposed that could be so. Fellow had damp, earth-colored eyes; didn't appear moved by much, one way or another.

The second visitor, looking mighty high and aloof and looking mighty disdainful of Onofrio as a coffee-sipping partner, come to that, was Don Jaime Alvarez—no "Don" at all, actually, but certainly just as good as most real such, since he was *domo major,* or grand steward and domestic of Las Sabrinas—and appearing much more the hidalgo than the real Don Luis.

They'd come to see him, no doubt about it. Onofrio's thick gaze had been glued to him since the black came thudding down the alleyway.

Don Jaime didn't trouble to look up. He had very elevated airs. Was dressed as fine as a silver dollar, too—black charro suit, braided gold along his lapels, at his cuffs, a sombrero of fine hammered felt (black as night but for its trim of gold braid). Don Jaime looked the grand *haciendado* to the life—these fine clothes, a high-bridged nose as proud as Satan, tiny needle-pointed goatee, grey eyes as frigid as a Castille winter.

Hard to believe the fellow was simply a puffed-up servant, a housekeeper on the grand scale, Don Luis' butler-in-chief and overseer of the household. Not that these were unimportant roles. They were not. Even as Don Luis' shadow, the fellow swung more weight than most in Sonora ... would have no trouble getting an interview with the Governor himself, come to that.

Not an inconsiderable fellow, for all his charro airs. And, of course, there was Miguel Onofrio. Also, in his way, a considerable fellow.

Lee booted the black over to the raised porch and found himself, with some embarrassment, lifting his sombrero to "Don" Jaime. Mexican ways were catching and the fellow's fine airs had some effect after all.

As he made the courtesy, Lee noticed the girl, Florenca, standing at the kitchen door, watching him. Young fool probably thought he was a dandy dasher, greeting such a lordly acquaintance.

"Good afternoon, Don Jaime," Lee said, making no sport of the title.

"Evening, surely," Don Jaime said, looking out over his coffee cup at the shadows stretching across the yard. "We see you well, I suppose, *Senor?*

"Very well, thank you."

Onofrio had nothing to say. He sat facing Lee, his plump hands relaxed in his lap. Lee got that picture of the fellow in his mind and held it there. Any sudden change in the fellow's way of sitting . . . any sudden movement of his hand . . .

For a few moments, Don Jaime had nothing else to say. He and Onofrio sat like frogs at the edge of a pond, Don Jaime sipping, Onofrio doing nothing at all.

After this pause, Don Jaime put down his cup with a tiny click of china against china. Luz had served this grandee on her own dishes.

"Would it please you to join us, *Senor* McCann?"

"A pleasure indeed," Lee said, and keeping Onofrio in mind, swung down from the black's bare back, went to the porch steps, walked along the planking to them, and took the chair Don Jaime indicated across the table.

Onofrio, Lee found, had a not unpleasant odor of manure about him—odd, since as far as Lee knew, the man pushed no stock at all.

"The Don," Don Jaime said—and there was no doubt as to whom he referred—"is most pleased with your actions in Canyon Rojo."

Pesos saved, bandits dead. And the Don

demonstrating how much he knew, and, thanks to the telegraph, how soon.

Lee said nothing to that, maintained a modest silence. He'd noticed some time ago that people preferred fighting men to remain as silent as possible, assuming, he supposed, that that betokened determination. People who assumed that, he thought, had never met Harvey Logan.

Miguel Onofrio, now—here was a classic of the silent sort of *pistolero*. Fellow sat still as stone, smelling of manure, his hands quiet in his lap.

"I am now," Don Jaime said, "*en route* to La Sabrinas, on a mission of some importance."

French linen bed sheets; Mason jars for the pantries; sacks of Kentucky grass seed; a payroll of several thousand pesos; denim material by the hundreds of yards; German serving platters; Saltillo *serapes;* Colt's Best Revolving Firearms by the case; ammunitions innumerable; liquors and wines by the tun; a purchase (forced or voluntary) of an additional grazing space of some 50,000 hecteres . . . it was matters such as these that constituted Don Jaime's domain, and all in service to Las Sabrinas and its lord.

"All the more the honor you do me in making this visit," Lee said, "in interruption of more important matters."

Don Jaime considered this, found it a

reasonable attitude, and nodded pleasantly. It was always a surprise to discover a *gringo* with any delicacy, any courtesy at all.

"And yet," the Don said, "there is some slight affair that might be usefully brought to your attention, I suppose . . ." He picked up his coffee again, sipped at it, and finding it cool, made an unpleasant face. "Some slight affair . . ." he said, setting the cup down again. "The manager . . . the 'engineer' at Los Gatos has purchased a ticket on the express to Tampico, intending, we presume, to mount that express tomorrow night at the station in Hermosillo or at a nearer stop."

"A long trip," Lee said.

"Yes—but not as long as the next, for this 'engineer' has also purchased by Federal mail a steam-ship ticket from Tampico to Buenos Aires."

"A very long trip, then," Lee said. "Extremely long. I hadn't known it was his time of leave from the mine."

"It is not," said Don Jaime, "his time of leave from the mine."

Lee was not foolish enough to wonder how this Don and the other far more important Don had discovered Max Thornhill's travel plans. He could wonder how Thornhill, a tall, disagreeable German-Scot, born in Mexico but considering himself in no way part of it, could have been stupid enough to assume that the manager of one of the richest small silver mines in Sonora would not be under observation by the owner of that silver mine.

The man was worse than an ass.

Likely, he was dead.

"A robbery of some kind?"

"So we assume," said Don Jaime, staring down into his coffee cup as if the stuff might turn hot again.

Lee glanced over to the kitchen entrance, saw the girl, Florenca, watching him, and lifted his hand as if he had a cup in it, then indicated the Don.

The girl popped out of sight.

"*Senor* Thornhill has become too ill to travel?"

"He has not," the Don said. "He is still in perfect health, as far as I know. Has made new friends, also, it appears."

The Don seemed after a few moments to have nothing more to add and was only roused when Florenca, approaching the table with a good deal of hesitation and one awkward curtsey, placed a fresh cup and a small flowered China coffee pot before him. The Don nodded to acknowledge the service, said, "Clumsy thing," of Florenca, and poured and commenced to sip at his coffee.

"That she is," Lee said, "though, I believe, an honest girl. I doubt if even you, Sir, could train her up to Las Sabrinas standards."

The Don, like many foolish-seeming men, was no fool at all.

"Is that some whore of yours, *Senor,* that you think to foist on the service of Don Luis?"

Miguel Onofrio stirred ever so slightly in his chair. His plump hands hadn't moved. His shoulders had moved a little.

Lee, pinked once, decided against fencing with a fencer.

"I have been with her once. She was a virgin, a girl sold from the hills into this place. She is a good girl, nonetheless, and a Christian. She wishes to leave this place for some other place both decent and peaceful."

Having said that much, Lee shut up.

The Don stared down his long nose at Lee, as if in renewed astonishment at the ways of the savages of the north.

"What a romantic tale," he said, "and too nonsensical not to be true." Another sip of coffee. "We will take her with us when we go. She can ride on top of the diligence with the baggage. She will learn our ways at Las Sabrinas . . . in the linen room, I think, to begin . . . or she will prove herself a fool, or lazy, and so be given to the vaqueros for their amusement."

Lee had no notion the Don would forget

this favor owed nor fail to request repayment in his own good time.

"An act of Christian charity, Don Jaime."

"What, in the name of Our Lady," said Don Jaime, "can a Protestant know of that?" and so closed the subject.

Onofrio spoke up then, his voice as slow and sleepy as he seemed. "This Thornhill met three *Tejanos* in the pueblo at Tecochli. Two *gringo* men and a boy."

Having spoken his piece, the *pistolero* subsided into a lump still whiffing slightly of manure.

"Just so," said the Don. "It might be useful if you were to choose to visit *Senor* Thornhill as soon as possible. To inquire, perhaps, what might be the . . . intentions . . . of this Thornhill, and of those three of your countrymen."

Not much doubt about intentions. Intended to rob the damn mine, is what they intended, and Thornhill likely already paid well for his information.

"It is of interest, I believe," the Don added, "that the Bank of the Republic in Cuidad Juarez was robbed of thirty-seven thousand pesos seven weeks ago."

"Yes," Lee said, "I heard of that."

"And the thieves . . ."

"Yes . . ."

"Two men, and a boy as lookout."

Silence on the side porch of Mamacita's.

Nothing much more to say. Max Thornhill looked to be getting, say, thirty-five thousand pesos to set up a nice robbery of his employer's silver mine. Which meant that the mine office strong room must at present contain at least fifty to sixty thousand pesos' worth of refined silver bars.

More than enough to bring some very hard cases south from Texas. And longheaded thieves as well, to have robbed a bank very successfully and only to finance this present even more profitable venture.

"Why not send police up to the mine?"

The Don rolled his eyes slightly at such a *gringo* suggestion.

"My dear *Senor* McCann, the 'police' of this section of the Province are not 'police' in any ethical sense. They are, shall we say, servants of certain corrupt political groups, cabals, influences . . ."

So Lee hadn't been mistaken about Captain Gonsalves' speculative stare. "Certain corrupt political influences" surely included men like the Lieutenant Governor, a grim thug named Chavez, and just as certainly did not include friends of Don Luis. That wheel would turn, of course, but apparently not yet.

"Let us say then," said Don Jaime, "that it would be . . . unwise . . . to invite the police into the strong-room of the mine at Los Gatos."

And so, Don Jaime's visit to Mamacita's. Lee was, it appeared, to be the angel of salvation for Don Luis' silver at the Los Gatos mine. The angel of retribution as well, of course. In fact, the angel of death.

No use playing coy about it.

"I'll go to the mine directly and do what has to be done."

Don Jaime nodded, satisfied, and poured himself another cup of coffee. "I expected no less," he said, a considerable compliment from that source.

"One matter—these Americans . . ."

"I regret to say, very fierce. Savages. At Cuidad Juarez, they shot to death two men. It is our understanding that they killed a man at the pueblo of Tecochli also, and he himself had been a man of some reputation with firearms."

Worse and worse.

Not just a passel of border roughs with big eyes, then. The genuine article, they sounded. The McCoy. Hard cases driven south by the Rangers and the telegraph, by the county posses, the Federal Marshals and the Pinkertons. Driven south into wilder country. Country as wild as their country had been not too many years ago.

Three of them.

Wouldn't be like potting those sad, raggedy-ass *banditos* at Canyon Rojo. Wouldn't be like that at all . . .

Lee noticed that Don Jaime was scurrying to Las Sabrinas fast enough—taking his *pistolero* with him, too. Well, it wasn't fair to blame a man for being sensible.

Lee stood up from the table.

"My apologies," he said, "but it is a long ride to Los Gatos, and I had better be on my way." He held out his hand, and Don Jaime looked surprised, but took it.

"God go with you, *Senor*," Don Jaime said, "I will see that the young woman is. . . properly situated . . . at Las Sabrina."

God almighty—the old sissy thought Lee was for the bone-yard sure!

Chapter 10

Say what a man might of the black horse's looks, he was a locomotive for going; and just as well, for he had a piece to go before full dark, then a piece to go by moonlight before they were benighted.

And up and going again at dawn . . . then the last long climb up to Los Gatos. And make that before Thornhill left for his railroad train. Must get to Los Gatos before Thornhill left for his railroad train . . .

The girl had made no fuss at Lee's going, had understood she was to travel with Don Jaime and his people, had understood there would be work . . . a place to live.

Lee had kissed her. Her mouth was as soft as gardenia petals.

He swung up on the black—rifle and roll, war-bag and saddle-bag all tied to, canteen

fresh filled with cold water—had waved to
scrawny one-eyed Luz up on the porch, bent
to lightly stroke the girl's soft black hair,
then had spurred on out of the yard in a
cackle of scooting chickens and had not
looked back.

No call to. No use to.

The black had the damndest trot. If it
weren't so steady a gait, a man would swear
he was low-bucking.

Lee reined him down off the rock-strewn
road and off into a stubbled cornfield, heading northeast by the sun. It was easier
riding through the fields. Horse wasn't
such a pounding ride.

This was pretty country, if you didn't
mind it parched. Long as you didn't try to
look long up into the hills for rich green, for
big trees, pines and such . . . As long as you
were content with scrub flowers, little
juniper shrubs, that sort of stuff.

The evening was fine, though. Cooler
than some. Night would be coming down
before he was up into the hills at all. Lee
was damned if he could accommodate to the
black's gait. "You damned iron-leg son-of-a-
bitch!" Lee tried booting the beast into a
canter and the black did as he was bid, but
wouldn't hold to it, slacked back into that
grinding trot. Lee finally gave up on him. If
the black wouldn't alter, then Lee's ass
better had. He tried sitting looser, limper,
rocking to the trot, and that did help some.

It appeared that with this horse, twenty-five years of riding, some twenty years of that work-riding, and some fifteen years of *that* breaking and training . . . Appeared that none of it was enough to deal with this damn horse.

Lee's back had commenced to ache like a boil.

At moonlight, higher in the country, Lee rode through a no-name village of little adobe whitewashed houses. Didn't look too bad, these little houses, unless you went inside. Then you wished you hadn't. Then you saw how poor the country was despite all the sunshine and the oranges easy to buy.

Nobody came out to see the wayfarer when the black's stone-hard hooves rang on the stones. These were not the villages, and night was not the time to be coming out of doors when a horseman came riding through. These *pueblos* had suffered in the Revolution—had seen their sons lined against church walls and shot. Had seen much worse things than that. No one from this nameless village cared to come outside to see who might be passing.

Lee rode through and rode on out by moonlight, riding higher all the time.

An moon-down, on a spiny ridge sharper than a toothed saw, Lee pulled the black up. The animal had kept to that grim gait of his for hours, and jarred Lee's guts near to entirely loose. But had not faltered, not mis-stepped. If it weren't for the pain of it, the black would be a considerable traveling horse.

Lee groaned aloud when he swung down out of the saddle. Felt his backside near skinned, his backbone a sore stick indeed. Cost him something to get the black hobbled, though the horse was well behaved enough. Just so damn sore.

He sat on a patch of a gamma (or at least the grass felt like gamma in the dark) and wolfed tortillas and handfuls of cold beans out of an oilskin package. Tasted damn good, too—almost took his mind off his aching butt.

Finished that, which didn't take long, he stumbled off into the dark to try and piss downhill, then stumbled back to his possibles, guided by the black's loud munching on the gamma or whatever. He tugged loose the Saltillo blanket, wrapped up in it as tight as any squaw, and lay down on the grass or whatever—felt mighty like rocks, in fact—and drifted off to a dire sleep and uneasy dreams.

He woke to the first of the light, saw through a drifting morning haze the narrow spine of the ridge stretching off north, up into the mountains, and sat up with a grunt —his rear still sore as spanked, the Saltillo

jeweled with myriad drops of dew. The
black stood, munching at pebbles
apparently, a good distance off. It seemed
to have broken its hobble in the night.
Might stand still to be caught or might
decide to lead Lee a little chase.

Looked to be a long day coming.

Whether it was the angle of the climb, or
simply numbness in Lee's hindquarters, the
black seemed easier riding today. They
were up in real mountains now, for all there
was no forest to ride through, and Lee's
belly was grumbling for breakfast as he
rode. There'd be no breakfast . . . no midday
either. These mountains had odd streaks of
ochre red running down through the rocks.
Copper ore, perhaps. It was not a matter
Lee cared to investigate. He'd had his run
at copper years before.

Cooler up here, too.

This mountain, and then another—and
then Los Gatos.

If the black didn't break a leg, which appeared unlikely from the way it had of
stomping along like a donkey engine
driving pilings. Lee leaned forward in the
saddle, leaning into the climb as the black
took a narrow pitch upslope. Would be a
pleasure to get to the top of this one.

It was, of course, possible that Don Jaime
and his information on Thornhill was so
much horse shit. Thornhill might have

family business . . . personal business . . . in Tampico. Might even have personal business in Buenos Aires.

Not likely, but possible.

Possible, also, that the wandering *Americano* hard-cases had had nothing in mind concerning Los Gatos. Might well have already wandered on. In which case, this damn ride was for nothing at all. In which case, Lee would be more than glad.

Hard to think another man could really put him down. Hard to think—but not impossible to think. Lee had known a couple of men who could certainly have put him down with knife or pistol. A couple of men . . .

You have the name, you can expect sooner or late to have to play the game. Had played it in Canyon Rojo, he supposed. And, he supposed, would have to play it at the mine in Los Gatos.

He reined the black right, higher up the slope. Perhaps an hour to the top of this shoulder . . . another two hours, or three to the reverse slope of the next mountain. Then another hour climbing to the top of that.

Maybe more than an hour.

He'd be lucky to ride in by the afternoon. Catch Thornhill there or at a switchback by Tenochli, if the fool had already caught the train. Catch Thornhill, and get the truth out of the son-of-a-bitch.

And then perhaps kill him? Perhaps. Don Luis would certainly be surprised if he didn't. Max Thornhill. No great loss—one of those foreigners who liked to lord it over the Mexs, made no nevermind he'd been born in the country himself. Spoke Spanish better, probably, than he did his father's German, his mother's English. Tall, ungainly fellow. Lee had met him once in Tenochli delivering a package of some kind —samples of silver ore, likely. Tall, awkward man with mild blue eyes . . . wore spectacles. Man had been pleasant enough to Lee at the time; hadn't pretended to be tough as so many men did who met Lee, made uneasy by him. Had been unpleasant to his Mexican assistant, though. Had made that fellow hop . . . made him look small before Lee.

It would be hard lines to take the fellow off the train. Could be done, but not easily. Much better to take him at the mine.

The black rumbled up and over the pitch at the mountain's shoulder, and Lee pulled him up for a breather, sat looking out at the second mountain. smaller, thank God. Less steep to it.

The black farted, bent its head, and started chewing on dwarf shrub of some kind. Greasewood, maybe. Creosote. Black didn't seem to give a damn. Chewed into it like bluegrass.

* * *

By afternoon—some twenty minutes after three o'clock by Lee's stem-winder—he rode the black up into Los Gatos. The black had been a fine grinder, one of the toughest Lee had ridden, but even this thick-boned nag was thoroughly worn out now, sweat- lathered and blowing. Lee's backside felt like a chunk of wood. He could reach back and pinch his butt and not feel that at all.

Los Gatos was a ruined village. It had been a small farming stead at one time, apparently. Now it was hutches and hovels for the mine workers, the *peons* who sweated in the refinery, the stamping mill. These men lived in Los Gatos as dogs lived in their kennels—going there to sleep, to eat some soggy trash or other, to get up at still dark and get to working.

Not a pueblo at all, really.

Some men, off-work, were standing in the narrow street today, gazing gap-mouthed as Lee urged the weary black along the cobbles. Took Lee a few moments to take these fellows in, to take in as well the silence of the place. No rythmic thud of the hammers up in the mill. No regular rumble as the ore was smashed to rubble.

Silence.

Sunday.

Of course—Thornhill would have planned the robbery for Sunday. Thornhill, or the others.

The men on the street stood or sat as still as near dead men, only their eyes, the slow turning of their heads showing otherwise as he rode by. They seemed barely curious.

No children. No women, either, though there were *cantinas* in the place—nasty, hot, tin-roofed sheds. A couple of them, the last time Lee had ridden through. There were women in those places, if you cared for toothless old women, other women so ripped and raddled with disease it took a very drunken man indeed to have anything to do with them. Some of these sad creatures had no noses, those members having rotted off or collapsed into the women's faces.

The liquor, the entertainments in these places, were of a primitive sort even by the standards Lee had known at the edges of the Rocky Mountains in deep winter. Fights between dogs and naked men . . . fights between drunks armed with broken bottles, the results wagered on.

He rode on up toward the mine . . . found himself wishing for another day, somehow, as if he were becoming shy . . . becoming more and more afraid of a fight. Of trouble. Better not be so. This was no time, no day for it.

He turned stiffly in the saddle, looking back at the men lined like statues along the streets. They would know, of course, of any three *Tejanos* in the place; no way those

three could bury themselves deep enough
not to be marked and remarked. These men
would know, but they wouldn't be telling—
certainly not telling another *gringo* (Don
Luis' *gringo*) about those new *gringos*.

Pillars of silence, they would be, until it
was over. Then they'd be pleased enough to
mutter over it in their dens, get vomiting
drunk on foul *mescal,* and stagger back to
their sheds to dream of better villages,
women, wives, children and other times.

Men who died in this place were not
buried. They were escorted in shouting,
stumbling processions, always at night
between shifts, by small crowds of laughing
drunks in torchlight. Carried out to the
steep washes that drained the mountainside in the winter rains, carried out on plank
doors, prayed over by mock priests with the
marks of the *penitentes* still laced across
their backs.

They carried the fortunate-unfortunate
out to one of these washes and dumped him
down, cheering the fall. No scavengers but
animal needed to crawl down to rob the
corpses; that had long since been accomplished.

Tonight, very late, there would likely be
another such parade. A celebration by
moonlight . . .

Lee rode on out of the settlement, up the
long, winding incline of the mine road, the

black walking mighty slowly, out of steam at last.

Lee pulled the horse up and with some effort swung down from the saddle, lighting very stiff and stick-legged in the dirt. The black snorted, shook its head, and stood four-square and still, getting its breath.

"Well, you nail-gaited son-of-a-bitch, you got us here; damned if I know whether to thank you for it."

He led the black horse on up the mine road, trying as he walked to stretch his muscles loose, get some feeling back into his butt and legs . . . ease the reins-stiffness out of his fingers and hands.

Well, by God, if he didn't end by paying for this ride, someone else was surely going to do so. His painful ass was calling for vengeance of some sort, that was sure!

Chapter 11

He tied the black by a watering trough beside the settle-slide in the mine's lower yard. Slid the Winchester up and out of its scabbard, dug a box of ammunition from his saddle-bag and put it in his jacket pocket. Noticed then the buckskin was looking mighty worn. Not much the dandy, now. No wonder that grandee-steward had peered down his nose.

Standing there in the warm sunlight, he drew the Bisley, checking its loading, checked as well to see the cylinder spun free. Odd things seemed to happen to weapons sometimes on hard rides. Piece of road dirt, piece of turf kicked up, dust, mud. Stuff would seem to fly into the work-ings of a weapon to jam and slow its action. Not this time. The Bisley Colt's maintained the action of a Switzerland watch.

Lee stooped a little to draw the broad-blade double-edge dagger from his right boot. Nothing to go wrong with that razor-sharp steel . . .

He slid the knife back into its sheath, then unstrapped his war-bag from the saddle cantle, reached in, and tugged free the coils of his whip. Draped those supple slender loops of braided black leather over his left shoulder. Never knew when a fine blacksnake lash might come in handy . . .

The mine building was a four-story tower, forty feet on a side. A considerable structure, this tower crowned the heights above Los Gatos as a castle might have done. It was pierced by windows here and there; at the top floor, the mine offices, and some places on down the rough plank walls, wherever the workings of hoists and chutes, steam engines and machinery required at least some good light.

A considerable building. Still and silent now. Sunday. No holiday since the revolution. Don Luis must have decided that one day's holiday at least was the better for production throughout the rest of the week.

A considerable building. And Thornhill's apartments on its fourth floor, behind the mine offices. Fellow had cared to be close to his work . . . .

Lee looked and finally saw a man standing in deep shadow up on the second level—

shadowed by the iron arm of a great crane. Man was watching him but not, it seemed, with much interest. Had a shotgun over his arm.

With such protection as this, no wonder Thornhill and his friends had planned a taking. Man up there looked barely awake.

Lee waved to the man to come down. Fellow stood still up there . . . moved not an inch as far as Lee could see. Lee picked up the Winchester. Waved again with that, and seemed to have an effect. Man with the shotgun turned to the long, angled flights of wooden steps to climb down to Lee's level and, to Lee's surprise, another guard, who must have been sleeping in the crane's shadow, stood up to follow his comrade.

Two guards, then. Two lazy fellows with shotguns to watch over a fortune in silver. Damned if he could blame Thornhill and the others. Too juicy a strike to pass up. Showed the weakness of the ways these people went about their business. Sooner pay a pack of spies to watch Thornhill than pay an extra two or three guards to make a robbery too risky.

Lee stood by the black, which had drunk some water from the trough, but not enough to founder itself (a knowing horse) and watched while these two guardian dragons shambled down the steps to him. A fair climb.

Then, at Lee's level, the two men padded

barefoot across the sun-baked yard to him —stupid, incurious as any of the work-broken men of the town. Round, flat Indian faces. Hooded, dull black eyes. Chosen, Lee supposed, for lack of any initiative, lack of the wit to comprehend the value of what they guarded, lack of the wit to plan to take it.

He didn't trouble to ask their names. Cared only that some fellow from Los Gatos didn't wander up to steal his goods off the black, steal the black itself.

"Do you know me?"

No answer. They stared at him like cattle.

"I am Don Luis' man." Lee put his hand on the coils of the whip at his shoulder.

What he said—or what he did—made some difference to them, and they nodded, attentive.

"You are to take this horse to the stable stalls behind the cracking shed. Do you understand me?"

Nods. Their eyes were on the coils of the whip.

"Do that, then resume your posts. If you sleep, I'll beat you. You understand that?"

Energetic nods—a muttered "*Si, Senor.*" Sad, ridden-down men, to take such threats, and them with shotguns in their hands.

Lee considered something, for the little good it might do.

"Have you seen other *Americanos* here?"

"No—no other *Americanos.*"

"If you see such," Lee said. "They are *banditos*. If you kill them, you may have their boots, their time-pieces. You understand?"

They nodded, looking uneasy. Not likely to be of much help. Still, as watch dogs, they might do to bark. Might be useful, just getting killed.

"*Senor* Thornhill—is he up in the building?"

"*Si.*" The "Patron" was in his building, the best news so far. No spurring the weary black downslope east to the switchback, then trying to climb that damn moving train.

"Go then," Lee said. "And do exactly as I have told you."

And off they trailed, looking more than a little worried, pausing to untie the black, to lead him away, apprehension in every line in their backs. Might have been a mistake to mention *Yanqui* banditos. New and sudden trouble was a thing no inhabitant of Los Gatos cared to hear about.

Hard to blame them.

Lee hefted the Winchester and walked over to the first long flight of wooden steps. A long climb to unpleasant work for the men of Los Gatos. Now, for him as well.

"I recall very well meeting you, Mister McCann. Though I can't conceive what might have brought you to Los Gatos. Surely not the nonsense you've been talking!"

A difficult interview.

Thornhill had been alone in the office, one large, square, sunny room lined with shelves of ore samples, heavy oak cabinets of files and other paper. Rows of high tables stacked with entry sheets, ore tags, weighing records, and pay receipts. The afternoon sunshine shone clear through this big room from side to side, turning slow, faint clouds of dust to gold.

Thornhill had, from the start, played so innocent and busy a fellow, so astonished at some nonsense about railroad tickets and steamship tickets, that Lee might almost have believed the Don's spies to have been sadly mistaken had not Thornhill mentioned Buenos Aires (in amused contempt at such a notion) before Lee had had a chance to do so.

So the foolish fellow had his plot indeed. The question now was the others.

The strong room was on the floor beneath this. Lee'd seen it. Heavier planking. Strips of iron spiked into the wall and door. Nothing, to be sure, to keep out a man with a charge of blasting powder. Not strong enough to keep out some determined men with axes, if it came to that, and they had time enough.

"Thornhill," Lee said, "I would surely

prefer not to kill you."

Thornhill, who had until then been rattling on like a barker at a county fair on the subject of trust and nonsensicality . . . the great difficulty of dealing with a primitive people of no real culture, no background in Europe whatsoever . . . suddenly shut his mouth.

Lee had never, so far as he knew, taken pleasure in seeing a man frightened. It was easy enough of a stunt, after all. Any fool with a revolver or a knife could accomplish it.

It gave him no joy, therefore, to see Thornhill (not a man of violence, after all) turn pale. No pleasure to see the man's hands tremble, resting on his desk top. Tall man, stooped now, his spectacle lenses reflecting the sunshine, the filing cabinets.

"I would prefer not to kill you but I certainly will do just that if you don't tell me where those hard-cases are right now."

Lee stood, waiting to see if the fellow was sensible.

Thornhill said nothing at all. Sat like a jackass in a cool mud pond. It was disturbing. It meant he was at least as scared of those fellows (whoever the hell they were) as he was of Lee.

"Now, now," Lee said, "don't be foolish. Don't force me to do what I'd rather not do . . ."

Thornhill reached up and took his spectacles off, held them in both his hands clutched close to his chest, as if Lee was bound to break them. The man then closed his eyes.

If Lee had not been so worried about those others, he might not have done what he then did, so soon.

He reached up to tug the whip free of his shoulder, drew his arm full back, and struck Thornhill across the face with the braided coils as hard as he could. Such an odd thing to do in a sunny business office.

Thornhill was knocked sideways out of the chair, still managing to hold his spectacles as he fell, and lay on his side on the floor, a stipple of bright blood appearing to bloom out of his face like tiny hibiscus blossoms. He drew a shuddering breath, opened his eyes, and stared up at Lee like an injured child as Lee stepped over above him to hit him again.

Lee struck down hard and Thornhill shouted something in some language— sounded like German to Lee—and with blood running from his nose as from a faucet, writhed and kicked in his fine grey suit, and rolled to hold onto Lee's right boot with both hands as if that would prevent him from being hit again—as if Lee might somehow protect him from Lee.

As much from shame as from exasperation with the man from being so uselessly stubborn, Lee kicked his boot free (striking

Thornhill in the side with the toe of it—
not meaning to) and bent to beat the
shouting fellow with the whip coils as a
cowpoker might beat some trespasser with
the coils of his lariat.

Scrambling away on his hands and knees
under this punishment, trailing spatters of
blood as he went, Thornhill again cried out
in that foreign language and hustled full tilt
into the side of a paper cabinet so that his
head made a solid cracking sound against
the oak.

Injured thus even more than Lee had
injured him—likely thinking it was Lee had
done it—Thornhill lay weeping, clutching
his head where it had met the cabinet.

Lee bent over him, took him by his suit
lapels heedless of the blood smeared on
them and shook him out of his tears. Thornhill opened his eyes, lifted a shaking hand
to wipe at them when Lee let him go, and
then lay back on the floor, resigned, snot on
his chin.

"Tell me," Lee said, "before I lose my
patience."

Thornhill cleared his throat, then turned
his head to the side and spat onto the floor.
Lee saw that the man still had his spectacles clutched to his chest, still unbroken.

"They are camped east of Los Gatos," he
said, sniffling as some drops of blood ran
from his nose. He put up his hand to pinch
at his nose to stop its bleeding. "And they

162

will soon be here to kill you," he said with not a little satisfaction.

"Soon?"

"Soon enough," Thornhill said thickly. His nose was continuing to bleed a little.

"Who are they?"

Thornhill rolled an eye at him but didn't answer. The thought of Lee being murdered by those men had apparently given him courage.

Lee drew his knife, leaned down, and put the tip of the blade just under Thornhill's left eye. He pressed the blade tip in there, but only the smallest bit. "I surely will have your eye out of you like a mulberry if you don't give me any answers I ask for," Lee said. He had lost his patience.

"Pony Deal," Thornhill said. His eye was turning this way and that above the knife tip, as if it might manage somehow to escape its socket entirely.

"Deal?"

"Yes . . . a red-haired man."

Lee had heard of Deal, and nothing good. An Arizona gunman. Had been one of the Clanton people. And, Lee believed, had shot two men to death in McAllen, Texas. He'd heard of Deal.

"The others?" Expecting this time to be told that Wesley Hardin was out of prison and had come south to shoot Lee's buttons off. Hardin and Ben Thompson?

"Keller." Thornhill said. "A man named

Keller—and a boy. I don't know the boy's name." His eye looked wild.

At least it wasn't Hardin and Thompson.

Chapter 12

Lee sat at a window, looking out over the four-flight outside staircase—spidery wooden members laddering down, turning at a landing, then laddering down again, turn by turn, to the wide loading yard four stories down. The shadows were longer now —light would be going in an hour or two. Then dusk, then dark. It would be very unfortunate if those people came up to the mine by night. That would make matters very difficult.

It seemed unlikely, though. His own sad attempt at robbery had been at night and the result had been a dead deputy by lantern light.

The strong room, and its silver (Lee had gone downstairs to be certain the hen-house had not already been robbed) were on the

165

floor below. Thornhill, bruised and swollen-nosed, all dignity fled, now sat on one stack of small silver bars, his hands tied behind him with office twine, his ankles tied together, and his ankles connected to his bound hands by another lashing. He was certainly uncomfortable but he was alive.

Don Luis would not approve.

It was barely possible for Lee to shoot a man to death and that man unarmed, and helpless.

It was certainly not impossible for him to beat a man until he broke.

Sadly for Don Luis' approval, however, Lee had found that he could not beat a man to flinders and then shoot him to death. So Thornhill, a stranger to the country he had been born in, now sat beaten on top of silver dug from its earth. Poor fellow was a ruined man and no mistake about it. A ruined man —and when his clerk and office staff, when other men who served the Don appeared with the new work week, would likely be a dead man. Someone would certainly seek to please the Don by taking Thornhill's head— and possibly in fact. Lee had heard of more than one *patron* who had demanded a very real head delivered to him in a basket.

A dead man perched on a stack of silver.

Unless his confederates came soon, unless they were able to kill Lee. Then, that done, if they were honorable men, they might free him. Might give him his share.

Might escort him safely to his train . . . see him off on his way to Tampico, the steamship, and Buenos Aires down in Argentina.

They might do that for Thornhill, but Lee wouldn't have cared to bet that way.

Lee had thought of staying down on the strong room floor, then had thought again. Here on the top floor he had the outside staircase under his gun—held the top of the inside staircase, too.

Good men with guns might well win their way into the strong room below. They'd play hell getting any silver out.

Don Luis would approve of that.

Time to wish Los Gatos was more than a company kennel. Time to wish it had a police post, friends of the Don or not. Even Captain Gonsalves would look good this afternoon. Gonsalves and his clever sergeant would both look mighty good.

Lee sat at his window, looking out, noticing the gleam of sunlight on the Winchester's barrel. Handsome weapon. Short ranged, though. Not like that old Sharp's.

An odd sound . . .

Odd sound.

It took Lee a moment to realize it was a human noise. It had sounded like machinery . . . whining . . . unoiled. Not that, though. Not machinery.

A man screaming down in the yard.

A high, thin, screeching noise. A trapped rabbit's scream.

Lee levered the Winchester and stepped back out of the window light.

Silence. No more screaming from the yard.

They must have caught one of those sad, stupid guards. Played at him with a knife, it sounded. Lee didn't doubt the poor fellow had said all he knew before they cut his throat for him—let him shriek out that last scream for Lee to hear.

Some relief they hadn't waited till night. Some relief, but not much. For the guard, no relief at all.

Someone shouted in the yard, voice echoing from the buildings' sides. Something in Spanish. Shouted again.

Lee was ashamed that he jumped a little when a shotgun went off down in the yard. No doubt about that hard slamming sound.

A revolver shot came right after.

Both guards down. Lee was surprised the second man had made any showing at all. There'd been a man behind that dull stare, after all, a man who could hear his fellow die screaming like a rabbit and still come on.

Lee stepped back to the window and saw, down in the yard, a man in cowhide chaps standing looking up at him. Man had a Stetson hanging down his back on its chincord. Had a shock of red hair. Sunburned face, with a lank, jutting jaw. Too far to see the color of his eyes. Wore two revolvers—

looked like Remingtons from the butts—holstered high at his sides.

Deal, Lee supposed.

Man waved up at him. Seemed to be smiling.

"Sent for the cavalry, did they?"

Odd, that the first thing Lee should feel just for an instant was pleasure at hearing an American voice. It lifted his spirits, no question of it.

He stood to the side of the window, carefully, and called back down.

"Sent for—and come! You Deal?"

Though he was watching, Lee didn't see Deal draw. Saw the powder-smoke at the American's left hand, and flinched away as the side of the window frame splintered, smashed.

Lee leaned out fast with the Winchester to squeeze off his shot just as Deal skipped back under the shadow of the stairway. Saw the round kick dust just behind the man's heel.

Silence then for a while.

Lee levered another round into the Winchester. If Deal had made a slightly better shot than that, Lee would be cold meat. Son of a bitch was every bit as good as Lee had worried. No sign of the other men, though. Man and boy.

"Say!" Deal called from below, "Sorry about that cheap shot, McCann. It is

169

'McCann,' ain't it?"

"It is!" Lee called back, and heard Deal say something to someone else in the yard.

"I suppose," Deal called up again. "—I suppose you've seen that old elephant, McCann!"

"I have, and walked 'round it and kicked its ass."

"So I thought . . ."

Lee leaned to the window again, saw that Deal was staying snug out of sight while he did his shouting.

"And that being so," Deal called, "you must surely be an open-minded fellow. Open to . . . say . . . thirty thousand pesos? Just to arrive here the littlest bit too late?"

"And what about Thornhill?"

Deal laughed. Lee again heard him say something to someone in the yard.

"You don't say that dude is still kickin'?"

"Still waiting for his *compadres*," Lee called.

Deal laughed again. "Sorry to cross a pal," he shouted, "but I'll just pass them pesos over to you, McCann—do you earn them!"

Lee was a little surprised that Deal and his men hadn't made a harder try. Was not surprised that they knew his name, at least the name he was using. Thornhill must have stooled his guts, mentioned Lee as a possible tripping block. For whatever reason, perhaps some notion that Lee might be stupid enough to trust him, Deal had tried his first shot—and a fair enough shot it had been—and then gone to talking.

Deal apparently took silence for encouragement.

"Say—McCann?"

"I'm here."

"I suppose you wouldn't care to have me come up an' talk to you. I could bring that passel of pesos with me . . ."

"Come right on up."

Deal laughed. A merry man, apparently. "I do, an' you'll plug me. Right?"

"That's right," Lee said.

"Didn't hear yuh!"

"I said, *you're right!*"

Deal thought that over for a moment or two. Then Lee heard him call, "Matty!" to someone down there.

Lee leaned to the window, seeing if there might be a shot to take while Deal was so busy chatting. Saw nothing at first. Long shadows stretching across the yard. Then a moving shadow at the base of the outside stairs. One of them coming out.

Lee leveled the Winchester down.

Saw a white piece of cloth. A tow-headed kid waving a white piece of cloth. This boy came stepping right out under Lee's gun waving that foolish piece of rag in both hands. Came out and walked to the bottom of the staircase and started climbing right up as if he was going to a barn dance.

171

There'd been an instant there when Lee should have shot him, and damn that white cloth. But the boy had no gun showing. Had looked mighty young to be in such desperate company. It crossed Lee's mind that Deal and Keller might be forcing the kid along.

Mister Keller seemed to be a little shy.

The boy had reached the second landing now—looked up at Lee and waved the silly scrap of cloth again. Appeared some sort of Reuben farm boy, fifteen years old, if that. Yellow hair and a face full of freckles. Homely as a hedge fence.

Boy was carrying a small canvas bank sack. Lee could see some printing across the canvas. That, he supposed, would be the pesos Deal intended to buy him with. It was no temptation, particularly since Deal would certainly back-shoot him at the first opportunity thereafter and take those pesos right back.

Time now to shoot the boy, if he was going to.

Kid was coming up the last flight of steps, leaving a long late-afternoon shadow behind him.

"Take it easy now, McCann . . . !" Deal worried about that timely shot. "Matty's just got your cash money there. No need to be pluggin' a kid."

Lee said nothing.

"No need to go jumpy, now . . ." Deal

sounded some jumpy, himself. Liked the boy, apparently.

"Mister . . .?"

The farm boy stood just below Lee's window on the last landing, ten feet away, and dead meat.

"I got your money, Mister. Pony wants you to come down and get off this place. We won't bother you none do you do it . . ."

The boy was dressed mighty poorly for having been in a big bank robbery. Likely the three of them hadn't had the chance to buy much in the way of pretties, hustling down here for the bigger score. Boy was in worn blue-jean trousers and baggy flannel shirt, skinny wrists and ankles sticking out like a scarecrow's.

Not a rich target at ten feet.

"Kid," Lee said, keeping to the side of the window in case Deal tried his luck again, "kid, you'd better get your butt back down those steps . . ."

"I got your money," the kid said, dumb as a dog, and started up the last flight of steps to the door, still waving the white rag at Lee as if it was magic.

Lee stepped over to the door, turned the knob, and pulled it wide open. Might do to knock the kid silly . . . tie him up . . .

The boy stood squinting in the sunlight. He held the bank-bag out to Lee as if he'd been sent for, was handing over a bucket of beer.

"You come in here," Lee said. "You won't be going back down those steps."

The boy heard him out, then shook his head as stubbornly and stupidly as a horse, held the bank-bag out for Lee to take. The boy had light grey eyes.

Lee started to take the long step out onto the landing to get his hand on the kid and haul him in—and stopped. There was a noise . . . something . . . behind him.

Lee half turned, heard a ticking . . . something back in the office. A sound down the inside staircase.

Keller. And the reason for all the talk.

He glanced at the boy to judge him for a stroke of the Winchester's butt and saw him standing as he had been, but now the bank-bag falling to the planking. The boy was still clutching the white cloth with his left hand and reaching behind his back with his right.

Lee leveled the rifle and shot the kid through the belly.

He had almost turned back into the office when a slight young man with long black hair to his shoulders, dressed like a drover —a blue bandana 'round his neck—came up the inside stairs and into the office firing revolvers right and left.

This man's first shot caught Lee along his left side and spun him into the door frame. The second struck the Winchester's receiver and blew the rifle from Lee's hand.

Felt as though his wrist was broken.

Lee threw himself down behind a row of sample tables, trying to reach around to get his left hand on the Bisley Colt's. The long-haired young man came across the office at him at a run—boots sounded like thunder on the floor.

Lee got the Bisley out of its holster cross-handed, knelt up and shot the young man high through the chest. But Keller—ex-drover, bank robber, whatever—was the McCoy. He went back-stepping 'til a desk stopped him, and fired left and right as he did. The sombrero was snatched from Lee's head as if by a hasty wind, and he stood and fired back, shooting left-handed into a cloud of gunsmoke. The round struck Keller at the side of his forehead and seemed to blow a piece of his skull away.

The long-haired man fell sideways in a quick bright spray of blood and, lying on the floor, raised his right-hand gun and fired at Lee again, as if his injury, looking so desperate, was nothing much after all.

Lee shouted . . . something. He stooped as Keller fired again, the bullet snapping past Lee's left ear, stooped lower still to get a clear shot under the powder smoke, and caught that surprising fellow up on his knees, clutching the side of an office desk, trying to get to his feet.

Lee, frightened as he had ever been in a fight, then shot Keller once through the middle to hold him still, then a second time, this round striking Keller in the head with a sharp whacking sound and killing him.

Lee stood upright, staggered and almost fell. His left side hurt like blazes. Felt like that young son-of-a-bitch had shot a rib out of him. Damned if Lee had ever seen a fellow more determined in a fight. Damned if he had!

The office was full of smoke. They'd done some shooting, no saying they hadn't. That Keller—and who had ever heard of him—pure poison in a fight.

Someone screaming like a woman.

Not Keller, please God. That son-of-a-bitch was finally dead as any man ever had been.

Someone screaming, though.

Lee walked to the door. He could see through the smoke to the landing outside. Tried to reload the Bisley one-handed as he went—an awkward business. Felt as if his right wrist was broken from that second shot. The Winchester surely a dead loss. Don Luis could fucking well pay for a replacement.

Screaming . . .

Lee stood in the doorway, off to a side so that Deal mightn't get a shot from below, and saw the boy standing down on the second landing. He had apparently torn his shirt open to get at the place where Lee had shot him and now stood wailing, both hands fumbling at his bright red belly where a thick, soft tube of red and blue came bulging out, spattering blood down his blue-jean trousers. At his narrow chest, revealed by the opened shirt, two small long-nippled breasts trembled at each scream.

A girl, of course. "*Mattie.*" And Lee should have known it. Thin, fragile wrists on a farm boy . . .

The girl, her hands clenched in the complications of her guts where the rifle bullet had undone her, put her head back, staring up as if some mercy might be expected from the sky, and called out, as regular as a clock, the same high trilling shriek.

There were clots of brown down the steps, the way she'd gone, her torn bowels releasing what they'd held.

A little nickel-plated revolver lay on the second step. Kept it behind her back, tucked into her pants as she held the bankbag out. The bag lay on the landing at Lee's feet.

"Oh, Mattie . . . *Oh, Mattie!*"

Deal was getting his reward, shouting up at the screaming girl. There was that in his voice was worse than the agony in hers. And the only way up to her was into Lee's gun.

Smoke came swirling out of the office behind Lee, thicker than it had been in the fight and smelling of wood and paint and coal oil, not gunpowder.

Keller had set a fire down below—or Deal had, once Keller was climbing. Had figured to smoke Lee out, if shooting didn't do the trick.

The mine building was burning up its four stories like a chimney. Deal and Keller must have thought there'd be just time enough to get the silver out once Lee was flushed.

But Lee wasn't flushed.

The girl stopped making her noise and sank to her knees. Her hands were full of herself now. Blood everywhere down there.

Lee cocked the Bisley to finish her, but Deal got in first from below. One shot up and through her heart, it seemed. Knocked her over and gone, and not a kick.

"Oh . . . Mattie . . ."

Should never have sent her up—should never have brought her to Los Gatos. Lee felt sorry for the man. Hard not to.

"Sorry, Deal," he called down. *"Bad business all 'round."*

Deal came out and up the steps like a cougar, a revolver in each hand, but only the left one firing. Must be a lefty.

Lee fired a fast shot and missed Deal plenty. Then Deal was at the second landing, fired that left-hand Remington twice, clipped Lee through the calf of his right leg, and knocked him down.

Lee landed as if he'd been dropped some

distance, landed hard enough to knock his wind out—the shot leg didn't pain at all—and fired from there and missed again as Deal jumped past the girl's body, leveling that Remington for a finisher. Jumped almost past the girl's body. Deal's boot slipped in the blood.

Deal went to one knee—had to drop his right-hand gun to steady himself, to lever himself up again, quick as a cat. He didn't drop the left-hand gun.

Lee, still stretched out and out of breath, sighted along the length of his hurt leg and shot Deal through the throat as the red-haired man came lunging up the steps again, cowhide chaps flapping, the left-hand Remington coming down to the level.

The bullet struck Deal just under his long, pale sunburned jaw to the right of his Adam's apple, and knocked a small black hole clear through his neck, front to back.

The small hole turned immediately red as an angry eye, and spurted a thin squirt of blood before Deal as he kept coming and fired at Lee as Lee rolled left for his life.

A plank split and brushed out splinters with a crash as Lee's head jerked just enough away, and Lee raised the Bisley and shot Deal again, straight into the man's chest as he came on.

Deal stumbled and drew a great whooping breath. Then he seemed to recover and came up the last two steps, but slower. Got to the landing and tripped again. Said, "No . . . no," and staggered toward the staircase railing as if Lee wasn't lying there at all, close enough to reach out and touch.

Deal drew that noisy breath again, opened his left hand and let the revolver fall out of it. The heavy weapon made a heavy sound striking the planks.

Deal, his back to Lee, clung to the staircase railing with both hands, and drew another long, noisy breath. His dirty checkered shirt was half soaked with blood from the wound through his neck.

Lee, propped up on an elbow, lifted the Bisley Colt's, cocked it, and fired into Deal's back and broke it.

Chapter 13

It took a while for Lee to get up.

The leg had had no feeling to it for a time —couldn't make the thing work. Lee would have preferred pain to not being able to stand at all.

But that didn't last. Soon enough, he could make the leg answer him. The pain came with that, though, and then Lee would have preferred crawling.

The smoke was rolling out onto the staircase landing. A soft, continuous thumping sound like a dull roll of drums sounded from inside the building. The Los Gatos mine was burning. Lee, supporting himself on the stairway railing as Deal had, looked down the building's side and saw flickering red at the lower windows. He put his arm out, rested his head against the building's

side. Warm—warmer than the dying sunlight would have made it. Eddies of smoke
drifted past him, over him—over the two
dead ones, too. Deal at his feet was
stretched out as if he was asleep, having
bathed in red. Man was not as tall lying
there as he had been coming up the steps,
shooting. Might have done better standing
still to shoot rather than firing as he had, on
the climb. Had he done any better though,
Lee would be stony dead instead of just
crippled up and hurting.

The girl lay huddled down on the second
story landing, dead in a tangle of her guts.

Lee looked down there once and didn't
look again.

Not my fault. Not my fault . . .

Smoke, rich and dark grey as unmilked
chocolate, was rolling out of the fourth floor
doorway now like a thunderhead, with a
soft, roaring sound, as if the smoke was
being breathed out by a beast somewhere
inside. There was nothing welcoming about
it.

Inside, one full floor down and barred
behind strong oak doors banded with iron
straps, Thornhill would be sitting on his
stack of silver bars, hearing the fire coming
up around him, smelling the smoke, seeing
the first hazy tendrils of it drifting under
the weighty doors. Would be hot down
there, now, growing swiftly hotter as if

some great furnace door was slowly swinging wide.

In a short while, the strong room would be broken by the fire, the iron bands turning dull cherry, the thick oak panels charring, glowing their own cheery crimson in the flames.

The doors, the walls would then buckle like a drunken woman to a man's embraces, and the fire would come in upon Thornhill and torment the bound man to squalling. Torment him into something much less than human before his brain baked hard as a hard-cooked egg, the stack of silver molten beneath his roasted corpse. Spectacle frames running in bright drops of liquid gold.

Lee had tied him. Lee had left him there.

Lee turned from the rail, the splintering wood already hot beneath his hand, and limping wonderfully (dipping and swaying at each step as if he were at sea in very heavy weather) he managed to get to the doorway—drew in as deep a breath of air as he could—and dragged his furious leg along into smoke and the mine office.

It was a long walk to the inside stairs. A blind walk. Lee had heard of the darkness of fires; this was his first experience of it.

The world was dark, velvety grey, a single sheet of that color wherever he chose to look. Lee put his hand up to his face and could not see it. Couldn't see it when his fingertips were brushing his eyelids.

He felt his way across the room, his boot soles growing hot enough to burn him, his shot-through leg giving him fits. His side, where Keller had clipped him, hardly bothered him at all in comparison. Lee felt his way across the office (and a damned wide office it seemed) by crashing into desks and tables, by nearly tripping over this chair and that file-box—did trip over Keller all of a sudden, and almost fell. His hurt leg, his aching lungs were both telling him not to fall. Not to fall down and lose his sense of where the staircase was . . . not to fall and forget where the door lay behind him . . .

Not to forget that.

Keller had felt companionably soft to the toe of his boot when it struck him. Even a dead man was good company in this grey world of no breathing, though Lee's chest had begun an odd sort of trying to breathe whether he wished it to or not.

Lee reached the inside staircase—and knew it because a savage wind of heat was pouring up from the stairwell, all unseen in the cool, cool grey.

The heat burned his face as scalding water would have done; Lee smelled his hair as it began to burn . . . the softer stink of scorching buckskin as his jacket began to char.

"Walk in to me, and die," that strong wind said.

Lee stood for a moment, blind at the top of the stairs—tried to turn his face from the heat, and felt the skin begin to blister on his cheek, his ear.

"Walk on down . . . and die."

The building trembled beneath him, the fire shaking it as a cat might shake a chipmunk it had caught among spring grasses.

Lee leaned into the wind as best he was able, fumbled for a hold on the stair railing, and jerked his hand away from rounded wood hot as any stove lid.

"Thornhill!" He shouted the man's name again. Screamed the man's name down the thundering well of fire, bright enough now to lighten even the perfect grey to a brighter shade.

"THORNHILL!"

And turned away, not knowing whether it was the fire or the wound in his leg that pained him so. Felt as if a pack of dogs were tearing at him.

But turned away.

Not such a champion, after all . . .

Man could never have heard him, of course. Was, more than likely, already dead. Been foolish, no doubt, even to come in to try for him.

A foolish gunman. Happy enough to be shooting girls; not so pleased, however, to go down into fire to save a man he had left bound and helpless. Not so pleased to be doing that . . .

Lee was sure he had properly turned around, had properly retraced his path. It was puzzling how long it took a man with a dreadful leg to drag it through brightening grey toward a door that better be there.

It took the longest time a man could think of.

Lee tried to take in just a little breath— the smallest sip of a breath. Just once.

The grey slipped into his lungs and tore at them like a gardening rake. Lee whined in his throat, then. Whined like a dog begging to be let in from winter.

Perhaps it was the pain of his leg that helped him a little, kept his mind on what he was doing. On where he was, and what was happening. His leg kept him from dreaming in the grey while he spent a long, long lifetime crossing thirty feet of planking. The planking hissed and spat, popped and cracked beneath his boots as he limped along, stumbling from this smoking table to that charring chair.

Never bumped into Keller going back. Thought at the time that the dead bandit had gotten up somehow and walked out of the fire and on out a window perhaps. On out into the cool air.

Lee found the door as he was dying, tripped over the sill, staggered onto the landing, and fell full length into a vagrant draft of clear wind blowing hard into the welcoming flames.

Senor Saumarez had been a *regulator*, a conductor and inspector of the wheels and carriages on the railways of the Republic for some twenty-three years. Had, of course, seen extraordinary sights in that long time, sights that the average peasant, stuck like a mole in his little piece of dirt, could hardly imagine. It was quite correct, what some Englishman had said about travel. It did broaden a man, enrich him, make him more of a man.

There were rich men who hadn't seen of the Republic what Miguel Saumarez had seen. Nor was landscape, town-scape, city-scape all of travel's pleasures. Not nearly.

Men—women—children. Here were land-scapes that a wise man could never fail to profit from.

Were there many who had seen Juarez writing in his notebooks in the public car on the Sinaloa grade?

Not many.

Not many who had been shot twice by varieties of bandit-politicos, both wounds being received in attacks upon the railroad by men too ignorant to perceive its most essential value to a civilized state. Shot twice, and awarded medals for each wound.

Men, women, and children. Not many men (and they could thank God and His

Mother for it) had seen a child crushed under the great flanged wheels for playing unwisely in the grand Station at Mexico City. Not many—and they could thank God again—who had seen that child's mother go mad at the sight.

An official, a man of honor and responsibility, speaks to no-one of more private visions—of innumerable matters of sexual intercourse in this carriage or that, and by no means always in the third class.

And a murder, still unsolved. A Brazilian, speaking a very comic Spanish, a generous tipper and a gentleman, found lying quite dead, a knife driven into his back so thoroughly that the policeman, later, had had to plant his shoe between the poor fellow's shoulderblades and heave him like a black to free it.

A bad business. The Brazilian had offended no-one, as far as a man could recall . . .

Strange events and much traveling—but few stranger than this of tonight, when an undoubted *Tejano,* stinking of smoke, his trouser leg a column of blood (more blood still at the left side of his jacket) had hauled himself aboard by moonlight at the switchback ten miles from Los Gatos. Had left a fine if somewhat stocky black horse trotting free behind him also, and not seemed to care.

A dentist named Fernandez had been

smoking on the platform, and had, to his surprise, received from the night air—saddlebags (from one of which, he confided, a corner of a more official canvas sack appeared, which jingled in a way that only pesos do.) He then received right after a call for assistance, which he gave, helping to pull this bedraggled *gringo* (obviously having been up to much less than good) off his sturdy black horse and onto the rear platform of the *Especial.* And fortunate he had not attempted this at a straight-away where the train might have been speeding to fifty kilometers an hour.

This much the dentist had seen and done, and Saumarez had not.

The rest of the matter, however, was railroad business and no business of the dentist who, it seemed, lacked a little in the understanding of proper procedure and private communication.

Once this importunate dentist, however, was shut out of a compartment in the first class, the *Yanqui* was able to establish to a *regulator's* satisfaction a fine sense of the fitness of things, requesting permission to stay on board (apologizing handsomely for his unorthodox method of mounting) and offering immediately to pay both for that very first class compartment and for the undoubted inconvenience to the *regulator* of this surprising style of commencing a railroad journey.

The fellow had looked sadly used enough, after all, and Miguel Saumarez, while he knew his duty, was also a Christian.

The gringo appeared drunk at first, though it soon became apparent that he was only sad, and sadly scorched and wounded. Had something to say about a dog, and the removal of a dog's collar, then asked if a *medico* might be traveling. Asked also the names of shipping companies that might own vessels out of Tampico for the Argentine trade.

An odd fellow, even for a *Yanqui*. A bandit of some sort, Saumarez had supposed, though in these troubled times, who was there who was *not* a bandit of some sort?

The *medico*, a physician named Lopez traveling with his wife from Hermosillo, was very rude when asked later for information perfectly proper for a railroad official to possess.

It could only be said with certainty— since just before morning, passing the compartment, it had accidently been overheard—that this *gringo* had wept.

From the pain of his injuries, no doubt.

A man of violence, a foreigner, and a Protestant must surely expect some punishment for the error of his ways.